Wildcat Dome

YUKO TSUSHIMA

Wildcat Dome

Translated by Lisa Hofmann-Kuroda

PENGUIN BOOKS

PENGUIN CLASSICS

UK | USA | Canada | Ireland | Australia
India | New Zealand | South Africa

Penguin Classics is part of the Penguin Random House group of companies whose addresses can be found at global.penguinrandomhouse.com.

Penguin Random House UK
One Embassy Gardens, 8 Viaduct Gardens, London SW11 7BW

penguin.co.uk

Penguin Random House UK

First published in Japanese as *Yamaneko Dōmu* by Kodansha Ltd., Japan 2013
First published in the United States of America by Farrar, Straus and Giroux 2025
First published in Great Britain by Penguin Classics 2025
001

Set in 11.25/14 pt Dante MT Std
Typeset by Jouve (UK), Milton Keynes
Printed and bound in Great Britain by Clays Ltd, Elcograf S.p.A.

The authorized representative in the EEA is Penguin Random House Ireland, Morrison Chambers, 32 Nassau Street, Dublin D02 YH68

A CIP catalogue record for this book is available from the British Library

ISBN: 978–0–241–64946–6

Penguin Random House is committed to a sustainable future for our business, our readers and our planet. This book is made from Forest Stewardship Council® certified paper.

MIX
Paper | Supporting responsible forestry
FSC® C018179
FSC www.fsc.org

Wildcat Dome

I

A dry, restless sound. Insects, each alone barely audible, covering every branch, large and small, down to the tips in heavy clusters, some slipping to the ground, perhaps a hundred, no, hundreds, fervently gnawing away at the leaves, emitting a sound that builds in layers, a whirlpool, a wave, expanding in ever-widening circles around the tree. The insects gleam, metallic in the light, a dark emerald green.

pish pish pish pish

Crowded together on every branch, they push and shove in greedy hordes, inching past each other as they devour the leaves – an ordinary shade of early summer green – which have been whittled down to bare veins, all but replaced by the metallic green carapaces of the insects. The whole tree seethes with their movement, glittering in the light. For them, time never stops. They churn in the light, squirming and wriggling in one continuous dark emerald motion.

*

Mitch, you stood near the tree where the scarab beetles clustered together, their light so bright it hurt your eyes. You listened closely to the restless sound they made as they devoured the leaves. But perhaps there was no such sound. After all, the swarming beetles terrified you. You stifled a scream, bracing yourself with all your might.

pish pish pish pish

Mitch, perhaps you'd put it something like this: Time has stopped, except in that tree, where the insects gather all at once, flaunting their enormous appetites. There, time flows on and on, a river of emerald. But over here, time stands still. And the friction between these two planes of time sounds something like the drip of ice melting.

Perhaps you watch, petrified, as one of the insects lifts its head, spreads its wings, sprouts human limbs. A face takes shape, the smile of a boy with curly black hair floating emerald in the light.

Shh, don't move. Be quiet.

That's Kazu's voice. Kazu was part of you, Mitch – or rather, he *was* you, and you were him. Even after he died, you still heard his voice wherever you went. In truth, it was your own voice you were hearing, but Kazu never strayed far from your thoughts, even after all these years.

Isn't that right, Mitch?

Yonko wishes she could cling to Mitch's arm, whisper softly in his ear. In her mind, he becomes a little boy again, the skinny kid who never left Kazu's side, running swiftly alongside him. The two look nothing alike, and at the same time so alike that she can barely keep them separate in her mind. She can't think of one without thinking of the other. Of course, by now the real Mitch is an old man who walks with a limp. But it's as children that she still thinks of them both.

The insects swarm, scattering light as they devour the leaves. One nearly slips and falls from the cluster, the emerald light illuminating it briefly before it disappears back into the squirming mass. Kazu laughs, his black eyes sparkling, and Mitch laughs with him.

⋆

I can't believe it. My head is reeling. Never seen anything like it. Something terrible has happened. All the trees in Tokyo have gone haywire. I can't help but think it's the radiation. After the nuclear accident in March, the anemones started sprouting huge leaves, garishly huge – and the leaves of the crab apples, well, those turned to ugly rust. And then there's the beetles. Maybe I'm overthinking it, but they've been breeding like crazy lately. The tap water, and the ocean, all of it's contaminated now. And the roses I've been tending, and the lawns, and the trees, and the soil . . . It's terrifying. How am I supposed to do my job?

⋆

No, there's no way Kazu would talk as fluently as that.

His voice echoes inside Mitch's head, overlaid by the *pish pish pish* of the insects. Maybe Mitch tilts his head anxiously, knitting his brow. He puts on a mask, hooking the loops around his ears.

Oh no. This is bad. What if I've been breathing in the air this whole time and now it's stuck somewhere inside me?

He feels a dull pain behind his eyes. The ground shakes, wobbles, sways. He can't tell if it's an earthquake or his own dizziness. He can't believe people are still going about their normal lives as though nothing has happened.

To Mitch, Tokyo seems essentially unchanged. The only perceivable difference, now that summer is approaching, is the signs plastered all around town urging citizens to conserve electricity. People hurry through the shopping districts and train stations. Passengers stand waiting on the Yamanote platform, their faces expressionless. Trains arrive and depart. The calm voice of the station employee announces something over the speaker system. Storefronts crowd together, young mothers wheel their children in strollers, uniformed schoolgirls chatter excitedly in cheerful, high-pitched voices, as old people with sullen expressions brush past them. Flower shops, bakeries, bento stores, bicycle repair shops, banks, drugstores, convenience stores – so many they seem superfluous – all calmly go about their business. The aroma of steaming oden fills the air. In the cafés and restaurants, there are customers, as usual. Mitch enters one, orders a coffee and his favourite meal of curry and rice, and eats in silence. But then he wonders – what if the food is contaminated, too? Come to think of it, the flavour does seem a little off . . .

He looks out the window, weighed down by the tedium of his own anxiety. A normal cityscape. A normal, unaffected time. But to him it is a ghost world, soundless and stagnant. Dim shadows float over it. He had boarded a plane only to arrive in this dead, otherworldly world. Was it the frightening footage he'd seen on TV that brought him back? Or the fact that unthinkable things had happened in this place where he was born and raised, to the point that he could no longer feign indifference?

*

In any case, Mitch, you've returned. You saw it on TV in some other country: footage of a tsunami so big you couldn't believe your eyes. Four nuclear power plants exploding. You must have been scared. Maybe you stiffened in horror, wanting to look away. But your eyes were glued to the TV. You bought a newspaper and stared at the photographs on the front page: surreal images of large fishing boats scattered all over the shore after the tsunami retreated. Cars washed up on the rooftops of buildings, lodged in the walls of houses. Aerial photos of the wreckage. Snippets of voices talking excitedly: *Hard to believe this is Japan's third nuclear disaster, after it already had atomic bombs dropped on it twice!*

⋆

So this was the prophecy Mitch had heard all those years ago. Perhaps he thinks of that strange curse now. His eyes flash green, his body trembles, in his back he feels the pressure of the tsunami. The hard stone pavement melts away beneath his feet.

For years, Mitch had denounced Japan, wishing this hateful country would disappear from the face of the earth. Before Kazu died, he had been able to stand it somehow – but since then, his hatred had only grown stronger and more violent.

If only Kazu had stayed away from Japan, Mitch thinks, maybe he wouldn't have died so young. Mitch didn't want to go back to Japan. He wanted to forget all about it. But now, learning of the tsunami and the nuclear accident, he realizes that his hatred of Japan only reveals how much it means to him.

Distant memories, long submerged inside him, begin to wriggle and squirm as though irradiated. However much he tries to deny it, images of the tsunami and the nuclear accident remind him of the bombs during the war. The newscasters call the surviving children *tsunami orphans*. The moment he hears the phrase, a part of Mitch's brain collapses, leaving a small but deep hole inside him.

Hey, that's not true! I was already planning on coming back to Japan, anyway.

Is that what you'd say, Mitch? Yonko pictures Mitch nervously boarding his flight, dragging his left foot behind him.

Whatever the reason, you chose to come back to Japan in May, when everyone else was leaving because of the radiation.

⋆

When he boarded his flight, Mitch left behind a world of reason, where time flowed calmly and smoothly, and landed in another, where time had stopped altogether. Radiation hung over everything like a silver mist. But he couldn't just stay on the plane. Beyond the door, the silver mist made everything look distorted, as though it were suspended in jelly. He squeezed his eyes and mouth shut and stepped decisively into it. And then, ever so cautiously, he opened his eyes. He was surprised to find he could breathe normally, and even see and hear clearly, inside that radioactive jelly. Passengers came and went, employees hurried about their work.

(Perhaps it was all a bit anticlimactic for you, Mitch. Maybe you wondered what all the fuss was about. But immediately you must have backtracked, thinking, No, it's because we can't physically sense it that radiation is so dangerous, and immediately covered your nose and mouth with a mask.)

After that, Mitch headed downtown to Kazu's apartment, the one he'd inherited after Kazu died; he stayed there whenever he came to Tokyo. He still kept an urn with Kazu's ashes there, which he handed off to Yonko for safekeeping whenever he left Japan.

Why don't you just put Kazu in Mama's vault? There's space for three in there, anyway. I think it'd make her happy.

How many times had Yonko said this to Mitch over the years?

You can put his ashes in there with mine after I die, but not before then, Mitch would reply stubbornly.

Mitch, how many days were you wandering around Tokyo by yourself? Just a day? Or was it three?

★

At last, Mitch worked up the courage to call Yonko. He hadn't expected her to pick up immediately, which caught him off guard.

Yonko – is that you?

Mm.

He laughed timidly, his voice hoarse and shaky. Yonko chuckled, too. She knew it was him right away. That unforgettable voice, as sweet as melted ice cream, words slurring a little at the ends.

I didn't think you'd still be at this number . . . I wasn't sure if I'd get through. I didn't bring my phone or laptop.

Mm-hmm, Yonko said again.

So, you . . . ah . . .

There was a mixture of affection, hesitation and anxiety in Mitch's voice, making him sound awkward.

What?

Aren't you . . . trying to leave?

Yonko laughed again.

Mitch, where are you right now?

Tokyo.

So you came back. Why? Because you remembered the prophecy? Did it come true?

Who cares about all that. You need to get out of here, soon. Aren't you scared?

Yonko took a deep breath before answering him.

Where have you been all this time?

It doesn't matter. Look, I'll come get you, let's just get out of here.

No, really. Where have you been? What have you been doing?

Please. Come on, we have to leave.

You've just come back to Japan from God knows where and now you're telling me I need to leave? Yonko said, laughing. Besides, what about Kazu's ashes?

Well . . .

And then, Mitch, in obvious distress, you described how you'd found a Stewartia tree, its leaves ravaged by a flock of scarab beetles.

Scarab beetles? Wasn't there a song about those? I don't think I know what they look like. Oh, wait, you mean the ones the ancient Egyptians prized so much?

No, no, those are dung beetles. Scarab beetles are just . . . scarab beetles. They live in colonies and eat the roots and leaves of trees, so they'd be natural enemies for gardeners like Kazu.

The Stewartia tree stood in a corner of a municipal park that Kazu used to like. The park had a variety of trees and shrubs – not just the usual azaleas, but daffodils, lilies and roses, too, all in healthy bloom. As a gardener without his own plot of land, Kazu had tended to the park quietly, in his spare time. Sometimes he'd complain about people stealing his flowers. But they've probably all wilted away by now. After all, it's been ten years since he died.

Mitch stands transfixed by the insects squirming in the emerald light. Maybe it's a good thing Kazu died before all this happened, Yonko thinks as she pictures Mitch with his left shoulder slightly drooping. If Kazu were still alive, he might have shut himself away in his room in mourning. And the plants, held captive, and the soil that nurtures the plants, and the water that flows beneath the soil, and the water that falls from the sky – all of it would be contaminated, along with the insect larvae sleeping in the earth. And after breaking through the soil, they'd eat the contaminated leaves, scattering irradiated pollen. Even the mosquitoes, which have begun to flit around the park, wouldn't be immune. How could Kazu, who always loved to play in the dirt, have survived the despair? The very ground that he had such faith in was shaking and trembling, and he was helpless to stop it.

It really is just as the prophecy foretold, isn't it?

Is that what you thought, Mitch, as you gazed at the emerald insects? You've never been afraid of scarab beetles, or drone beetles, or caterpillars, or anything like that. You used to catch drone beetles with your bare hands and twist their heads off, brush scarab beetles off of branches and crush them underfoot. Scarab beetles aren't nearly as tough as drone beetles. But that May, after the disaster, you found a whole swarm of them, so many they seemed to spill out of the tree where they gathered, making a *pish pish pish* sound as they devoured the leaves. You were overcome by a rush of dizziness and felt your body split open. The emerald light scattered and pierced you. You braced yourself against the sharp pain.

It hasn't even been a year since Yonko last saw Mitch, but to her it feels like an eternity. He must look like an old man by now. There's still some hair left on his head, but most of it has gone grey. He wears reading glasses. Yonko knows all this, but still, it's difficult for her to imagine him this way. When she was a teenager, she used to wonder how a plain-looking girl like herself had ended up with two boys as dazzlingly good-looking as he and Kazu.

Kazu had been a big, muscular, brown-skinned boy. He always kept his eyes lowered, his head down, and his shoulders slumped, as though his body were unbearably heavy. But his curly black hair danced in cheerful spirals around his head, and sometimes he'd look up, as though lifted by those springy curls, and turn his large, shining eyes toward Yonko. His long eyelashes would flicker shyly, and a soft smile would appear on his lips. Yonko loved that smile and could never resist smiling back.

By contrast, Mitch was small and thin. He was quick and agile too, at least until he hurt his leg, running wherever he went, which always set the grown-ups on edge. Yonko used to tease him, saying he looked Spanish. Not that she knew any Spanish boys – it was his sharp, upturned nose and the curious colour of his eyes that gave her that impression. His eyes were brown but occasionally shone an emerald green.

Mitch had always hated cutting his hair. Instead, he'd let it fall in dark waves around his face. He would sneer at everyone he met, twisting his thin lips into the meanest expression he could muster. Eventually this habit left a permanent wrinkle that began just above the right corner of his lip and extended across his right cheek in a deep arc. But the sneer was always offset by a fragile light in his eyes.

Mitch, you chose to come back to Japan now of all times, transfixed by those insects as you stood beneath the Stewartia tree.

Yonko listens along with Mitch to the ceaseless *pish pish pish* of the insects inside the emerald world. It is the sound of insect time colliding with human time, which has come to a standstill. The radiation has caused the insects to overbreed, and they go on devouring time with their voracious appetite. They crowd and jostle each other on every branch, sometimes falling to the ground. From far away they look like clusters of rough, green fruit swaying in the wind.

Yes, it was windy there, too, Yonko remembers. The branches rustle in the damp, sluggish air, and her field of vision flickers in shades of green, making it difficult to tell who is hiding where. Kazu is crouched down, enveloped in green shadows. He is eight. Mitch is hiding in the same bush, feeling the movement of the wind on his face. Beyond the green is a wide expanse of water, glimmering white. Small waves ripple the surface each time the wind blows. An emerald green droplet borne on the wind lands on the water, reflecting the light. For a while, the glowing, dark green insect whirls around and around on the surface of the pond. At last, it begins to transform into the body of a girl floating face-down. Her orange skirt sways in the water, her hair undulating around her head.

No, you've got it all wrong!

pish pish pish pish

Yonko's head feels like it's splitting open. She frowns, tearing up.

No, I didn't get it wrong. I just don't want to remember. I can't.

Still, the memory calls her back again.

Look, there's Mitch and Kazu, in that bush over there.

Suddenly Yonko wants to run to them. But of course, she can't.

The two boys hold their breath as they crouch in the bush, staring at the white light reflecting off the water. They know how to hide themselves anywhere. Curling up, not moving a muscle. They open their mouths slightly, eyes wide and shining. From time to time, they look at each other and grin. Then Mitch notices another child hiding a short distance away from them. A little girl with bobbed hair.

Is that Yonko? What's she doing here?

It looks like someone else is with her, too, but he can't be certain.

Keep still, will you? Shh, quiet.

Beyond the bushes, the pond brims with muddy water after several days of continuous rain. Surrounded by a large grove of trees, it glitters at the bottom of a hollow, a stone bridge stretching across it. It looks like it might once have formed part of the garden of someone's estate, though now it lies in ruins. The neighbourhood children keep their distance from this damp and gloomy place. Oil pools on the surface of the pond. A dumping ground for all kinds of trash, it exudes a strange smell.

Come to think of it, a lot of radioactive material has probably accumulated in that pond by now – that's what you'd probably say, Mitch, Yonko thinks, addressing the absent older man.

A girl stands near the pond, alone. Yes, that's Miki-chan. Mitch and Kazu watch her as she stands at the edge of the water. Yonko, too, is crouched in the bushes, keeping perfectly still.

To this day, she doesn't understand why the boys stayed hidden in the bushes like that, watching Miki-chan from afar. Neither do Mitch and Kazu. Was it supposed to be a prank? Were they curious what she was doing in a place like this, all alone? Were they planning to jump out of the bushes and surprise her if they'd had just a few more minutes?

Yonko had always been enthralled by little Miki-chan's beauty. That day, she looked like a little French doll as she stood poised at the edge of the pond. Maybe that was why Yonko, Mitch and Kazu had been hiding in the bushes: to keep watch over her. Was that how it happened – or not at all? Was the whole thing just a child's fantasy? Even if they could ask Miki-chan herself, she would probably have no idea, either. It was as though she'd suddenly been swept up in a strong wind, and then . . .

At some point, the children spot one another hiding in the bushes. They could have stood up, or given up hiding and gone out to play, but they didn't. Every time the scene replayed in Yonko's mind, her chest would constrict and she'd feel faint. If only Miki-chan had been one step further from the edge. If only one of them had come out of the bushes. If only Miki-chan had been wearing a grey or a black skirt, or any other colour.

pish pish pish pish

The drone of the emerald insects envelops Yonko.

Tabo, an older boy from the neighbourhood, approaches Miki-chan from behind. She is wearing a short orange skirt. She tries to turn around but falls headfirst into the pond. The sound of something hitting the water. Her orange skirt disappears in a white splash, then fans out around her. The splash becomes a cloud of metallic green insects, which begin to flit around the pond. Mitch's eyes flash like scarab beetles, leaping from the bushes toward the pond. Kazu's hair stands on end. The whir of insect wings ripples the muddy surface of the pond. There, standing all alone in the green light, is Tabo.

Do you remember, Mitch? How many minutes passed before we crawled out of the brush, trembling as we approached the pond? Was Tabo still there? Or is that not how it happened? Even after all this time – or precisely because so much time has passed – we don't remember any of the crucial facts. What did we do? Who was there, really?

2

The old mother opens her eyes just a crack. Her eyes are heavy, creased with wrinkles, already wet with tears. In her dream, she'd heard the same sound over and over – a wave, someone sobbing. She always feels like she's wandering around inside the same dream, and just as she is on the verge of waking up and her eyelids begin to flutter open, it dissolves, disappearing without a ripple.

She lets out a long sigh. Her lower back hurts. So do her shoulders. She is used to pain and has developed a knack for living alongside it.

So I've made it through another night without dying, she thinks.

Every morning she is surprised to find she is still alive. And every evening she feels relieved when she lies down and closes her eyes, thinking, At last, I can die now. But evidently, she's managed to evade death yet again. She has no choice but to pick up where time left off yesterday. This empty time that might extend for decades, centuries even.

She puts on the eyeglasses she's had for fifteen years, the ones whose temples she's duct-taped to the rims; reaches for the thick zippered jacket she keeps folded beside her bed; and slips her arms through the sleeves. She long ago stopped bothering to undress before bed. But this jacket, the one with the ragged hem that used to belong to her son, is the only exception, as it's too uncomfortable to sleep in. She used to change into pyjamas before bed, but at some point she got into the habit of sleeping in her undergarments, then she'd stopped taking off her socks, and finally her pants. Now she doesn't even put away her futon in the morning, so she can collapse right back onto it at night. She never sleeps long anyway.

She crawls across the tatami floor toward the window and opens the faded curtains. Through the dirty panes, she can just make out the wall of the neighbouring house, illuminated by a streetlamp. There is no reason to open the curtains other than habit, since the dirty window mutes the light like frosted glass. Still, she looks up at the sky, waiting for it to grow light.

It's April, so the nights are getting shorter. That much she knows. But the chill of winter still clings to the old mother's body. She spends most of the year sunk in the depths of winter, the freezing darkness seemingly interminable, until the brief moment when a strange orange glare descends upon her before giving way again to the darkness of night. Today, the old mother hunches her shoulders against the cold. If she opened the window, it would be even colder. When the orange light came through, the cold clinging to her back would begin to melt into sweat, dripping down and pooling around her feet. For the old mother, that was the extent of the short season called summer.

Her mouth is parched. She groans as she drags her aching body to the bathroom. She never closes the door, since she lives alone. Back when her son used to live with her, she would lock the door, but now there is no need. She lowers her pants and underwear, then straddles the shaky toilet seat, surrounded by stacks of toilet paper. After her son died, she'd bought a lifetime supply. She figured that a 'lifetime' for her wasn't that long anyway, so she'd bought as much as the room would hold. The fact that she was still alive after her son had died such a miserable, lonely death made her so angry and disgusted with herself that she wished she could bury herself in toilet paper – as though she were trying to convince herself that she was worth less than a roll of toilet paper.

That's what she'd probably say, at any rate, if someone were to ask why she had so much of it. But thc young woman who visits her from time to time never asks anything of the sort, just eyes the mountain of toilet paper suspiciously. She always seems to be searching for proof that the old mother is losing her mind. Maybe she did have a screw loose – with the constant pain in her back, it would only be natural if her mind, too, had begun to break down. She had already accepted it. After all, look how long she'd lived. If only her mind would give way completely, things would be much easier. Unfortunately, she is still lucid enough for the woman to get on her nerves.

The old mother can't tell whether she's actually peed. After she's straddled the toilet for a while, she uses a modest amount of toilet paper, then pulls up her pants. She yanks the cord that hangs from the tank to flush the water, which always sends drops of water flying beyond the toilet bowl. She touches the toilet with a trembling hand. The wetness reminds her of melted snow running down a mountain. Instinctively, she scoops some water up from the toilet bowl and brings it to her mouth. She groans and dips her hand in again. This is death water, she thinks, the kind of water you're given on your deathbed. It tastes unexpectedly sweet. Everyone is born from water and dies in water.

Just then, the old mother becomes dizzy and slumps against the toilet, her head narrowly missing the bowl. As she crawls on her hands and knees, she sees the plastic lampshade swinging from the ceiling in the main room. She hears something, though only faintly, since she is hard of hearing now. It sounds like the entire apartment building is screaming. The windows rattle dramatically. Must be another earthquake, she thinks. But the stacks of toilet paper in the bathroom haven't fallen over, and no new cracks have appeared in the windows or walls. The old mother looks at the butsudan, the altar across the room. The room is dark, the altar small, and her glasses unfocused, so she can barely see. Still, the altar looks undisturbed. Only the six kamaboko boards, left over from packaged fish cakes, seem to have fallen over.

The old mother's eyes fill with tears again. There has been a series of big earthquakes lately.

Once, the young woman who came by the apartment to take care of the old mother asked whether she had heard the news.

Don't you ever read the newspaper? she'd said. You don't even have a TV here, do you? There was a huge earthquake, and then a tsunami. It was the worst one on record, a lot of people died or were injured. No, it didn't reach Tokyo, but that's not all. Do you know what a nuclear power plant is? Four of the ones in Fukushima exploded, spewing radiation everywhere. People were told to evacuate immediately, dairy farmers had to abandon their cows. Yes, some people even killed themselves out of despair. Radiation is a scary thing, you know. I want to move somewhere where there's no earthquakes or radiation, but I can't just abandon everyone I'm responsible for. I mean, without us, you wouldn't be able to survive. Still, to think something like this could happen in Japan . . .

The young woman had rambled on and on excitedly as she rubbed the old mother's feet with a damp towel, in what was apparently supposed to be a massage.

It's scary, you know, really scary, she repeated.

The old mother had let the woman's words wash over her, paying her no mind. The voice of her son as a little boy came back to her, and the smell of rain falling on the parched earth.

It's ra-di-o-ac-tive rain. They say your hair will fall out if you get rained on. So you have to buy an umbrella, okay, Mommy, you don't wanna go bald, do you?

Later, he'd brought home a broken black umbrella he'd picked up somewhere, or maybe stolen. It was an adult-size umbrella, and the mother had painstakingly mended the ribs and patched the holes in the fabric. Her son was delighted, and though the umbrella was too big and heavy for a child, he took it to his room and spun it around and around, accidentally shattering the light bulb that hung from the ceiling. It must have happened during the day, because the room hadn't gone dark even after the bulb broke. The mother just stood there in shock, staring at the shards of grey glass scattered all over the tatami. She could still picture the expression on her son's face as he held the open umbrella. The sight of his mouth hanging open was so funny, she'd forgotten to be angry and just laughed instead.

The old mother had heard the young woman rattling off a string of familiar words – *plutonium*, *strontium*, *Geiger counter* – so that the past and the present began to meld together. How old had her son been then? She herself had been young, too. It was always just the two of them, living a quiet life together. They were poor, but they never starved. She had no memories of the boy's father. They might have lived together, but only briefly. From the beginning, she'd raised her son on her own. As a young mother, she'd assumed that when he grew up, he'd find a job somewhere, get married and have children. Instead, they'd continued to live together on their own. Then her poor son had died all alone, and she had survived. She'd never thought she'd live this long. She'd always assumed she'd die before him. She'd lost track of how old she was – she knew only how old her son was when he died. He was just about to turn fifty-two.

*

No matter how much the young woman carried on about the tsunami, the earthquake and the nuclear disaster, the old mother showed no reaction, and from this the young woman concluded that the elderly woman was probably senile, that even if she had enough wits about her to manage her day-to-day affairs, she likely couldn't handle much more. Why should the old mother care, anyway? And with that, the woman had gone home. But the old mother understood. Every time there was an earthquake, the windows rattled and the whole building swayed so hard it threatened to collapse. Once, the tremors were so bad that the mortuary tablet, the six kamaboko boards, and the rice bowl filled with water had fallen off the altar. The plates and bowls in the kitchen had smashed to the ground. Grit fell through the ceiling. Cracks appeared in the walls. Somehow the windows had remained intact, except for a small crack in one corner that the old mother had patched with some paper.

Someone had stopped by after that, a man wearing black-rimmed glasses, perhaps the owner of the building, she wasn't sure. He inspected the crack in the wall but did not repair it. And it had been that way ever since. Another two or three earthquakes would probably do this apartment in. The old mother hoped that when the time came, she would be crushed along with the building, so she could finally leave this world. No doubt the super, or the owner, or whoever that old man was, was also hoping for another earthquake, so he could tear the building down and sell the lot. Of course, it wouldn't matter by then, since the world would have ended. But foolish, greedy people would always go on waiting and scheming.

There were no newspapers or televisions in her apartment, but the old mother had her son's radio, and after the last big earthquake she'd listened to the news about the tsunami assailing the entire Tohoku region. From the static and confusion among the newscasters, even she could tell that something terrible had happened. She was only a child during the Great Kanto Earthquake, so she didn't remember anything about it. Besides, she had been living in her rural hometown back then, not in Tokyo. A town in a basin, surrounded by mountains. It had been a long time since she'd heard from her family. After she left, there had been a war, years when bombs rained down from the sky. And after the war, she'd given birth to her son.

Even after the Kanto earthquake, even after the war, the world had somehow gone on. This time, however, it wouldn't.

So this is how the world ends, the old mother thought. If her son were still alive, he'd probably be afraid. At least she didn't have to witness that.

Most of the people who had been swallowed up by the tsunami had drowned, and those who survived were left to imagine what the dead had suffered. Although the old mother supposed there hadn't been enough time for them to feel much pain. She'd told her son this long ago: it's not the dead who suffer most, but the ones who go on living.

As long as we are alive, we can't escape the flow of time. On the banks of the river, the dead stand quietly swaying, unblinking, watching the people get swept away by the current of time. To the dead, the current seems terribly fast, but in fact, nothing is moving. The dead grow more and more numerous. The old mother and her son count them together.

After the earthquake subsides, the old mother walks over to the sink beside the toilet. Without realizing it, she's begun to cry again. Saliva is dribbling down her chin. She wonders just how much water is inside her body. Her mouth always feels dry, and though she didn't mean to cry, the tears and saliva seem to flow of their own volition. She wets her face at the sink, rinses her mouth, and drinks the water. For decades, this has been her little morning ritual. She'd been a mother, after all, which means she is always meticulous about her routine. She hadn't wanted her son to be a slob. And even though he is gone now, that motherly part of her remains. Her son led a meticulous life indeed, and died a meticulous death. In fact, he was so meticulous that his mother was the only person he could bear to live with. In the end, he had more grey hair on his head than she did.

Of course, she hasn't forgotten her younger self, nor the way her son looked when he was a baby. His little round nose. How soft his cheeks felt. How smooth his little arms and legs were. She'd continued working; she was a well of energy back then. She didn't care much about her appearance, but once in a while she'd put on a little lipstick. She'd even fallen in love with a man. He had thick, glossy black hair, and not a single wrinkle on his body. Year by year, her son grew bigger, bringing her an unexpected happiness.

That was a long time ago. So long ago, in fact, that it almost seems like someone else's memory. It depresses her that she still remembers. She wishes she could leave the past behind entirely. But when her life finally comes to an end and she reaches the gates of hell, when she is asked what was most important to her, she knows she will answer without a second thought that it was being the mother of her son.

The old mother approaches the window and looks out at the sky again. The darkness is beginning to lift. She watches it gradually fade to blue, then carries the rice bowl from the altar to the kitchen and changes the water. She can't fill it too much or it will spill. Slowly she carries it to the altar, then lights a stick of incense. Just picking up one of the sticks with her dry fingers requires enormous effort. As does lighting it with her hundred-yen lighter. For a long time, she'd used a different lighter, one that her son had left behind. When it finally expired, she thought about using matches, but couldn't bring herself to part with this trace of her son. So in the end she'd just bought another lighter. Someone had once told her to be careful with incense. Just like candles, they could start fires. Though what would it matter if this old apartment burned down, the old mother thinks, clicking her tongue. If she burned to death, so much the better – it would save someone the time and energy of having to cremate her. Still, it would be a shame if the fire didn't run its course and she were left liable for the damage, so she is careful to break the incense sticks in half whenever she leaves the altar.

It can hardly be called an altar at all – just an old tin box with a lid. This, too, is something her son had picked up somewhere and brought home with him a long time ago. The mother had polished it with a rag, then wrapped it in a floral-patterned cloth. Originally, she'd made it for the little girl. Little white and pink flowers, perhaps chrysanthemums, danced around the box. She'd made a mortuary tablet out of a kamaboko board and placed it on the lid. This had been the first tablet and was now the oldest. There is nothing written on it except a small red dot. She'd drawn it on with one of her son's coloured pencils. When it came time to add more mortuary tablets to the altar, she'd had the idea to differentiate them with coloured dots.

After her son died, she'd placed the urn with his ashes inside the tin box and put the mortuary tablet made of plain wood that the police officer had given her behind the other wooden tablets. The urn fit so perfectly inside the box that it seemed specially designed for it.

The makeshift altar the mother calls a butsudan has no connection to any priest, but that doesn't make it any less real to her. Every morning, she stands in front of it, chanting her sutras so the dead can rest easy as they enter nirvana. For decades since that fateful day, she's joined her hands in prayer at the altar in the morning, and again before going to bed. When her son was still alive, she'd forced him to pray alongside her. At first, just sitting in front of the altar had made the mother's whole body tremble and tears trickle out of her closed eyes. The son refused even to look at the tablet, cowering on the tatami instead.

But no matter how much he resisted, the mother forced him to read sutras in front of the altar twice a day. They had to. They were still alive. After a while, she stopped trembling, and the sutras grew longer. But every time they had to add another tablet, the trembling returned. Their shared solitude deepened, the darkness thickened. After her son died, the mother braced herself for some kind of change, but nothing happened, except that she now had to bear the loneliness of two people alone. It weighed on her, bending her back even more.

Nanmaida, nanmaida, kanjizai bosatsu gyō jin hannya haramitta . . . Fushō fumetsu fuku fujō fuzō fugen . . . Hannya haramitta ko toku anokutara . . . Gyatei gyatei haragyatei harasōgyatei . . . Gyatei gyatei haragyatei harasōgyatei . . . Kanjizai bosatsu gyō jin hannya haramitta . . .

The old mother doesn't know what the words mean, nor does she want to know, but she recites what she can of this sutra from memory, her lips moving automatically. She doesn't remember all of it, but she cobbles together the parts she does and repeats them over and over. Meanwhile, her thoughts continue.

Finally, the world is ending. Mercifully, it is ending. Everything will disappear. The end of the world is here, now. My son, I wanted us to be together on this day. But now I don't care. After all, the world has already ended. The tsunami. The radiation. I can rest easy now. I hated you, pitied you, feared you. I hoped and prayed we would die an early death together, believing there was no other choice. But you went and died all on your own. Leaving your mother behind. Leaving nothing but hurt, pain, and curses in your wake. I'm afraid, so afraid I can hardly breathe. But everything is coming to an end now. Thankfully, the world is vanishing. Mercifully, it is vanishing.

A little girl begins to dance in front of the old mother's eyes, spinning around and around. An older girl appears, too, smiling and waving, then opens her mouth as though to say something. But the old mother can't hear her. As she continues chanting, more and more girls appear. Not just children, but adult women too. As they twirl, their hair fans out around them. Her son is a child again, curled up underground like a cicada larva. He begins to shrink and contort as the girls go on trampling the ground. They leap and stomp vigorously over him. Some are tall, some are short, some have round faces, or square faces, or gaunt faces, but when they smile they all have the same expression. They each turn toward the old mother, calling out to her.

The old mother's face crumples with pity for her son. Every girl is wearing an orange skirt. The vibrant colour floods the mother's voice, her mind, her entire body. She writhes in anguish. The sound of her son sobbing surrounds her. For a long time, the wailing permeates the floor, the walls, the ceiling. The ground becomes sodden, then turns to mud before her eyes. The mud splatters the girls' feet, and her son sinks into it. The mother begins to writhe even more violently. Her breathing falters, she collapses on the tatami and lies there, unmoving.

When she finally gets up, the world outside is beginning to grow light. The darkness of the night is giving way to the darkness of morning. Once again, another day begins. It dawns as it always does, though the world might disappear at any moment. The old mother looks out the window, her cheeks wet with tears, and sighs deeply.

3

Why? Because it was a midsummer morning. (It occurs to Kazu that if he put it this way, perhaps Yonko would understand, even if she looked angry.) Because it was a midsummer morning. Because no other time of day feels so good. The sky was a cool, radiant blue, not a cloud in sight. It was a midsummer morning, and the temperature was rising by the minute. The transparent blue sky seemed to promise that something wonderful was about to happen. I was captivated by it, I opened my mouth and took a deep breath. Then my body became light, and for a moment I felt like I'd become a winged bird. That's why, you see?

Maybe if he'd said it like that, Yonko would have laughed in spite of herself, wiping the tears from her face as she murmured: Oh, Kazu, you never change, do you?

Kazu can almost hear her voice, picture her face contorting with grief. Whenever Yonko cried, she looked like a child again, and Kazu would get the urge to nuzzle her soft, round cheeks the way he used to. But then she might protest, complaining about his scratchy beard.

But the person nestled close to Kazu now is Mitch, not Yonko, and it's Mitch's voice Kazu hears – that much he can tell without opening his eyes, he knows that everything will be okay as long as Mitch is nearby. Besides, Yonko is supposed to be here soon.

Hey, I finally got a hold of her. She said she'll be right over. Nod or move your mouth if you can hear me, will you? You can't even do that?

Mitch sounds annoyed. Kazu could have sworn he'd been nodding in response to Mitch's questions, but evidently Mitch hasn't been picking up on it. Maybe he is just tired of talking to himself.

Kazu's thoughts drift back to Yonko, whom he is seeing for the first time in a long while. Though, when he thinks about it, he realizes it's only been about two years. But how long ago that seems now. The truth that Mitch and Hide had stumbled across was so frightening that Yonko and Kazu stopped talking, unable to look at each other or even talk on the phone. They tried to forget, since there was nothing they could do, no matter how much they wished otherwise. For two years, they tried to convince themselves: I've forgotten, I've forgotten. All this time, enveloped in an unnatural silence. As they continued to avoid talking to each other, they hoped their connection might fade on its own. Though perhaps what they really wanted was to escape their own past.

Kazu imagines Yonko running through the city, livid.

Why do you only call me at times like these? I told myself I wasn't going to have anything to do with you two anymore. I wanted to forget all about you!

The harsh summer sun glints off her glasses, her straight hair – although, Kazu realizes, he has no idea what her hair actually looks like nowadays. Her sweat glistens. He knows she must be in Tokyo somewhere, but for some reason he pictures her surrounded by a vast forest. The wind blows through the summer forest, and leaves rustle. Above her, little birds chirp, and wild rabbits and squirrels look on in astonishment as she runs past them. Sometimes she trips and nearly falls.

Careful, Yonko! If you fall and hurt yourself, too, we'll all be in trouble. You're already a ripe old lady.

So what? Yonko mutters to herself as she runs. I swear, you and Mitch are so selfish. Don't die, okay? Just hang on. You'll feel better when you see me. Wait right there.

Kazu nods repeatedly as he pictures Yonko running.

Of course I'll wait for you. I wish I could have seen you under better circumstances, but for some reason it never occurred to me. Don't get angry when you see me, okay? I promise I didn't do it on purpose. It's just that it was a beautiful midsummer morning and then, before I knew it, I ended up like this. That's all. I honestly don't know what was going through my mind at the time.

The reason I can't help thinking of all the excuses I'll make when she gets here isn't that I'm scared, Kazu tries to say to Mitch, who is sitting beside him. It's because I don't want her to worry about me.

But the words never materialize.

Kazu can perfectly picture Yonko's shocked expression when Mitch broke the news to her. Mitch had been surprised when he'd got the call from Tokyo, too. They had always assumed Kazu would outlive them both. To them, he was strong and sturdy, not likely to keel over at the slightest thing, and they'd expected he would take over their responsibilities when they passed and go on living forever.

A familiar scent drifts toward Kazu. He can see the sharp leaves of a holly tree. Raindrops, glimmering white, slide off each leaf, the sound of the drip, drip striking his eardrums like a song: a quietness that could only be called a raindrop song, a cheerful song. It was coming from the small holly tree visible through the glass door in the hallway, at the end of which is a bathroom and a sink with an enamel washbowl containing disinfectant.

Use this every time you wash your hands, okay? Mama always used to say to Kazu and Mitch. *That way you won't catch anything.*

Thinking back on it now, Kazu can confidently identify the scent as cresol. But as a child, he'd had no idea what it was called. The sound of rain and the smell of cresol, the sensation of the wood floors against his feet come back to him all at once. There were fine cracks in the wood, so you had to walk carefully to avoid splinters.

It's because they use cheap wood that these floors fall apart over time, Mama used to complain. I'd like to refinish them, but there are too many places to fix. I do want to get them to make less noise, at least. It's already loud as it is, but when you kids run around with no consideration for me, my headaches just won't go away.

The floors would squeak and groan when Kazu walked on them, the air would smell like disinfectant, the holly tree was visible through the glass door, and, on rainy days, he would be transfixed by the raindrops running off the leaves. On winter days, snow would pile on those leaves and they would droop under the weight of it, until finally the snow would slide to the ground and the leaves would snap back as though returning to life. On sunny days, those same leaves would glisten like a crow's feathers. In midsummer, the light reflecting off the glass door would be so bright it hurt his eyes.

Yes, light can be a weapon, too. Midsummer mornings are beautiful, but they can also kill. The atomic bomb was dropped on a midsummer morning.

Don't you get it, Yonko? If it hadn't been a midsummer morning, this never would have happened.

Kazu takes a deep breath. He wants to believe that he remembers Mama's house, where he'd lived with Mitch until they were twelve years old, but all that's left are fragments of memories. And when he tries to piece those fragments together, they don't add up to a whole house. If only he could stand in front of the real house again, he might be able to say with confidence: Yes, that's our house, see, there's the grime on the door, and the slant of the roof, it's all just as it was.

But now that the real house is gone, those memories aren't proof of anything. This was the house where ten-year-old Mitch had gotten trapped beneath the kerosene heater, leaving him with burns and a permanent limp, though the house itself never caught fire. Kazu remembers Mama tending to Mitch, asking herself why they'd ever bought that old thing in the first place.

He remembers the light blue curtains fluttering in Mitch's hospital room, the smell of medicine that followed him even after he was discharged. Luckily, his recovery was quick. He hadn't lost the ability to walk, but he did develop a bad temper. He'd always had something of a contrarian streak in him, but after the accident it became even worse.

Forty years have passed since then. Kazu suddenly has the urge to cry. What a short thing a human life is. He smells cresol, though this is the hospital, of course, not Mama's house. He pictures himself laid out on the clean bed. Mitch is sitting next to him, looking worried.

Now it's Kazu's turn to be in the hospital, Mama would probably have said if she were alive. He feels like he should be in pain, but he isn't. He can't seem to figure out what's wrong. Could it be that he's completely paralysed, or perhaps knocked out from anaesthesia? He wants to ask Mitch, who is going on and on about something. But he's not telling me what I want to know, Kazu thinks. Is it possible he could be brain-dead? No, that can't be. After all, here he is, having these very thoughts, thinking about Yonko, recalling specific memories.

He wants so badly to remember what happened when he fell from the tree, what he was feeling, but the crucial moment eludes him. It had been a conspicuously tall chinquapin tree, probably more than ten metres high. Maybe as he was moving from one branch to another he'd been captivated by the blue sky spreading out above him and suddenly lost his footing, falling to the ground headfirst. Then again, maybe that's not at all what happened.

He does remember thinking he was in trouble.

Kazu had heard that when people die their life flashes before their eyes in a fraction of a second, like a sped-up movie. But it hadn't been like that for him. Did that mean he wasn't in danger? He'd seen a flash, and he'd sensed that the flash was mocking him. And then, for a brief moment, he'd locked eyes with Tabo, who had been dangling from a tree branch. Or had he? He should have felt the impact of the fall, but he had no memory of that. Did that mean he'd lost consciousness before he hit the ground?

Mitch had been in Hokkaido when it happened, near Lake Shikotsu. He'd been staying at a guesthouse there, helping to record a song by two female singers he knew. They'd planned to broadcast it on a small radio station in Chitose, and though he'd initially wanted to record in a studio to minimize the amount of background noise, it had been a particularly hot day, so he'd wanted to go somewhere cool, and besides, he thought, singing by the lake might help set the mood. They were about to begin recording when one of the staff members at the guesthouse told Mitch there was a call for him from Tokyo.

Immediately, Mitch knew something bad had happened to Kazu.

Kazu had always carried a card with him that listed Mitch as his emergency contact. They were each other's only family. There were other people they considered like family, of course, including Yonko, but there were certain boundaries they couldn't cross, like asking for money.

Mitch and Kazu had been adopted by Mama when they were three years old, and raised like twins. In a way, they were more alike than actual twins. They never knew their biological parents, and they didn't want to know them, either. All they knew was that their fathers had been American soldiers. Which meant that they could have applied for American citizenship and been raised in the United States. But they'd refused. They had Mama, so why would they do that?

That was how they'd felt when they were young, but there was also a certain desire to flatter Mama as well. As long as she was there, they weren't afraid of anything. But Mama herself wasn't immortal. When she died, they had only each other. They had hoped to live together at one point, but eventually they'd given up on that idea. Even actual siblings have different personalities, and different things they want to do with their lives.

Mitch told Kazu that the person who found him had called an ambulance. Someone at the hospital had gotten hold of the card with Mitch's number and called him at the apartment in Chitose. But no one answered, so they'd called the other number written on the card, the one for the radio station, which then directed them to the guesthouse near Lake Shikotsu where Mitch was staying. Mitch had debated whether to postpone the recording or let his assistant take over, and in the end he'd opted for the latter, since it was unlikely he'd be able to get the singers to come out to the lake again.

I thought it was a solid plan, Mitch had told Kazu. They're only going to play the song on a local radio station, so it might not make a big splash, and we definitely won't make money from it, but still, it's better than nothing, right? They're supposed to send me the tape soon, so we can listen to it together. If it gets good reviews, I'll turn it into a CD and sell it. Though at that point I'll have to record it again in an actual studio, of course.

One of the female singers was someone Hide had introduced Mitch to when Mitch was in France. Hide had become interested in ethnomusicology in college, first for research and then as a hobby, and now he knew people in the field. The woman he'd introduced Mitch to lived in Brittany, in a little town in a department called Finistère, which meant 'end of the world', and Mitch had enjoyed a few meals with her, first with Hide and then just the two of them. She was only a local singer, but she was quite beautiful, with chestnut-coloured hair and eyes, and she had a rare talent for singing old Breton ballads.

Hide had told Mitch the singer was spending the summer in Japan, and that she wanted to go to Hokkaido and hear some Ainu songs while she was there. Hide had already made arrangements with a young Ainu singer, and all he needed was for Mitch to interpret for her.

Mitch had just managed to get a job at a local radio station, and it occurred to him that he could take advantage of his position to broadcast a recording of the singers there. He didn't want to spend all his time interpreting. Just recording the Breton singer would generate quite a buzz, but if he could get the Ainu singer to join her, it would be even more meaningful. Though he had to admit he was also motivated by the prospect of getting into the good graces of his workplace. He ran the idea by the two singers, letting them know that he wouldn't be able to compensate them. But they were happy to do it all the same.

The Breton singer was around forty years old, a beautiful woman, coquettish, with a cruel streak.

She looks like a young Anna Karina, Mitch had whispered to Kazu.

Let me guess, something happened between you two, Kazu wishes he could say to Mitch, teasingly. But he can't speak or move. All he can do is continue listening.

You think you're just a nobody from nowhere, don't you?

the beautiful female singer from Brittany had said to Mitch. I bet that's why you come up with ideas like this. But that's impossible. Take me, for example. Technically, my nationality is French, but my lineage is Breton. I used to not care about that kind of thing, but eventually I came back to it. Since there are so few people who can sing Breton songs, I thought, Why not sing them myself? My family was against the idea. They said people in Paris would laugh at me for being from the backwaters of France. That I should consider doing something more serious.

The young Ainu singer had told Mitch something similar: I don't even know the Ainu language. But if you want to become a singer, you have to brand yourself in some way. And the closest thing I had to that was being Ainu, so I thought, Hey, why not go with that. A lot of interesting things happened to me after that, and I'm enjoying life now. You know, I like that you're mixed and an orphan, and the odd colour of your eyes. There's something mysterious about you.

Had the two female singers really said all that to Mitch? And if so, how had he responded?

Kazu imagines Mitch looking perplexed, blinking rapidly behind his glasses. He smiles to himself. Of course Mitch would have secretly been happy. In any case, he was definitely exaggerating what the singers had said when he relayed it all to Kazu.

That morning, Mitch's group had met at the radio station in Chitose and headed toward Lake Shikotsu in a rental car. The call from Tokyo came in just as they were finishing up a leisurely pasta lunch at the guesthouse and were getting ready to head out to the lake. Mitch got on the bus alone, made his way to the airport, and was at Kazu's hospital by that evening.

I couldn't believe how fast I got here, Mitch had said when he arrived. Traveling at that speed would have been unthinkable when we were growing up. It almost made me dizzy, going from cool, relaxing Lake Shikotsu to this hot, noisy city so quickly.

The first thing Mitch did when he got to the hospital was check on Kazu, who was asleep at the time. Then he spoke to the doctors. Kazu had no idea what they discussed, since Mitch refused to tell him anything. The only thing he knew for sure was that he wasn't getting out of there anytime soon. Mitch paid Kazu's hospital bill and stayed in the apartment Kazu had been living in, never leaving his side except to eat and sleep.

Hey, what about your job? Kazu wants to ask Mitch. You aren't planning to stay here forever, are you? You have to leave eventually. Or are you not leaving because I'm going to die soon?

He certainly didn't feel like he was dying.

And today, Mitch had reached out to Yonko. Kazu supposed it had only been about a day since Mitch had got to Tokyo. What had he said to her, in their first phone call in two years? How had his voice sounded?

Yonko had been shocked to get Mitch's call, and she immediately dashed out of the store where she worked. It wasn't so much a store as a showroom in Hibiya that sold fancy beds. The interior was elegant, and the store clearly catered to rich people. Kazu, at least, remembered being impressed when he saw it. Yonko had got the job through someone she'd met at the hotel where she used to work – a job, in turn, that she'd got through someone Mama knew. Yonko had seemed to enjoy working at the hotel, but from the start, she'd found the job at the showroom boring, complaining that it had put her to sleep all year round.

But the minute Yonko got the call from Mitch, she was suddenly wide awake.

I'm going home early today, she called out, then took off running through the streets of Hibiya, telling herself, Run, run, then hopped on the first train to get to the hospital where Mitch and Kazu were.

I wish I could toss these heels, perhaps she thought as she ran. I can't run in these. Why is this train so slow? Wait for me, Kazu.

Is Yonko remembering what happened two years ago as she waits impatiently? Even if she wants to pretend like it never happened, wants to snip the past off clean, she can't. It always catches her off guard, comes back to life, clings to her as though to say: No, it's not over yet.

Is Yonko frightened as she runs?

So nothing's changed, then. What's going to happen if you die, Kazu? Back then, just thinking about you and Mitch made me sick. I couldn't take it anymore. I decided there was no point in forcing myself to see you. So why does this connection we had as kids keep coming back, no matter how much I try to run from it? You'd think that traumatic experiences would feel less intense the further they recede in time, but no, they only become larger and more frightening. To think that we were nursing this dread together the whole time.

As Yonko runs, a scream rises in her throat. Trees appear around her, the trees become a forest, the forest deepens, the branches of the trees sway. A large deer looks up, stunned at the sight of her, then bounds away. The birds fuss and cry. This time Yonko is the one who is startled by them.

It's strange, isn't it, Yonko? Kazu thinks. Why am I picturing you running through a forest? You're pulling the forest around yourself, but you go on being frightened of it. You always were a scaredy-cat.

It's true. Kazu remembers. When they'd first met as children, Yonko's eyes had grown wide. Her jaw dropped at the sight of the two boys, and she immediately turned away. She was only three years old then. Kazu and Mitch were four. She'd had a little bowl cut, and when she turned around, the hair on her nape was clipped so close to her skin that Kazu had the urge to place his hands over it to keep her warm. But Yonko probably would have cried and run away if he'd done that.

She'd given them the same look of astonishment when she'd come to the hospital with her mother to see Mitch after his accident, and when she'd seen Mitch and Kazu off at Haneda Airport as they were leaving to go to a boarding school in England, and when they'd come back to Japan at fourteen. It was a look that seemed to say: Who in the world are you?

And two years ago, Yonko had been so taken aback by what she'd heard that her mouth hung wide open. I can't breathe, she'd gasped. Hide and Mitch, who'd gently broken the news to her and Kazu, were just as distraught, their shoulders and hands twitching from time to time.

Of course you remember, don't you, Yonko? You were crying then. It's too painful, you kept murmuring to yourself. I don't know what to do. I didn't want to know all this. It's too much.

Kazu had wanted to hold Yonko close then, but he'd felt unable to. Eventually he noticed Mitch embracing her from behind.

As she runs, frightened, Yonko remembers seeing Kazu's trembling hands on that day two years ago and wishes she could grasp them now. The skin on his hands was always thick and rough from gardening, and he could never get the dirt out from under his nails, no matter how many times he washed them. And his fingers would always tremble. He would put his hands in his pockets or curl them into fists out of embarrassment, but within seconds they would be visibly trembling again.

It's like time has suddenly leapt across from then to now . . . and to hear that you've been injured like this, Yonko thinks bitterly as she runs. If you end up dying, Kazu, I swear . . .

No, you can't die now, Kazu, not you, too. What was I doing for the past two years? Those are two years I can never get back. Years when fear permeated my dreams.

I used to cry out in my sleep: Kazu, help me! Mitch, where are you? Please, come quick. But when I woke up, I'd convince myself that seeing you two was out of the question. That it was all over now.

Is Yonko recalling that time two years ago when Mitch had just come back from Brittany, completely uncertain of his future, how he'd followed her and Kazu around everywhere, critical of everything and everyone around him?

If you can't handle Japan, why don't you go somewhere else again, Kazu had snapped at him. You're the one who refuses to settle down.

After that, Mitch had disappeared for a while, and Yonko began to worry.

He's not a child, Kazu had said. He's in his fifties. Honestly, it's embarrassing.

In Brittany, Mitch had been taken in by someone he said was a 'sorcerer'. He took care of the livestock, helped with the farm-work and housework, and gathered driftwood from the shore, which the sorcerer would use to make sculptures. Mitch wanted to learn sculpture, too, at least the basics, but that never came to pass. The sorcerer was always telling him to listen to 'the voice of the driftwood', but he could never hear it. He didn't understand his teacher's ideas about beauty. The reason the man was called a sorcerer was that he was known for his ability to cure illnesses. People came all the way from England to see him, and he made quite a bit of money from that. Sculpture didn't pay, but medicine did.

If that's the case, why don't you focus on your 'sorcery', Mitch had suggested to him one day. When it comes down to it, isn't sculpture a bit self-indulgent?

In response, the sorcerer had flown into a rage, firing Mitch and even casting a spell on him. At which point Mitch had had no choice but to go back to Japan for a while.

At least, that's how Mitch had explained it to Yonko and Kazu.

Just when Kazu, too, was beginning to worry about Mitch being unemployed and not having a stable place to live, he'd shown up out of the blue with Hide in tow. Hide had lived in the same orphanage as his mother, Joyce, so Mitch treated him as his adopted child. Hide adored Mitch. Perhaps it was because Joyce had always told him how fond she was of Mitch, or how the first time she'd ever prayed in earnest was when Mitch went to the hospital after he burned his leg. Before that day, Hide hadn't told Yonko or Kazu, or even Yonko's daughter, Sara, that he was still seeing Mitch. Nor had he told them about the two newspaper articles that Mitch had found – which is why everyone had kept their distance from Hide for a while afterward.

That day, Mitch had turned to Yonko and Kazu and gotten straight to the point. When the sorcerer from Brittany kicked me out, he made three prophecies as a parting gift. Unfortunately, they seem to be coming true. The first one is that, in the near future, a person who has harboured a fear inside himself for a long time, a fear he could never tell anyone about, will die, and that fear, released from his body, will spread to those around him. The second prophecy is that I or someone close to me, so close as to be inseparable, will die a sudden death. I can only assume that's you, Kazu – meaning one of us is going to die. Keep in mind that the bastard probably just made this up to get back at me, so don't worry too much about it. After all, everyone dies when the time comes. And then the final prophecy. This one is much grander in scale. He said that one day, the Japan where I was born and raised will be swallowed up by the sea, and that a mysterious evil spirit will take up residence there. Can you believe it? The old geezer wasn't content to put a curse on me alone, he had to curse the whole of Japan! An evil spirit, he said. I almost laughed out loud. Anyway, you don't have to worry about this one, either. It might happen someday a hundred, maybe a thousand, years in the future, of course. The first prophecy is the one we need to worry about.

When Mitch finished talking, he took out a cigarette and scowled at Yonko and Kazu over his glasses. His eyes giving off a faint green light. Because Mitch was prone to exaggeration, Kazu had assumed he was making most of this up. How much of this had the 'sorcerer' actually said? Maybe the sorcerer himself was a figment of Mitch's imagination. But why would Mitch invent such an elaborate – and ominous – lie?

Mitch, I still can't make up my mind about it. I want you to tell me, but is it too late?

The four of them – Mitch, Kazu, Yonko and Hide – were at the local park, the one where Kazu's garden was. One corner of the park was fenced off with wire netting, and several boys were practising basketball there. It was a lovely, clear autumn evening.

Wait. That's how I remember it, but I'm not sure that's how it really was. There's something wrong with my brain. I went to that park so often that all my memories of it are bleeding into each other.

Do you remember, Mitch? It was an autumn day. I think Yonko was wearing a soft, fluffy, cream-coloured cardigan.

An image of Yonko's hair, straight as ever, strands of grey coming in here and there, appears in Kazu's mind. He's pretty sure she was wearing a scarf then, but he can't remember what colour it was. Not to mention what Mitch and Hide were wearing – that he doesn't remember at all.

Mitch had narrowed his eyes, paused to take a drag of his cigarette, and gone on. Hide wrinkled his forehead, glancing at

Mitch uncertainly. Mitch read the newspaper every day, from front to back. He had to, as long as he was in Japan. That day, he'd bought several from the kiosk as usual, combing through them carefully, and eventually found a short article. That was the first one. It was from ten days ago. It said that the body of a nineteen-year-old girl had been found on a road in Toshima Ward, in Tokyo. She had been strangled with a torn skirt, which had been left around her neck. A passer-by mistook the orange colour of the skirt for blood and ran to a nearby store in a panic, saying there was a corpse with its head cut off.

This again.

Mitch felt completely alone. Tears rolled down his face. How many times did this have to happen? It had been years since the prior incident. He kept hoping and praying that each one would be the last, but every time he'd be proved miserably wrong. The same event, repeating itself over and over, till it made you sick.

Two days later, Mitch had called Hide and told him about the murder. Hide had already heard the whole story from Yonko, beginning with Miki-chan's death, but he went pale as he listened.

So it was all true, then, Hide murmured. It's not that I doubted it, but it didn't feel real until now. Should I call the police, say I'm a friend of the victim? I want to know exactly what happened.

The next day, Mitch found another article in the newspaper. He wasn't going out of his way to look for murder cases involving the colour orange. After all, it was highly unlikely that such similar cases would occur so close together. He just happened to come across it. He hadn't wanted to find it, but when he did, he told Hide right away.

You don't have to call the police anymore. Did you already call them?

Thankfully, Hide hadn't. Every time I tried, I couldn't bring myself to, he explained. What's wrong, did something else happen?

Mitch handed him the article. Hide took his time reading it, and by the time he was finished, he was in tears.

I can't believe this . . .

It was an article printed in the News Tidbits section of the paper. A fifty-one-year-old man had been found hanging from a sakura tree in a corner of Yanaka Metropolitan Cemetery in Taito Ward. He'd left no will. He was single, unemployed, on welfare, and had been living with his elderly mother in an apartment in Toshima Ward.

Rumour had it that forty-two years ago, when the man was a boy, he'd pushed a little girl into a pond and killed her. When police looked into the incident, they'd discovered that there really had been an incident in which a seven-year-old girl had died by drowning in a pond. The girl was a mixed-race orphan who'd been abandoned by an American GI. For the older residents and the local police, her death recalled Japan's wartime defeat.

Mitch looked at Yonko and Kazu. Both of them were already trembling, their faces frozen in horror.

You get it, right? This is about Tabo. The prophecy came true. When I discovered the first article, I wasn't sure what to do. But talking with Hide convinced me that we needed to tell you right away. Waiting wouldn't change what happened, and besides, we couldn't carry this knowledge by ourselves. I guess Tabo's fear swelled up so big inside him that it eventually killed him. And now that fear is going to invade our bodies, too, at least according to the sorcerer. We've felt so much fear up till now, but the fear we're about to encounter will be much more concrete. What could we have done? I feel like we kept doubting and doubting, until finally we drove Tabo into a corner. We even asked ourselves, over and over, if we were the real murderers. No matter how many times we tried to convince ourselves it wasn't true, that uneasiness never went away. But we won't go to the police. What good would that do? He'd already died.

Really? You're sure there's no point? Yonko had moaned.

Yesterday we went to this person Tabo's house, Hide added quietly. The apartment from forty-two years ago had been torn down, but Yonko's mother knew that Tabo and his mother were still living in an old apartment nearby. She'd caught a glimpse of Tabo's mother once and followed her home, which is how she found out where they were living. It was a run-down building that looked like it was about to fall apart.

Mitch knitted his brow and continued where Hide had left off.

Tabo never was able to leave, even though it must have felt like the scariest place in the world. And his mother, of course, is still living in the same place where her poor son died.

It was then, or perhaps a little before, that Yonko's daughter, Sara, appeared. She was the spitting image of her mother. She gazed shyly up at Kazu and Mitch, her straight black hair swaying.

A wave of nostalgia comes over Kazu, as though he's suddenly been thrust back into that time, and he shivers. If he didn't say something, he felt like the fear would swallow him whole.

And then? he whispered to Mitch in a hoarse voice. What happened after that? Did you see Tabo's mother?

Of course not. What do you think would happen if she recognized us? It would be even riskier for you, Kazu.

Are we going to be killed? Kazu whispered.

Did I really say that, Kazu thinks. Two years have passed since then. A bitter taste rises in the back of his throat.

Do you remember, Mitch? I'm sure the story in the article

was real, but what about the sorcerer's prophecies? Did that really happen? The first one was spot-on, and the second, well, I guess it's happening to me right now. But you know, Mitch, it's strange: when I think about dying, I don't feel scared. I was way more afraid two years ago. In fact, you might be more scared than me right now. Mitch, what's going to happen to you if I die? Are you going to go all the way to Brittany and kill the sorcerer? Promise me you won't do that.

Kazu looks at Mitch, who is sitting on a chair next to his bed. Mitch tries to say something to Kazu, stands up, paces across the hospital room, sits back down.

Yonko's late, Mitch mumbles to himself. She always was a bit slow, wasn't she, and besides, it's sweltering today, you feel like you're suffocating when you step outside, Lake Shikotsu felt like being in another world, how great would it be if we could all go together . . .

Kazu knows Mitch must be thinking of Tabo, too, but if he is, he doesn't say it aloud.

Two years ago, Mitch hadn't tried to answer Kazu's question, just flashed his green eyes at him.

. . . What were we even doing at that pond? Yonko had said, avoiding Sara's gaze as her daughter approached her. To this day, I still don't know. That's why it never ends.

Sara looked quizzically at her mother's drawn expression, as though to say, What are you talking about? What do you mean?

Yonko was hanging her head, reaching her hands out in front of her and moving them through the air as though searching for something. Mitch grasped her hands, then embraced her. Tears fell from her eyes.

Two years had passed since then. Yonko should be coming through the hospital entrance any minute now.

Kazu thinks of the heat outside. She's probably bathed in

sweat. She can't run through the air-conditioned hospital, so she walks quickly down the hallway, gets on the elevator. She wipes her face with a handkerchief, catches her breath. What floor is this? The display in the elevator flashes 2, then 3, then 4. Kazu isn't sure what number the elevator stops at, but Yonko watches for a certain number, then waits for the doors to open. She presses her right hand to her chest, bites her lip.

Mitch, Yonko's almost here.

Kazu gets the urge to push Mitch. Yonko's going to walk into this room, with the scent of her sweat, he wants to say to him. At first, she'll sneak in here quietly. Then when she realizes you're here, she'll break into a smile, slowly approaching my bed one step at a time.

Kazu focuses on the nerves in his ears and nose.

See? The air in the room just changed. That familiar forest smell is flooding the room.

The smell of cresol fades away.

Because it was a midsummer morning. Kazu practises forming the words in his mouth so he can answer Yonko as soon as she asks him the question.

There wasn't a cloud in the sky. It was blue, and shimmering. The kind of midsummer sky that promises something wonderful is about to happen. A midsummer sky. That's why I felt like I'd become a winged bird. You get it, don't you, Yonko? A midsummer morning – beautiful, but frightening, in that it can kill a person. After all, the atomic bomb fell from a midsummer sky, too. That's why, you see?

4

Kazu was the one who saw Mama crying, not me.

A cold rain is falling.

Oh.

The tiny raindrops turn to white light, whizzing so fast they make Yonko dizzy. One after another, countless raindrops scatter through the air, then fly off. Mitch's voice disappears into the rain, and Yonko can barely hear him, though she is walking right beside him. They have to whisper so Mama doesn't hear.

Yonko and Mitch are huddled under a blue umbrella and trailing the others – Kazu, with his backpack, and Yonko's mother, who is carrying a big cloth bag and talking with Mama about something. Mitch drags his left leg a little as he walks. I wonder if it still hurts from the burn, Yonko thinks. Mitch hates when people comment on his leg. Yonko doesn't want to anger him, so she pretends not to notice. She consciously matches her pace to his. She doesn't want to hurt his feelings by walking too quickly.

I couldn't believe it . . . , Mitch mutters, as though to himself. Yonko nods along. Kazu occasionally turns around to look at them. He knows what they're whispering about. Maybe Mama and Yonko's mother know too, Yonko thinks.

It has been drizzling since morning. The early spring rain is cold, and Yonko is disappointed that she and her mother will have to go back to Tokyo in this weather. How warm the light was that poured over us just yesterday, she thinks. If only the weather had held up for just one more day, Sachi might not have struggled to hold back tears when we were saying goodbye, and Mother Asami might not have given us such a melancholy look.

Yesterday, Saturday, Mitch and Kazu had been spellbound by the sea, which glittered silver far below them, and by the little buds on the trees just beginning to open, and by the faint spots of green appearing among the wilted grasses, and, above all, by the scent of soft dirt, something they'd never encountered in Tokyo. How Kazu must have longed to break away from the group and wander off without a care in the world! But of course, each of them had been assigned a task, and he couldn't make an exception for himself. Gentle Kazu didn't pout or do anything of the sort. But Yonko imagined that every time he had to deny himself in this way, a dream was growing a little bigger inside him – a dream of having a garden of his own.

In the morning, Yonko's mother took a group of them to go shopping near the train station, while the rest stayed behind to clean and do laundry, and in the afternoon the children in the orphanage raced each other and went treasure-hunting on the hill out back, and at night they had a farewell party for Sachiko, who was going to America. The farewell party also doubled as a birthday party for Mitch and Kazu, since that was the day they'd been brought to the orphanage.

It's not like we were sickly babies on the verge of death, Mitch had told Kazu long ago. They said we were healthy and slept through the night.

But Kazu was sceptical. Say what you want, he mumbled, turning his face away from Mitch. It's not something we can know for sure. The fact is that we were abandoned at birth.

Yonko imagines the two infants with different skin tones

wrapped in clean blankets, brought to the orphanage with great care. They must have slept soundly, their long eyelashes fluttering from time to time. Where they had been born, and under what circumstances, who had brought them here – there is no need to think about any of that now. Surely no one had wished misfortune upon them, surely their mothers would have raised them if they could have. You see – Yonko wishes she could say to Mitch and Kazu – the important thing is, you didn't die. You became Mama's children. And you became part of my family. Isn't that a beautiful thing?

But the words sound forced, and she can't bring herself to say them out loud. Maybe she was the only one who was really happy about it, and anyway, how could she possibly know what it felt like to be a mixed-race orphan? When she thought about it that way, there was really nothing she could say.

The day the two babies finally arrived at Mother Asami's home in March became their official birthday. They were given the names Michio and Kazuo, Mitch and Kazu for short. Yonko didn't know what they had been called before. They'd taken Mama's last name when she'd adopted them. Yonko's mother had told Yonko that, since Mama wasn't married, she'd had to jump through endless bureaucratic hoops. And after all that, the state decided it would recognize Mama only as Mitch and Kazu's legal guardian. Of course, this didn't affect anything about their actual lives. Mama was their mother.

And yesterday had been Mitch and Kazu's twelfth birthday.

Mama normally didn't cook much, but that day she went all out, buying a cookbook and enlisting the help of Mother Asami and Yonko's mother to make a feast so magnificent it was like Christmas: a whole roast chicken, sandwiches, potato salad, and for dessert a cake coated in fluffy white cream. The children ate so much they were full to bursting. They took turns singing and dancing, and by the end of the day, everyone was so boisterous that an observer might have thought they were drunk. Everyone laughed at Mitch's stupid jokes till tears rolled down their faces, and Sachi's and Yonko's impersonations were a huge hit.

Yonko imagined that Sachi's talent for impersonation would help her in America, since it meant she'd be able to get by without English. The white couple who were supposed to adopt her were arriving next week. They would travel around Japan with Sachi before taking her back home to somewhere in America. If Sachi was scared, she didn't show it. She followed Yonko around all day with a big smile on her face.

It was past nine o'clock by the time the children wore themselves out and dragged themselves upstairs to bed, hurriedly washed their faces, brushed their teeth and burrowed into their futons. Since they were the guests, Yonko and her mother were allowed to sleep in Mother Asami's room. But the women were grown-ups, and didn't need to go to bed just yet. They lingered in the dining room, where the lively laughter that had filled the room all day still echoed through the air. The three of them – Yonko's mother, Mama and Mother Asami – were old friends and were getting ready to have some drinks and adult conversation.

After the orphanage had quieted down, Sachi came into Mother Asami's room wearing her pink flannel pajamas.

Can I sleep next to you, Yonko? she called out.

Of course you can, come here, Yonko answered.

She was grateful Sachi had come, since she'd felt uneasy about sleeping in this unfamiliar room all by herself. Right away, she lifted the cover and motioned for Sachi to get in quick.

Come on, get in, you must be freezing!

As soon as she got under the covers, Sachi clung to Yonko, pressing her body close to her friend's. But she didn't cry. Yonko could feel her heartbeat. How fast it was pounding! All she could do was stroke her hair – this girl who would soon become an American child. She didn't want to think about how this was their final night together, nor was it something she could say to Sachi, who was still only nine. Sachi's hair was jet-black, silky-smooth. It felt nice to touch. Yonko wondered if it was her beautiful hair that the white couple had fallen in love with.

In the small hours of the morning, Yonko stirred awake. Mother Asami and her mother were still gone. The white fluorescent lamp on Mother Asami's desk was the only light in the otherwise deserted room. The damp, heavy air weighed on Yonko's chest. Outside, it had begun to rain. Sachi was sleeping quietly on her side, curled up into a little ball, both hands tucked under her chest. For a moment, Yonko wondered whether she was still alive and reached out to nudge her cheek. It was soft and warm. Sachi slept on. After tucking her back in, Yonko burrowed under the covers. This place, so close to the ocean, was much colder than Tokyo. She closed her eyes, waiting for sleep to come.

It was right around then that Mitch and Kazu were whispering to each other in their room – or so they told Yonko later. Mama hadn't returned to her room yet. It was the middle of the night, and she was still in the dining room with Yonko's mother and Mother Asami, crying. That's what Kazu had told Mitch when he'd come back from the bathroom.

What happened next? Yonko asks Mitch quietly, her head spinning as she watches the glistening white raindrops. Five metres or so up ahead, Mama is walking with Kazu along the muddy street in her fancy brown shoes. She staggers a bit from time to time under the weight of the bag she is carrying. She is immersed in conversation with Yonko's mother. Her stockinged shins are flecked with mud and sand. Everyone's shoes are dirty.

But my shoes are probably the dirtiest, Yonko thinks. Her

mother always scolded her, saying it was because of the way she walked that Yonko's shoes always got so dirty. On rainy days, not only her legs but her skirt would get covered in mud. Yonko didn't know how she was supposed to walk to avoid getting so dirty.

Mitch, who had worn long pants ever since his accident, is looking at the dirt around his feet. The dirt is mixed with sand, a sign that they aren't far from the ocean, and it crunches underfoot with every step. Little raindrops glisten like frost all over his hair and navy coat. Yonko sees Mitch's eyes glitter green as she walks beside him. Kazu keeps glancing back at them from up ahead.

Be careful! Mama hears everything. Don't make her mad. She's still feeling delicate, you know.

There's no doubt that Kazu is overhearing, however vaguely, everything that Mama and Yonko's mother say.

Tell us, Kazu, what are they saying? Yonko wants to ask. But Mama is right there, so she can't. What is your mama so upset about? Why is she so sad?

Mitch and Kazu had been whispering to each other in their room last night until the early hours of the morning. They'd tried to figure out why Mama had been crying, but just thinking about it made their chests hurt. Or maybe it wasn't that they couldn't, so much as that they didn't want to. Each wanted to hide his uneasiness from the other. The first thing they needed to do was find out whether Mama was actually crying. The rest they would worry about later. They pulled their coats on over their pyjamas and tiptoed toward the dining room, where Mama and the other adults were, Mitch dragging his bad leg behind him. The day's happiness still lingered, and the sight of Mama's tears had caught both of them off guard.

Caught you off guard?

Mitch nods slowly as he looks down at the mud.

Yeah. We were too busy celebrating to notice anything.

But it was your birthday, Yonko says gently. This was exactly the kind of trite consolation that Yonko's mother might offer. Mitch's face looks pale beneath his blue umbrella.

It was just a birthday, but we were so excited about it. Stupid, right? Twelve years old and still acting like children.

The previous night, Mitch and Kazu had been in a near-manic state, laughing and throwing pillows at each other even after they'd laid out their futons, laughing as they pulled on their pyjama pants, laughing at how hard and damp the futons were.

These futons are awful, they said.

They probably haven't been used in forever. They smell like cats.

Their birthday had filled them with such contentment that as soon as they crawled onto their futons and closed their eyes they immediately sank into a deep sleep, as though they'd slipped into a hole.

Kazu had drunk too much juice before bed, and he woke up after a few hours needing to pee. If he held it in, he'd probably wet his bed. How embarrassing that would be as a twelve-year-old – he'd never be able to face Yonko or the others again. He got up and walked toward the bathroom, still half-asleep. But by the time he returned to his room, he was wide-awake. Mitch was fast asleep, but Kazu shook him desperately, whispering in a shaky voice: Mama's crying.

The reason Kazu's voice was shaking had more to do with how cold it was than his actual emotional state. He was wearing only pyjamas, and he'd gone to the bathroom barefoot. Maybe it was their body warmth that made the room feel warmer than the hallway and bathroom, which was as cold as the dead of winter.

This time the two of them put on coats over their pyjamas

and slipped socks on their feet before tiptoeing out into the hallway. The dark hall went on and on, they were like explorers making their way through a cave. By this time, the rest of the children were fast asleep. They could hardly be called children, since the average child was now eight, and there were fewer of them each year. Now there were just eight-year-old Takeshi and three others. Sachi would be gone in a week. Before long, the rest, too, would be adopted by someone from America or sent off to a family in Japan. It was less likely for children to be adopted after the age of twelve, at which point they'd be taken in as apprentices at factories or shops. And when there were no children left, the orphanage would close and Mother Asami would have to move to a smaller house where she could live on her own.

It must be lonely now with only four children, Mitch and Kazu might have thought as they crept through the hallway. Back when they'd lived here, there'd been too many children to count. At least fifteen, probably more. But Mama had adopted them when they were only three, so their memories of the orphanage were hazy at best. Of course, they'd come back with Mama every now and then for special occasions, like Christmas, or when someone was going to America. It was always lively at the orphanage. There were three other children around the same age as them whom they were close to. And then there was Mu-chan and Eri-chan, the two older girls who helped Mother Asami. Mitch was fond of Eri-chan, with her round face and cheerful demeanour, while Kazu preferred the slender, quiet Mu-chan. Even after Mama adopted him, Eri-chan wouldn't hesitate to pull Mitch into her large bosom whenever he asked. Gentle Mu-chan taught Kazu the names of flowers. Sweet peas. Zinnias. Virgin's bowers. Four-o'clocks. Marigolds. Cosmos.

Yonko and her mother used to go with Mitch and Kazu when they visited the orphanage. Yes, she, too, remembers when it was still full of children. She hasn't forgotten Mu-chan's and Eri-chan's faces either. They looked to be about high school age. Yonko, whose mother was her only family, used to feel jealous of the children in the orphanage, who had so many friends to play with. Life with her mother made her feel trapped, stifled. But every year, at least one child would leave the orphanage. And then another and another. When she was eleven, Yonko finally understood: there were no more mixed-race children coming to the orphanage. Mother Asami was completely exhausted and had run out of money.

In the dining room, there was a window facing the hallway. The bathroom was next to the dining room, so if Mama and the others noticed Mitch and Kazu there, they could just say they were on their way to the bathroom. They peeked through the window. The glass had once been transparent, but now it was cloudy. The first thing they saw was Yonko's mother's back. She was wearing a dark red shawl over her shoulders. Behind her was the gas heater. Mother Asami was sitting at an angle that made it difficult to see her expression from the hallway. Mama sat on the other side of the heater. Her right hand was covering her mouth, and she was hanging her head. The room was big enough to seat twenty or so people, and they'd had many events there in the past. But right now, there were only three adults gathered in the corner, talking quietly. So quietly that Mitch and Kazu couldn't make out what they were saying. The overhead light was off, so that only the red light from the gas heater illuminated the women's bare faces. Mama adjusted herself in her chair and turned toward Yonko's mother. Yonko's mother nodded and said something. They could see Mother Asami's hands moving. Mama's cheek glistened. They could see the reflection of the light from the heater on her cheek, a glittering red spot.

Mitch and Kazu both saw the red spot at the same time and

looked at each other. Then they hurried back to their room. Mama hadn't noticed them. Probably. It was possible the three women had noticed but had pretended not to. Adults often did things like that. In any case, Mama had definitely been crying. For Mitch and Kazu, that was proof enough. When they got back to their room, they looked at each other again, but no words came to them. They were too tired to think clearly.

Let's just go to sleep, Kazu said as he crawled back into bed. There's nothing we can do. Maybe there are some things kids aren't supposed to know.

Mitch pulled the covers over himself, too. Mama still wasn't back. But when they woke up the next morning, there she was, sleeping beside them, her mouth partially open, snoring lightly. They couldn't bring themselves to wake her. Sachi and Takeshi were already banging on the door, yelling that it was time to get up.

So . . . that's it? Yonko whispers to Mitch, keeping an eye on Mama ahead of her.

Yeah, that's it. We obviously can't ask Mama about it, and we can't ask Mother Asami or your mum either. But I know she was crying. I saw it. Mama never cries unless it's something really bad.

Mitch wipes his runny nose. Kazu turns around to look at them and nods slightly, as though he can hear them from up ahead.

Yonko isn't sure which of them he's nodding at, but she nods back. Has Mitch caught a cold? Or is he crying? Why is he so concerned about Mama, even though he is only twelve years old? It seems strange to Yonko.

Maybe Mama just had too much to drink, she considers saying to Mitch. Maybe she was crying over something silly. But when she sees his pale, serious face, she can't bring herself to say the words aloud. What had Mitch meant when he said 'really bad'?

The rain begins to fall harder, the sludge on the road thickens. Only a little further to the station. When they get there, she'll have to say goodbye to Mitch and Kazu. They will get on a bus and go back home to Yokohama, to Mama's house, about thirty minutes up a hill. And Yonko and her mother will go back to Tokyo by train. Yonko's mother had to be back for work, but Yonko was on summer vacation, so she would have preferred not to rush back. But she knew her mother would never let her get on the bus with Mitch and Kazu.

Suddenly her mother turns around and looks at her. Yonko becomes frightened and looks down. Mitch glances at her, then at Yonko's mother and Mama. Kazu observes everyone quietly, carefully, then takes a deep breath.

Mitch has gone completely silent now, and there is nothing Yonko can do but hang her head and ponder what that 'really bad' thing could be. The sandy mud is on her sleeves now. Her red coat grows heavier by the minute. As soon as they get to the station, she is sure her mother will yell at her for not being more careful. And then Yonko won't be able to ask her anything at all. What were you all talking about last night, Mum, did something sad happen, she wishes she could ask. But children can't just go around asking questions of adults – especially questions that might cross the boundary of the innocent world that adults have constructed for them. Adults are always on guard against children, keeping them far away from their secrets. And children notice, careful never to get too close to those secrets, either.

As they approach the station, little stores begin to appear on either side of the road. The station is close to the ocean, so many stores here sell fish and fishing gear, and the restaurants serve fresh fish. Yonko and Mitch don't particularly like fish, so they aren't tempted to go inside. Yonko is still wondering why Mama was crying last night. Did it have to do with Sachi's trip to America? But Mama wouldn't cry over something like that. She'd been fond of Sachi, but she cared for her as much as any other child in the orphanage, and it was difficult to believe she had any special feelings toward Sachi in particular. Was she crying because she, or Mother Asami, or someone else, had got terribly sick and was going to die? No, that seemed too far-fetched. Of course, it wasn't entirely out of the question. But people die only once. And besides, real deaths don't happen the way they do in movies. It was useless to think about such things.

Or what if . . .

A chill runs through Yonko's heart.

She glances sideways at Mitch again. He is still sniffling. She looks at Kazu, ahead of them. He keeps turning around, caught between their conversation and Mama's. Yonko's mother and Mama are still discussing something. It certainly doesn't seem like a light topic. They are first cousins and look similar from behind. The slope of their shoulders. Their slender necks. The shape of their legs. They'd even lived together for a while as children. Mama had been like an older sister to Yonko's mother. She'd never married, but she'd had one child who had died young.

That's why she'd wanted to be Mitch and Kazu's mama, Yonko's mother had once explained to her.

Was it possible that Mama was remembering that dead child last night? Yonko wonders. Was that why she'd been crying? If she'd had a child, that meant she must have had a lover who had been the child's father. What had happened to him? Had he died in the war? Maybe Mama was thinking of her lover and child. No, it couldn't be, that had all happened such a long time ago, and besides, Mitch and Kazu were her children now, and yesterday had been their birthday. Why would such an old memory come back to Mama yesterday, of all days? Or was it because it was their birthday that the past had suddenly come flooding back to her?

Oh, I don't know. I don't want to think about anything anymore.

Yonko suddenly gets the urge to twirl her light blue umbrella. But then the raindrops would scatter everywhere and Mitch would get mad at her.

Hey, what are you doing, he'd yell.

Then she'd throw her arms around him and say, Mitch, I don't want to go home! Do we really have to go our separate ways?

But of course Yonko can't do anything of the sort. Every now and then she glances at his gloomy face and feels sad.

Mitch, what's going through your mind right now? Yonko thinks as she searches her memory. Kazu, are you thinking the same thing? So much has happened to us.

There was Mitch's accident, for one. She'd been sure he was going to die then. But he'd got better. Walking was a little inconvenient, but otherwise his life was basically unchanged. Come to think of it, maybe Mama had been crying over Mitch's leg. When he'd been taken away in an ambulance, they'd said she looked like she was dying. Maybe she had remembered that moment and begun to cry.

Yonko shakes her head. No, that seemed wrong, too. It was a terrible burn, but he'd got lucky and regained his ability to walk. Mama had been so happy, saying that he must have been blessed by a lucky god.

Yonko steals a glance at Mitch again, and continues talking to him in her mind.

Mitch, remember that time we played war? Back when the orphanage still had lots of kids, we played in the grove nearby, and then later Mother Asami and Mama got really mad at us.

Of all people, why would you make a game out of something like that? they scolded us. What were you thinking?

I was five and you were six. Mitch, are you thinking of that game right now, too? That was before you hurt your leg, and Mu-chan and Eri-chan were still there, and yes, even Miki-chan.

Yes, that's right. Miki-chan was there, too.

Mitch senses Yonko's gaze as she walks beside him, and suddenly he remembers, too.

I wonder why it's coming back to me now all of a sudden. It's not like the game was that special to us, but the adults got so mad, and we felt so bad after that, we didn't feel like playing war anymore. All those huge trees seemed to continue on forever, blocking out the sun so the ground was cold and soggy, and no bright spots of grass grew there. There might have been moss, though.

Hey, Kazu, you remember, too, don't you? Mitch calls out to Kazu in a voice that is not a voice. Kazu intercepts it and shakes his head.

No, that's not how it was. It's true there were lots of trees there, but the area itself wasn't that big. And it wasn't dark, there was grass growing there, and flowers, too. Purple bellflowers, and small yellow buttercups. Miki-chan was picking them.

Really? Mitch responds. Now that you say it, I'm less sure. Was it all just a dream? Who else was there?

Everyone, Kazu answers. Mama, and Nobu, and Tommy, too. And Ami-chan, and Kei-chan and Miki-chan. I wish I could see them all again.

Of course you can. Mitch's voice, slightly annoyed, echoes inside Yonko's head.

Ami-chan went to America and became Annie, and Kei-chan became Kate. Nobu became Jeff, and Tommy just stayed Tommy, I think. I hear they send letters from America sometimes. Not to us, though, because we left the orphanage when we were three. The kids who didn't go to America, like Mako and Fumi, write back to them. I hear they even come back to visit sometimes. They said they miss Mother Asami. Ami-chan was six when she left the orphanage, and Nobu and Tommy were seven. If you were three when you left, like us, you'd probably forget what it was like, but if you were six or seven, you'd probably remember quite a lot. Miki-chan was only seven, the same age as Yonko and Ami-chan, when she disappeared from this world.

I don't think it's possible to see them. The rain carries Kazu's quiet voice to Yonko. Miki-chan isn't here anymore, and America is so far away. But I bet when we're adults we'll be able to see some of them, at least. Though I'm not sure who.

Mitch's voice: That day in the forest, we split up into American soldiers and Japanese soldiers and pretended to fight each other. We used tree branches for weapons, and when one of our enemies poked us with their stick, we pretended like we'd been shot, and fell to the ground, dead, right then and there. Then we'd count to ten, and if one of our allies touched us before we'd finished counting, we'd come back to life, but if not, we'd become prisoners of war. We ran around in that grove as fast as we could, didn't we, hell-bent on trying not to get 'shot'. Then Ami-chan and Miki-chan tripped on a root and fell. Was it Ami-chan who got a cut on her forehead? Or Miki-chan? Anyway, as they were sitting there crying, they got shot by an enemy soldier, Tommy, and no allies came to help, so they got taken away as POWs.

We tried to rescue them, Kazu continues where Mitch left off. Right, Mitch? But we couldn't. The two of them were darker-skinned than me, so they were supposed to be Black soldiers. Hey, Jap, they yelled, smacking their pretend gum. Mama yelled at us for that, too.

Even callousness has its limits. Do you kids have a giant hole in your head, or what?

Kazu laughs, and a giggle bursts out of Yonko, too. She leans against Mitch as she walks, and her light blue umbrella tilts at an angle, causing raindrops to cluster together and roll onto her head.

It seems so stupid now. I mean, we're the children of American soldiers! Soldiers who did terrible things to our mothers. But we didn't know what any of that meant back then. Or maybe we did, but we didn't think it had anything to do with us. Even though I'm Black. At the orphanage, being Black was normal, and Mama never said anything about it.

Up ahead, Mama and Yonko's mother pause, duck under the wooden eaves of the train station, fold their umbrellas and set their luggage down. Mitch and Yonko approach them slowly. Mama and Yonko's mother shake the water off their coats and begin wiping the mud from their shoes. There is a bus parked in front of the station.

That must be Mitch and Kazu's bus, Yonko thinks.

The children look at each other silently, reluctant to part.

There's still more I wanted to talk about.

Once school starts, we can come visit you on our own, Yonko. I'm sure Mama will let us.

Maybe we can see each other in the summer. Don't forget about me.

Don't forget about us either, Yonko.

Yonko's mother goes to buy their tickets, then comes back.

Our train will be here in ten minutes, so we're going to head to the platform now, she says.

Mama nods. Okay. See you soon. Take care of yourselves.

Thanks for everything. Say your goodbyes, Yonko.

Oh, yes, um, thank you. For everything. Goodbye. And you, too, Mitch and Kazu. See you soon.

Yonko bows to Mama, and Kazu and Mitch, in turn, bow politely to Yonko's mother.

Thanks so much. Goodbye. Bye, Yonko!

Yonko slips through the ticket gate, still waving. Soon Mitch and Kazu are out of sight. She follows her mother glumly, dragging her light blue umbrella behind her, then descends to the platform. It's pouring now, and the other passengers are sitting on the covered stairs as they wait for the train. Yonko's mother sits down, too, holding her bag on her lap as she wipes her glasses with a handkerchief. Yonko sits beside her. A chilly wind blows around them. She is freezing. She thinks about the flecks of mud on her shins, her coat, her skirt. But so far, her mother doesn't seem to notice. She snuggles up close to her to keep warm, and her mother wraps her arms around her.

Look, Yonko, they're waving to you from way over there. See?

Her mother stands up, waving back eagerly. Yonko looks in the direction her mother is waving, searching for Mitch and Kazu. There is a fence around the station, and beyond it she can see the white bus. It has already started moving, and she thinks she can see a small light hand and a dark hand waving from one of the windows, but only for an instant. She can't be sure. Still, she turns toward the bus pulling out of the station and waves back, imagining that the light glittering from Kazu's black pupils and Mitch's green pupils is travelling straight toward her.

Apparently they're going to England, Yonko's mother murmurs, her lips freshly coated with pink lipstick.

England? Who's going to England? Yonko asks warily.

Them. She said it would be better.

When?

They still need to get ready, but . . . Let's see, well, they'll probably leave Japan sometime this summer, I suppose.

Finally, Yonko understands why Mama had been crying.

But immediately she doubts herself, thinking, No, perhaps that's wrong, too. If Kazu and Mitch went away to a school in England, of course Mama would be lonely, but Yonko has a hard time believing that Mama, tough as she is, would dissolve into tears over it. Besides, she'd probably made the decision herself.

But why? Yonko asks her mother, not expecting an answer.

Well . . . life is only going to get harder for those two from here on out. No need for them to be confined to Japan.

But . . .

Just as Yonko is thinking of what to say, the train pulls in. All at once, the people who had been waiting on the steps stand up and rush toward it. Yonko and her mother have no time even to open their umbrellas. They break into a run, along with the rest of the crowd. Their faces are getting wet, and their necks and hands. There aren't too many passengers, so they don't have to wait in line, just get in the car.

Quickly her mother opens the train door, panting, and steps inside. The air is warm and stuffy from bodies crowded together. There is only one vacant seat. Yonko's mother immediately sits down. She puts her bag down next to her on the floor and points, signalling to Yonko to sit on it. There are other passengers sitting on the floor, too. Yonko lowers herself onto the bag, her back turned to her mother. She knows that the mud on her legs and coat will get the bag dirty, and that her mother might scold her, but there's no point in worrying about it now. She folds her arms and rests her head on her knees. A white cloth falls on top of her. Her mother's handkerchief. Which is her way of saying: Use this to wipe yourself down. Reluctantly, Yonko lifts her head and picks it up. The train begins to move.

Still holding the handkerchief, Yonko looks out the window opposite her mother's seat and watches the rainy outline of the landscape collapse until only pure colour shines through. A colour somewhere between green, brown, yellow and grey. It's always the same. Yonko grimaces. Perhaps Mitch and Kazu are thinking the same thing right this minute as they watch the dull colours slide down the bus window. The train and the bus part ways, one carrying Yonko and her mother to Tokyo, the other carrying Kazu and Mitch and Mama to Yokohama. Nothing has changed, and yet everything has.

It rained a lot at Miki-chan's funeral, too. That's right, it had been an unusually stormy April.

When Yonko tries to remember Miki-chan falling into the pond, or even being pushed in, it feels like she dreamed it. She and Kazu and Mitch had been crouching in the bushes, hiding, and Tabo had approached Miki-chan, who was standing near the pond. And then the orange skirt, the white spray of water fanning out and out. But those were only fragments of disconnected memories.

Had they rushed back to Yonko's house after that? Told Mama and Yonko's mother in a panic what had happened, while the three of them cried and shook? Who had told Mama and the other adults about Tabo? Had it been Yonko? She can't remember. In any case, that was four years ago. Mitch and Kazu were only eight then, and Yonko seven, the same age that Miki-chan had been. Were they so shocked by what they'd seen as they squatted in the bushes that they'd had no idea what to do? Had Mama and Yonko's mother demanded to know how this had happened? Had they simply yelled: Tabo, it was Tabo that pushed Miki-chan into the pond?

But thinking back on it now, Yonko isn't sure whether it really happened that way. Miki-chan, with her long red hair. The orange skirt. Tabo had come, and pushed her. Miki-chan, floating face-down in the pond. Her orange skirt and long red hair undulating around her. It was scary, so scary, every time the image appeared before Yonko's eyes she began to cry. But had she really seen such a thing? As her eyes filled with frightened tears, she would be assailed by a strange thought: It didn't seem real. It was like she had seen it only in a dream.

What was it we actually saw? she wants to ask Mitch and Kazu. Why didn't we try to help Miki-chan? Were we afraid Tabo would see us? Is that why we took off running? Was Tabo really there that day?

But already four years have passed and she hasn't been able to say the words out loud. And now that Kazu and Mitch are going off to England, she won't be able to ask them.

Is this really what you want, Mitch? Kazu?

When had her mother told her that Miki-chan died? Yonko can't remember that either. She'd just known somehow. When her mother told her they were going to Miki-chan's funeral, she hadn't thought it strange at all.

It had been raining that day, and Yonko's mother had taken her to the orphanage. Kazu and Mitch came with them, too. Crouching in the bushes as she looked at the pond, going to the orphanage for the funeral – these two events simply didn't connect in Yonko's memory. Later, the other children told her that she'd gone to the funeral, and perhaps after a while she'd just accepted it as fact. All she could remember was watching the raindrops hitting the windowpane and running down the glass on the train ride back – and even that she could recall only with great effort. Why couldn't she remember anything about the funeral itself? It must have been a very sad event, not something she should have forgotten easily. Mother Asami and the children in the orphanage must have cried. Maybe Miki-chan, sleeping peacefully inside her coffin, had been surrounded by flowers, her expression so beautiful that it made everyone cry even more.

Kazu, you're a full year older than me. Don't you remember Miki-chan's funeral? And you, Mitch? Come to think of it, the three of us have never talked about what happened that day.

We vaguely acknowledged that Miki-chan wasn't with us anymore, but we talked about it the same way we talked about Ami-chan or Tommy going to America, so that sometimes I'd think maybe Miki-chan had done the same. Listen to me, Mitch, Kazu – doesn't that bother you?

Yonko spreads her mother's creased handkerchief over her knees and lays her cheek down on it. It smells like laundry detergent. The regular rhythm of the train makes her eyelids grow heavy. An image of Tabo from behind wavers before her eyes, then dissolves.

What would happen if we met Tabo? Yonko thinks. Back then, she'd had the impression that he was a rather large boy, but he was only in elementary school. Who had told her that Tabo lived alone with his mother? Was it a shopkeeper, or maybe the woman who lived next door? After all, Tabo did live nearby. What about the rumour that Tabo had pushed Miki-chan into the pond? And the rumour that some children from the orphanage had also been there? And the rumour that those kids had helped Tabo kill Miki-chan? No, that's nonsense, she wishes she could say, but she's not confident enough to refute them.

The only one who approached Miki-chan that day was Tabo. Can I be sure, though? What really happened that day? Had someone else been watching? Who was it? Or was it one of us that started the rumour about Tabo?

The sharp light reflecting off the surface of the pond illuminates Yonko's eyes. The rhythm of the train becomes the rhythm of Sachi's heartbeat, echoing in her eardrums. She might never see Sachi again. Everyone is leaving. Soon, the green light reflecting off the pond swallows Yonko's consciousness.

5

Once a rumour spreads, you're done for. It never disappears; it gradually permeates reality, eating away at everything around it.

Yes, I remember her saying that, Yonko's mother thinks, biting her lip as she recalls what Sister Yae had said on that night six years ago. And after that, Mitch and Kazu, they drilled you in English and sent you off to a boarding school in England.

Are you sure you want to do this? Yonko's mother had almost said to Sister Yae, seeing Mitch's and Kazu's miserable faces at Haneda Airport that day. England is so far away. But two years later, you came back, looking even more glum than you did when you left.

And then one day, when Sister Yae wasn't around, Mitch and Kazu had asked Yonko's mother: Why was Mama crying that night?

These two, I swear, Yonko's mother had thought, sighing to herself. They go all the way to England, and this is all they think about?

But when she looked at their faces, all grown up, hair sprouting on their chins, she'd changed her mind.

Your mama thought it would be impossible for you to escape the rumours. So she decided to send you away. She was ashamed of her own decision. That's why she was crying that night. But she was more frightened of the rumours. Frightened of the people who spread them. And she couldn't bring herself to confront them.

Yonko's mother had never actually said this to Mitch and Kazu. She didn't want to remind them now, not after they'd gone all the way to England. Besides, even she could only guess at the real reason behind Sister Yae's tears that night. And it didn't feel right to say something out loud that was just a guess. That's why she'd just smiled and given them a non-committal answer instead.

What are you two so worried about? Put all that behind you and just focus on your future now. Do you know how much it cost to send you to England? Yet here you are, back in Japan after only two years. Mama doesn't regret making you her children, though, not at all. So you have to concentrate on your studies so you don't disappoint her even more.

Come to think of it, Mitch's accident happened just two years after Miki-chan died, didn't it? Yonko's mother wishes she could say to Sister Yae, who is probably in the Omori hospital right now looking after Mother Asami. And it was after the accident, wasn't it, that you became more withdrawn? I don't blame you, of course. What parent wouldn't feel that way after finding out their child would have to walk with a bad leg for the rest of their life? Ever since then, you became even more protective of your children, wanting to dispel any ominous shadows lurking around them. So when I told you the rumours were still around, you furrowed your brow, clearly upset.

It wasn't those children's fault that they just happened to see it, you said, tears spilling from your eyes. They were just in the wrong place at the wrong time, and were so frightened by what they saw that they ran all the way home. Why do people think they were the ones who killed Miki-chan?

Now Annie and Joyce are on their way to Yonko's house, getting closer by the minute. They want to understand for themselves these distorted rumours they can't see with their eyes or grasp with their hands. They want to stamp them out with their own feet if possible. They're determined to find out why Miki-chan had to die, to get clear on what happened, at least for her sake.

Annie and Miki-chan have always been inseparable.

Don't forget about me, okay? Miki-chan had whispered in Ami-chan's ear in a slightly husky voice when they said goodbye.

And then, a year later, Miki-chan had died unexpectedly. Mother Asami had written to Ami-chan's adoptive parents to let them know what had happened.

It's a lie, Annie had whispered when she heard the news. Of course it is. I can't believe you're all falling for it. I have to go find Miki-chan, please, I know she's alive, please let me go back to Japan, she'd begged her adoptive parents. Ami-chan was seven then, the same age as Miki-chan and Yonko.

Joyce, however, was only five at the time, too young to understand anything. This was back when she was still Sachi and living at the orphanage. She loved Miki-chan, of course, so she was devastated to learn she couldn't play with her anymore. Ami-chan and Kei-chan had already left for America, so to lose Miki-chan on top of that was too much for her. She'd wanted to run away from the orphanage, but she just sat there in a daze. Even after she was adopted and became Joyce, she never forgot Miki-chan, who'd always cared for her in her own quiet way.

Now, ten years later, Annie and Joyce have boarded a plane back to Japan. Annie whispers something to Joyce, and Joyce nods.

Let's ask Yonko's mum when we get there. I'm sure Miki-chan would want to know why she died, too.

Annie nods, and continues whispering in Japanese.

I bet they didn't look into who did it, because she was just an orphan. If she'd had parents, they wouldn't have stayed silent about this. Well, we won't let them get away with it. We need to make Yonko and Mitch and Kazu tell us what really happened.

Jeff and Tommy are on the same flight with them. The four have been given special permission from their adoptive families to return to Japan to say their final goodbyes to Mother Asami. Annie had flown from Boston, Tommy from Detroit, and Jeff from Santa Cruz, and they had all met in Seattle, where Joyce lived, before flying together to Haneda Airport. They are allowed to stay in Japan for only a week, but all of them feel proud that they can travel unchaperoned.

Today is their fifth day in Japan. They'd planned on meeting at three o'clock in the afternoon. Yonko and her mother are waiting impatiently for Annie and Joyce to arrive. Kazu and Mitch said they would get there around five. For just this week, Yonko's mother and Sister Yae have put aside their usual worries about Kazu's and Mitch's problems at school, or Yonko's bad grades.

Just now Annie and Joyce must be walking uncertainly through the neighbourhood, which looks simultaneously familiar and strange to them. From inside the house, Yonko's mother pictures the two of them making their way, holding their breath instinctively. Perhaps the quietness unnerves them a little. The streets in Japan are much narrower and more meandering than the ones in America. They can't shake the feeling that the neighbours are watching them suspiciously.

Or perhaps Annie with her brown skin and curly hair isn't uneasy at all, but presses her lips together and walks ahead with long strides and a defiant expression, as if to say, If anyone tries to question us, I'll put 'em in their place. And perhaps Joyce keeps her gaze fixed straight ahead on her friend's back, never letting her eyes drift toward the houses around them, determined not to be left behind.

Were the streets always this narrow and winding? Annie might ask Joyce.

Alleyways lead to more alleyways, small houses are crammed together on either side of the street. None of them have proper yards but some are enclosed by concrete walls, which only makes them look more cramped. Many of the houses look like they've been rebuilt recently.

This is Japan, and the middle of Tokyo at that, Joyce and Annie think. Surely some people in America live like this, too, especially in big cities like New York.

From time to time, a dog sticks its face through a hole in the wall and glowers at them. One barks loudly. Yellow and red leaves crackle beneath their feet, the wind sends them skittering along the ground. There are no more dirt roads. All the streets are paved now, and though they vaguely remember rows of barracks held together with nothing but galvanized sheet iron, those, too, are gone. Some houses even have garages out front, with sparkling new cars.

This part of Tokyo sure has changed a lot, perhaps Annie says with a sigh. But it's strange, it feels familiar too, somehow. The smell. The damp air.

I wonder how many times we came to this house, perhaps Joyce replies, trying hard to remember.

Yes, that sounds right, Yonko's mother thinks inside the house.

Annie is older than Joyce, but she left Japan when she was still young, so it makes sense that Joyce, who'd stayed until she was nine, would have more memories of the place. Joyce and Annie must be picturing their younger selves walking along this road.

Back then, Annie was still Ami-chan, her hair as fluffy as cotton candy. She liked to wear a white blouse with a rounded collar and a skirt that came down to her knees, worn with suspenders. She always wore the same clothes, except in winter, when she'd wear a cardigan over her outfit, swap her summer skirt for a wool one, and wear long cotton socks. Joyce (then still called Sachi) and Yonko dressed similarly. Sachi had a habit of licking the ends of her straight hair. Her shirt-tails would come untucked from the waist of her skirt, and her suspenders were always slipping off her shoulders. Every day she wore the same sneakers, covered in dirt, with holes in the toes.

Yonko was the same way. She never cared much about her appearance, and often looked unkempt. Her long cotton socks, patched here and there, were always falling down.

Yonko's mother sighs, remembering how she'd mend her daughter's socks and umbrellas at night, half-asleep and exhausted from her day job.

I don't miss those days, unravelling old sweaters and using the yarn to knit a new one.

She puts a pot of water on the stove. I'll serve them some fancy black tea, not milk or juice. They're not children anymore, after all. Or will they want Japanese tea? Or coffee? Maybe I should wait and ask them first.

She peeks into the living room. Yonko is sitting in the corner. She's become nearsighted since entering high school and has started wearing glasses. She is squatting close to the ground, hugging her knees and resting her chin on them as she stares at the pattern on the carpet laid out over the tatami floor.

That look – she hasn't changed a bit since she was a child.

She would always curl up like that to calm herself down when she was depressed, or in a bad mood, or bored or worried or excited, or when she just didn't know what to do. She's probably feeling anxious now. After all, her beloved Ami-chan and Sachi are coming all the way here on an important matter. She must be excited, even if what they have to discuss isn't exactly fun.

A long time ago, little Ami-chan and Sachi, and Miki-chan,

and Mitch and Kazu, used to come and visit this house with Mama. Whenever Sister Yae came to Tokyo for a visit, she'd always stop by, bringing along some of the children from the orphanage. Usually it would be Ami-chan, Miki-chan and Sachi, sometimes Nobu and Tommy, too. She couldn't bring all of them every time, so she'd take turns bringing the girls, who loved to play with Yonko, and the boys, who were close to Mitch and Kazu.

These kids have never spent any time with relatives, so I want to leave them with you as often as possible, Mother Asami used to say to Sister Yae. Though Sister Yae had never known her own parents, she'd been raised by members of her extended family, who made sure she had everything she needed. She'd even inherited her grandmother's property, which is what allowed her to start her own business. So she understood Mother Asami's feelings completely, and after that, she would stop by the orphanage in Kurihama as often as possible and bring the children to Tokyo.

They say close friends are better than distant relatives, Sister Yae had said to Yonko's mother, laughing. But maybe close friends who you've known since childhood are even better.

Ami-chan and Miki-chan would walk timidly through these streets back then, clinging to Sister Yae's clothes. Sometimes it would be Sachi, not Ami-chan, who would cling to Mama. When the three of them would come over together, they would all hold hands. Then Mitch and Kazu would dart around them, dashing ahead toward Yonko's house, as if to say: This is our aunt's house, not yours!

The road was bright up ahead, illuminating the boys from behind, so they appeared only as dark shadows.

That's how memory is, perhaps Annie thinks. Like looking at a backlit object. We can't see it clearly, and all sorts of things might blur our vision.

The leaves on the hedges sway. Laundry flutters in the wind, as though inviting the children to come and play. Mitch's thin ankles, reddish and nearly transparent. Little stones fallen on the road. Kazu's voice blooming through the air like a spray of water. The sound of the girls breathing.

Only now Miki-chan is gone.

Where is she? Annie and Joyce wonder.

They stop in front of the house. Annie looks at Joyce as if to say: This is the one, right? Joyce smiles and nods. This old house, at least, they remember. The wooden fence. The sliding door. The nameplate, the dark lettering faded, nearly illegible.

Thank goodness we made it.

Mitch and Kazu had drawn them a map, and Yonko's mother had given them detailed directions over the phone, so there was really no way they could have got lost. Still, they had been nervous all the way here. They weren't sure how much Japan had changed since they'd last been here. But as it turned out, they had nothing to be afraid of. All that time they'd spent in Japan – look! It was still here, intact, in their bodies. That Yonko's house hasn't changed a bit helps them feel more assured. This style of house used to be ubiquitous in Tokyo but is a much rarer sight nowadays.

Both girls reach out to push the doorbell at the same time. They look at each other, then Annie presses the bell.

Brrrrrr, brrrrrr

Inside the house, Yonko looks up.

I'll get it, she calls out in a low voice. She gets up and runs to the door. The sound of the glass door opening. The sound of Yonko's sandals. The door opens. From inside the house, Yonko's mother strains to listen. She had expected to hear the bright laughter of girls, but it is strangely quiet. Perhaps the three of them look at each other in silence, then hug in the typical American way.

We're here! Finally. We wanted to come sooner.

You're here. I was so nervous, I could barely sleep last night.

We couldn't sleep either. But today was the only day we could come. A week goes by so fast.

Did your mum say anything, Yonko?

Inside the house, Yonko's mother waits one minute, three. Five minutes pass, and the girls still haven't come inside.

They must be telling each other all the things they can't say in front of their parents. But it feels odd to pretend I'm not here. I don't want to get in their way.

She wonders whether to go out or wait in the kitchen a little longer.

Are Annie and Joyce being careful not to let any English slip out as they speak in Japanese? Annie and Joyce have become Ami-chan and Sachi again. It would be understandable for someone who left Japan when they were six to forget Japanese, Tommy had told Yonko's mother once in the hospital courtyard. Though he was physically larger now, he wore the same mischievous expression he'd had as a child. But even after he'd gone to America, Kazu and Mitch had continued sending him letters from Japan. Don't forget Japanese, they warned him. Write letters in Japanese, read Japanese books. If international calls are too expensive, call Annie and Joyce, who are also in America. Listen to as much Japanese as you can, keep speaking it. If you find a Japanese person, talk to them, even if you don't know who they are. Otherwise, we won't understand each other anymore.

Mother Asami and the other adults didn't need Kazu and Mitch to tell them twice. They sent Japanese books and magazines to the children in America. They had to be shipped by boat, so sometimes it took three months, and often the packages were torn when they arrived. Sometimes they wondered if the children shouldn't just forget Japanese after all, give in and let themselves become American. But the desire for them to remember Japanese persisted.

If those children had stayed in Japan, people would have told them they were American, and in America, people probably tell them they are Japanese. But there are so many immigrants in America, surely it's a better place for them than Japan. At least, that's what Mother Asami believed. She was also encouraged by the fact that as the children of American GIs, they would be prioritized for adoption in American households. She'd heard that adoption was common in America, that they wouldn't be treated differently from anyone else. Of course, she couldn't be sure this was true, since the children who went to America never talked about that kind of thing.

Mother Asami is too good-natured, she's so optimistic about everything, perhaps Annie is saying now. But maybe that's what Christianity is. She's a dyed-in-the-wool Christian. She sacrificed herself for society, for other people, so much so that she never got married, but that's exactly why she couldn't just leave a bunch of mixed-race orphans like us out on the street. I heard there was a famous orphanage in Oiso, a fancier one with an on-site school and everything, but of course, there were so many of us that one orphanage wasn't enough. From the beginning she had no plans to make it a formal institution. The orphans who had lost their parents during the war were older by then, and she wasn't sure they would get along with the ones she'd already taken in. No matter how much they pleaded with her, Mother Asami always turned them down, insisting that she couldn't take in any more. But she did agree to take in the infants born after the war and then hand them over to a public institution when they turned two. But Annie didn't remember there being many babies in the orphanage.

Eventually Mother Asami became exhausted, perhaps Joyce says. She came from a well-to-do family, but taking in so many orphans depleted her savings, drained her energy. So now she has cancer and is on her deathbed. Mama, an old friend of Mother Asami's, had helped keep the orphanage running and accompanied her to medical treatments. Finally, in November, she decided she should contact the children from the orphanage and let them know what was going on.

When Joyce got the call from Kazu, she'd been overjoyed to hear his voice. But after she heard the reason why he was calling, she began to cry. She immediately called Annie, but Annie already knew, and they'd cried together over the phone. Then, a day later, they'd got a call from Tommy.

Tommy had said, Mama and Yonko's mother said they'd pay for some of our travel expenses. Why don't we take them up on it, and ask our adoptive parents to chip in, too?

Joyce agreed. We have to go back and see Mother Asami while she's still alive.

Thanksgiving break was coming up, so the children were able to take time off from school. But they were allowed to stay in Japan for only a week.

They contacted all the other former children they could think of from the orphanage. But the only ones who were allowed to go back to Japan, or could take time off to go, were Nobu (now called Jeff) and Tommy and Joyce and Annie. Yonko and her mother went to Haneda Airport to pick them all up. The children were exhausted from the long flight and the jet lag, but they didn't let themselves rest for long. The very next day they headed to the Omori hospital to see Mother Asami.

When Yonko first saw them, she was so stunned by how tall the boys and Ami-chan were that she almost forgot to feel happy. Though Ami-chan and Yonko were the same age, one now looked like an adult and the other still looked a child. Tommy and Nobu, now eighteen-year-old boys, were so tall that Yonko couldn't reach the tops of their heads even if she stood on her toes, and though Tommy was a full head shorter than Nobu, he was so big that wherever he went in Japan people mistook him for a rugby player. Kazu and Mitch were tall now, too, so she should have expected this, but it had been eleven years since she'd seen Nobu and Tommy.

Thankfully, Mother Asami was still alive when the children reached the hospital. From time to time she would wake up and smile as she looked around at each of the four children who had come back from America to see her. Or at least, that's how it seemed to them. Kazu and Mitch were there in the hospital room with their mama, and children who had stayed behind in Japan, like Takeshi and Fumi, took turns visiting the hospital, too.

Are they from the American school? the nurses asked, staring in amazement at the large children from the orphanage whose faces they couldn't help but see as foreign.

American school? said Mitch, who until recently really had been going to an American school in Tokyo. Please. Just between us, we attend a training school for the CIA, which reports directly to the president of the United States – you see, we're being trained to become America's most important spies. This woman who's sleeping in the bed here is our predecessor, a legendary spy who's practically a household name in America.

Annie and the others stifled a giggle as they listened to Mitch talk. Some of the nurses looked doubtful, but others seemed to earnestly believe what he said. As the Vietnam War raged on, so did the protests against it, so by then the CIA was well known even in Japan.

Did Annie and Joyce remember, in that moment, what Yonko had told them? That both Mother Asami and Mama were Christians? That once, they'd even helped carry out a secret project for a Communist organization, and that, during the war, people had regarded them with suspicion? In that sense, maybe Mitch's story about the spy wasn't a complete lie after all.

Unlike Mama, Mother Asami had never had a child of her own. Her dream had been to study hygiene, but the war put an end to that.

Doesn't Mother Asami have any relatives? Jeff asked. Doesn't it bother her that we're the only ones visiting her?

Takeshi and the other children didn't know anything about Mother Asami's relatives, but then again, neither did Mama or Yonko's mother. Mama thought that even if they did exist, Mother Asami must have cut ties with them a long time ago, since Mama had never heard of any relatives as long as she'd known her, which meant – the children realized with a sigh – that Mother Asami wasn't so different from them, after all.

In other words, Joyce or maybe Annie thought, maybe those who have no family unconsciously gravitate toward each other. I mean, even Mama and Yonko's mother don't seem to have a lot of relatives. And Yonko never had a father, though we don't know why. Maybe that's why she always wanted to be around us and Mitch and Kazu.

While the children visited Mother Asami in the hospital, they stayed in the apartment in Kanazawa Hakkei where she'd previously lived by herself. Three years ago, she'd closed the orphanage in Kurihama, then moved to this apartment with eleven-year-old Takeshi, the last child in the orphanage. A year later, Takeshi was taken in by the owner of a cleaning company in Saitama. The plan was for him to attend night classes, help out with the company, and if all went well, he would be given a job as a store manager. Takeshi was the one who had lived with Mother Asami most recently, so the news of her illness hit him the hardest. But it was difficult for him to take time off from school and work, so he came by the hospital only on weekends.

Mother Asami had moved into this apartment with Takeshi

a year after Mitch and Kazu came back from England. Sister Yae was at her wit's end, as Mitch and Kazu were struggling to adjust to school in Japan. Meanwhile, the children who had been adopted and sent to America were listening to Martin Luther King's 'I Have a Dream' speech and watching 250,000 people march on Washington, as were Kazu and Mitch and Yonko from Japan.

Mother Asami, ever optimistic, had sent the children to America believing that it was an open-minded, tolerant place where there was always plenty of food to eat, people were free, and everyone lived well. But the children, especially the ones left behind by Black GIs, were surprised to encounter a different reality. For wealthy white people in America, adoption was nothing more than an act of charity. They treated their children like pets, dressing them up in nice clothes and making them greet their guests. And if the children studied and did well in school, this, too, was just another feather in the parents' cap. Sending them to predominantly white colleges, though, was out of the question.

But at last, the children from the orphanage began to hear new phrases like 'Black Is Beautiful' and 'Black Power'. Around the same time as Dr King was giving his speeches, Malcolm X appeared, and for the first time the children felt grateful they'd come to America. It was him they identified with more than anyone else, because of his upbringing – for it was said that his mother was the mixed-race child of a Black woman who had been raped by a white man, and his father had been killed by a white man, and later his mother had been institutionalized in a mental hospital, and for a while Malcolm had been taken in and raised by a white family.

Then Kennedy and Malcolm X had been assassinated. The Vietnam War escalated, and the possibility that Jeff and Tommy might be drafted became more real.

Finally, Mother Asami fell ill and the children rushed back to Japan. There had been a string of major airline accidents recently, and typhoons all throughout the month of September, so Yonko and her mother waited anxiously to see whether they would all arrive safely at Haneda Airport. The minute Yonko spotted Sachi in her wide-legged jeans, she felt a mild sense of vertigo and grabbed her mother's arm. It reminded her mother of when Yonko had met Mitch and Kazu for the first time.

Yonko had only been three years old, and Kazu and Mitch four, when Sister Yae, now Kazu and Mitch's mother, had brought them to this house looking elated. Kazu and Mitch hid behind her, peeking out from either side of her skirt, scowling at Yonko and her mother suspiciously. They wore identical navy blazers, white shirts and dress shoes. Later, Sister Yae admitted to having splurged and bought them fancy English schoolboy uniforms from an import clothing store in Motomachi, justifying her purchase by saying that they needed to look nice for their first public appearance, and had forced the boys to wear the uniforms, even though they protested. Maybe this had also contributed to their nervousness that day.

When the two little boys first appeared before her with their unfamiliar clothes and faces, little Yonko had been frightened. But instead of crying, she immediately turned her back on them and buried her face in her mother's skirt. When her mother placed her hand on Yonko's head, it felt hot.

What's the matter, Yonko, she murmured before turning back to the boys. This one is very shy. Her name is Yoriko. But you can call her Yonko.

Kazu and Mitch nodded, but didn't come any closer.

Did the three children exchange some kind of greeting that day? The first thing Sister Yae must have talked about in the living room as they gathered under the kotatsu was Mitch and

Kazu, but Yonko's mother couldn't remember what else they discussed. Yonko's father, who had left when Yonko was one, must have come up at some point, and perhaps they had talked about Mother Asami's orphanage, too. Or the baby that Sister Yae had by herself before the war, the one who died tragically. Yonko's mother had still been a teenager when it happened, so she'd been very worried, and when she heard the baby had died, she'd been overwhelmed with grief for the first time in her life. Maybe they had spoken about their other relatives, whom they had almost no contact with now. Or about Sister Yae's work. Surely they'd had plenty to talk about.

Were the children sitting very quietly in a corner of the room, listening to the adults' conversation? Or were they nodding off at the edge of the engawa? Was Yonko cradling their black cat as she hid inside the closet?

Yonko's mother paces restlessly now between the living room and the kitchen, waiting for Yonko and the other girls to come back into the house. When had Yonko first met Ami-chan and Sachi? And Miki-chan? She was fairly certain that the first time she had taken Yonko to visit the orphanage was right before Sister Yae adopted Mitch and Kazu. She'd almost forgotten how Sister Yae hadn't mentioned anything about the adoption that day, instead telling her over the phone days later that she'd decided to raise two children and name them Kazuo and Michio.

Yonko's mother had been shocked, even angry, at Sister Yae. Why hadn't she told her about this at the orphanage?

They were all adorable, and it was difficult to choose, Sister Yae said. Call it intuition, I guess, but those two looked at me with those sparkling eyes, and I thought, Yes, they're the ones.

Yonko's mother couldn't remember which of the children were Mitch and Kazu, since there were so many of them at the orphanage. Miki-chan and Ami-chan must have been among them, too.

★

They were so small back then, but Mitch and Kazu are eighteen now. Yonko's mother listens for any sound coming from outside as she turns on the gas stove, then turns it off again. How time flies. Yonko has grown up, too, but she sees her daughter every day, so she doesn't always notice the changes taking place in her. If Sister Yae's baby had lived, she would have been a full-grown adult by now. But shamefully, Yonko's mother can't even remember what the infant looked like. How many times had she held it, changed its diapers, cooed at it? People often say that once someone dies, that's all there is to it, but the more time passes, the more she is confronted with the reality of its death. The dead child is abandoned in the past, growing ever more distant until it recedes from view.

And you, Miki-chan . . .

Yonko's mother says aloud, tentatively. Miki-chan appears faintly, smiles shyly and looks at her intently.

You'll always be seven years old. I still remember your face so clearly. Your big eyes, slightly blue, and your long eyelashes. Your pointed nose. Your lips, always drawn tight. The middle of your chin slightly dimpled. You looked like a little French doll. Sister Yae and I used to talk about how beautiful you'd be when you grew up, but you never did.

When you'd come over to our house, you and the other girls would play ohajiki and otedama. I think sometimes you'd play ishikeri, too, or compete to see who could knit the best. But you almost never played with Kazu and Mitch. As soon as they got here, you'd take off running somewhere. We were worried the boys would stand out in this neighbourhood because of the way they looked, but they never seemed to notice. They were always running around outside, bringing back lizards and grasshoppers – I don't know where they found them – annoying all the girls. Kazu loved plants, so sometimes he'd bring back weeds he would find by the road. Bindweed, four o'clocks, dandelions, white clover.

The girls didn't like being stared at by the neighbours, so they didn't go outside as much. But Ami-chan, always full of life, wasn't satisfied with that. Hey, c'mon, she'd whine. Let's go to the park near the pond, I want to play on the swings! And then everyone would feel sorry for her, and Yonko and Miki-chan, and Sachi when she was there, would get up and reluctantly head out together to the small park with the pond. They couldn't think of anywhere else to go, and besides, the park was the perfect distance, about twenty minutes from the house on foot.

If only you had stayed behind and ignored Ami-chan, you never would have attracted the neighbours' attention, you never would have met such a fate.

Who cares, Yonko's mother hears her daughter's voice say. If someone stares at us, we'll just stare right back at them.

No, we can't, Sachi's voice continues.

Why? Ami-chan's voice.

Yonko lives here, Sachi says. It's not the same.

That's right, I do live here. I've lived here my whole life, and I'll keep living here until I'm grown up. Yonko's voice. But it is no longer a child's voice.

That's why if anything ever happens, you're the one who would get the worst of it, Yonko, Ami-chan continues. Her voice sounds mature, but desperate. I don't want to talk about it either. I want to keep it our secret. But we need to tell your mum. I don't care if she gets mad at us.

Wouldn't it be better if Mitch explained it to her? Sachi's voice. She still looks and sounds like a child. Her long, straight hair falls in two loose braids. She reflexively brings the ends to her mouth and licks them from time to time as though confirming something, then looks straight ahead.

No! How are we supposed to look Yonko's mum in the eye and pretend like everything is fine while we wait for Mitch to get here? We can't. Let's get the hard stuff over with first. Then she can tell us what she knows. There's nothing else we can do.

Fine, Yonko says. I guess it's easier to keep the uncomfortable stuff a secret. That way we don't have to take responsibility. Maybe she pouts, averts her gaze a little as she speaks. But secrets never stay hidden forever. It's only a matter of time. That's the scary thing about them.

Even if it's not important, I want to know, for Miki-chan's sake. Sachi's voice, again. And I want to know why you weren't with Miki-chan that day, Yonko. Were you playing hide-and-seek?

I don't think so, but I'm not sure. It's true that I was usually with her. Sachi, you weren't there that day, were you?

I don't remember anything. When I think about being with you that day, I start to feel like I really was there. But I don't have any memories of it, so I wonder if I stayed behind at the orphanage that day. If Miki-chan was standing by the pond all alone and you were playing hide-and-seek, wouldn't that mean she was 'it'?

Oh, Yonko says, surprised. She has the same bowl cut she had as a child, but now she is wearing glasses and has pimples on her face. Is that why we were hiding in the bushes? And why we felt as if we couldn't approach her? It seems like each of us remembers that day differently.

Well, we were only seven, after all, says Ami-chan, sighing. At that age, you can barely distinguish reality from fiction. It's like living in a cocoon inside a dream.

Now I feel even more confused, Sachi says. But I think I remember hearing Miki-chan fall into the pond. It's strange, right? Maybe I imagined it happening after the fact, but the sound stayed with me.

Yonko holds her breath and shrinks back.

Oh, Sachi . . . I think you really were there, don't you?

For a moment, the three girls fall silent as they stand around a broken milk crate beside the door. Behind them, seven-year-old Miki-chan appears, watching them intently. A bright blue sky stretches out above her, reflecting in her eyes and intensifying their colour. Her hair falls in reddish waves around her. She is wearing a short orange skirt. The colour of oranges ripening under a California sun. Miki-chan never wanted to wear that skirt. But at the orphanage, children didn't have a choice in the clothes they were given. The skirt had been donated by someone, and though she didn't like the colour, it had plenty of flare around the hem, so when she spun it would whirl around her and cheer her up.

Ami-chan notices Miki-chan standing there and her eyes widen. Yonko's jaw drops. Sachi reaches out her hand toward the little girl. Miki-chan tilts her head, grins and floats into Yonko's house like a soap bubble. The three girls follow her nervously.

Yonko's mother, who has been in the kitchen, senses movement and looks up. Oh, she thinks, I barely heard them come in.

She makes sure the stove is off and hurries to the front door. Yonko has already taken off her sandals and is standing on the step, while Ami-chan and Sachi are standing in the entryway looking sad. Ami-chan's shoulders are drooping, her body shrunken. When she looks at Yonko, her eyes are ringed with red and she looks like she might cry.

What's wrong? Yonko's mother says. Well, come inside. I'll get the tea ready.

The girls cast their eyes downward, not saying a word. Yonko's mother hurries to the kitchen and begins to boil water. She's already boiled it several times, turning the stove on and off, so it doesn't take long. Yonko and the others file into the living room, still silent.

Yonko, come here and help me carry the tea, she calls out as she carries a plate piled high with kawara. She thought they'd like the kawara more than a Western-style dessert and had gone to the nearby senbei shop yesterday to buy them. Yonko reluctantly gets up and makes her way to the kitchen, and Ami-chan and Sachi bow to Yonko's mother, looking as though they've just woken up from a dream.

Thank you so much for having us, Ami-chan says.

Sachi opens her mouth to speak.

It was selfish of us to take so long. But we're very happy to be here. We have to go back to America tomorrow night, and we weren't sure if we'd have time to come by. We'd almost given up.

Yonko sits between Ami-chan and Sachi, saying nothing. Ami-chan looks at Yonko and Sachi, takes a deep breath, and begins to speak with great effort.

Ah, so . . . first of all, there's something we wanted to tell you. Um . . . we . . . we're really at a loss . . . and we wanted to hear what you thought . . . It's about something that happened three months ago. They found a woman's body in a subway underpass in Toshima Ward. Mitch was at Mama's office, browsing the newspaper, when he happened to notice the article – though he doesn't normally read the newspaper. Did you hear about this?

Yonko's mother furrows her brow and shakes her head vigorously. Her heart suddenly begins to pound. What were these children trying to say?

It seems the girl was strangled with a rope of some kind.

She was a thirty-year-old woman. It was definitely a homicide. It didn't seem like she was raped. She was wearing an orange skirt. The article said it was torn, but there wasn't a single cut or scrape on her entire body. This was three months ago, when it was still pretty hot out, so it was likely a thin cotton skirt of some kind. It was the orange fabric that caught the attention of a passer-by.

For a brief moment, Yonko's mother's vision goes blurry, and she feels like the wind has been knocked out of her.

You're probably thinking the same thing that Mitch thought when he saw the article that day, Sachi continues. At first he thought it was a joke. He told Kazu about it, and then Yonko.

Yonko stares into her teacup. Sachi looks alternately at Yonko and Ami-chan.

Kazu said it was just a coincidence, Ami-chan picks up where Sachi left off. That we were reading too much into it. Mitch and Yonko agreed. We just heard about all of this yesterday at the hospital.

Yonko's mother listens. She imagines Mitch standing in the hospital courtyard, the yellow ginkgo leaves swirling to the ground. She imagines him making sure that Yonko's mother and Mama weren't within hearing distance as he spoke to Ami-chan and Sachi, his face expressionless, only his green eyes flashing. Perhaps his voice shook as he spoke. Perhaps he said something like this:

The perpetrator hasn't been caught yet. It was probably a random attack, so it'll be difficult to determine the culprit. It just seems strange for a woman to be wearing an orange skirt. And this is the only thing the victim had in common with Miki-chan, so it's probably unrelated, but . . .

Then perhaps Kazu spoke as the yellow ginkgo leaves fell from above, one after another.

Mitch, let it go. You don't need to tell Sachi and Ami-chan all of this. It's not something we can treat casually. What happened with Miki-chan is over, it's in the past.

I know. That's why I'm not going to the police. I'm not even telling Mama about it. I want to pretend like I don't know it happened. But I can't. It's impossible – you know that, don't you? I'm scared. Really scared.

Yonko's mother trembles. Ami-chan's and Sachi's eyes are filled with tears. Yonko is still hanging her head. She wants to say they are overthinking it, but her mouth is parched, and she can't speak. Out of the corner of her eye, Yonko's mother can see Miki-chan standing in the corner of the room. She can see Tabo's dark figure approaching her from behind. Tabo is already nineteen, tall. He comes closer and closer, reaches both hands out toward Miki-chan. Her orange skirt billows up around her.

Suddenly Yonko's mother closes her eyes and moans.

After Yonko and Kazu talked to Mitch, Ami-chan continues, they went to the scene of the murder, in Toshima Ward. Mitch was against it, but Kazu said he wanted to see it for himself. So Yonko decided to go along with them. She was scared out of her wits, but thinking of Kazu wandering around by himself in that unfamiliar place made her uneasy. And Mitch wanted her to come.

What do you think you're going to find there? Mitch said. You're the one who said we shouldn't be too quick to jump to conclusions. There's probably no connection anyway. Yonko, you go with Kazu. Besides, it'll make him happy.

Isn't that right? Ami-chan asks.

Yonko lifts her head and nods. She seems incapable of speaking, so Ami-chan is telling the story for her. Yonko's mother wonders what Mitch had meant by 'Besides, it'll make him happy.' She turns her gaze toward her daughter, then quickly looks back at Ami-chan. She can't afford to miss a single word.

When Kazu and Yonko went all the way to the scene of the crime, they weren't able to find anything useful – though it had been obvious from the beginning that they wouldn't. Afterward, they went to the apartment where Tabo and his mother lived, which was within walking distance of Yonko's house. The pond that Miki-chan fell into, or was pushed into, was halfway between their apartment and Yonko's. None of them had ever returned to the park where it had happened. It no longer existed in their internal map. Miki-chan wasn't coming back, no matter how much they wished she would. But the place where Tabo lived? That would never disappear.

The building was still there, looking exactly as it had ten years earlier. One section of the outer wall was covered with galvanized sheet metal, like one of those barracks they'd built right after the war. It was bent and warped in places, its hue corroded and faded.

For a long time, Yonko and the others kept their eyes on that building. The children already knew where Tabo lived. At least, the ones who went to the local elementary school did. They went by it about a year after Miki-chan's death, then again when Mitch finally regained the ability to walk after his accident, and again after Mitch and Kazu came back from England. But they'd always get scared and run away. They couldn't bring themselves to run up to the plywood door and knock on it, or call out to Tabo. In fact, it never even occurred to them.

They'd run away before getting anywhere near the door, Yonko and Kazu said. The building was still in the same place, and through the window of the first storey, where it seemed Tabo and his mother were living, they managed to glimpse a pair of men's pants and underwear, which they thought must be Tabo's, hanging up to dry. In other words, they had managed to confirm nothing except for the fact that the building was still there.

Yes, I know that place, too, Yonko's mother murmurs.

She averts her gaze from the three girls sitting in front of her and searches the room for Miki-chan. But she isn't there. Yonko's mother shifts her gaze to the engawa. There she is, in a slanting ray of afternoon light, playing otedama all by herself. The sunlight reflects off her curly hair, turning it a deep red. She is moving her lips, probably singing an otedama song.

> *Ichi is for Ichi-nomiya,*
> *Ni is for Ni-kko's Tōshōgū*
> *San is for the Sa-kura's Sōgōrō . . .*

You didn't know anything about Tabo, did you, Miki-chan? Yonko's mother whispers to her in her mind. But Tabo knew about you. Just like Ami-chan stood out because of her dark skin, you stood out because of your blue eyes and light skin, and your face, which didn't look Japanese at all – even if you didn't realize it, you stood out.

Tabo had gone to the park to play by himself that day, as usual. And then you showed up, Miki-chan. The children were all playing hide-and-seek. You were 'it'. You stood near the pond, counting: Oooone, twoooo, threeee. Tabo was drawn to you, walked toward you, not understanding why you were all alone near the pond.

That's more or less what happened, right, Miki-chan? Right, Tabo?

Yonko's mother notices that Tabo, too, has appeared in the garden outside the house. He is standing there all alone, looking up at Miki-chan where she sits. Nine-year-old Tabo. His dishevelled hair looks whitish. His eyes droop a little at the ends, making him look perpetually sleepy. He came to school only when he felt like it, and even when he did, he'd just wander around the schoolyard. He would eat lunch, but never enter the building.

Maybe that was why a rumour spread among the mothers of the children at the school that Tabo was surviving on school lunches alone.

His mother works nights, so she's neglecting him, they'd say.

I heard that both mother and son were repatriated from China, that they were abandoned by his Chinese father.

All these rumours, of course, were based on nothing but speculation.

Tabo attended the same local elementary school as Yonko. He was two years ahead of her. His real name was Tamiya, but everyone called him Tabo. When the students looked out at the schoolyard during class, they'd often see him by himself, throwing stones at the fence, crouching in front of the jungle gym. They all knew who he was.

He was notorious at school, Yonko's mother thinks. He was always alone. Had Tabo ever had anyone he could call a friend? Maybe he'd wanted to be friends with Miki-chan, and Yonko, too.

Were you jealous of them, Tabo? You had such bad luck.

Yonko's mother nods to no one in particular, opens her mouth. She has to tell the girls that she knows nothing about where Tabo is these days. She doesn't want to believe that this nineteen-year-old boy has killed a random passer-by simply because she was wearing an orange skirt. She doesn't want to believe it, or even suspect it. Besides, Tabo might not have noticed the colour of Miki-chan's skirt that day. And even if he had, ten years to a child is practically an eternity.

Ah, but . . . Yonko's mother feels a sharp pain at the back of her throat. Yonko, you all remember the colour of Miki-chan's skirt to this day. Does that mean nine-year-old Tabo, too, was pushed into a place much deeper and darker than the pond Miki-chan fell into?

Yonko's mother takes a deep breath.

I have to tell them about the rumours surrounding Miki-chan's death, she thinks. They're still searching for a way to pull Miki-chan out of the whirlpool of mysteries.

The rumours mostly came from the parents' association at school. They were stories that the mothers had heard, and tended to fall into several distinct types.

One was that Tabo had targeted Miki-chan and intentionally pushed her into the pond, that he'd watched calmly as she struggled in the water. Someone had seen Tabo standing at the edge of the pond and watched as he ran home. Afterward, he didn't leave his house for several days or come to school for a long time, and when his homeroom teacher went to check on him, Tabo's mother wailed: Please forgive him, he doesn't know anything.

That was one rumour.

Another was that Tabo hadn't been alone that day, that he had been with a group of dark-skinned children. Miki-chan was a mixed-race orphan left behind by a white GI, and she had been raised in an orphanage. There were many mixed-race children like her there, all of them with warped personalities. Tabo was shy by nature, a gentle child, and must have been incited to act by those 'savage' mixed-race children. As Miki-chan was drowning, the other orphans had looked on, laughing. Among them was a girl who was friends with the orphans, the daughter of a single mother who lived in the neighbourhood. The mixed-race children of American GIs would sometimes go play at her house because they had a special connection to her.

There was even a rumour that a man who had been a victim of the atomic bombs had manipulated the children into committing this violent act. This person hated America, and had channelled his hatred toward the mixed-race children that the GIs had left behind in Japan. He couldn't stand the fact that these children even existed in Japan, and thought they should be eliminated for the sake of the country. After he moved to Tokyo, he'd noticed the orphans hanging around the neighbourhood. He knew he couldn't kill all of them, so he decided to get Tabo on his side and kill one of the girls to set an example for the rest . . .

Yonko's mother could never forget the shock she'd felt when the four children had come running home, crying, gasping for air, shouting: Miki-chan's going to die, she fell into the pond, come help, quick!

Children make such a big deal of everything, she'd thought at first. But it was obvious that Miki-chan hadn't come home with them.

Yonko's mother had left the children with Sister Yae and run to the park. A crowd of people had already gathered there, and an ambulance had arrived.

What happened? Yonko's mother whispered to the nearest person. A little girl fell into the pond, they whispered back. Poor thing, apparently she died.

Suddenly a siren began to wail, the crowd dispersed, and the ambulance drove off.

Yonko's mother rushed back to the house and quietly told Sister Yae what she'd witnessed. Sister Yae grimaced and closed her eyes. Give me the phone, I'm calling the police, she said after a moment. Take the children to the other room.

The police told Sister Yae which hospital Miki-chan had been taken to.

That was when Kazu murmured to Mama: Tabo was there.

Yes, Miki-chan and Tabo were there, Yonko and Mitch added shakily. Tabo was saying something. But it might not have been him. We're not sure.

Sister Yae and Yonko's mother looked at each other. For a while, they were frozen in fear.

Who's Tabo? Sister Yae said to Yonko's mother in a low voice, so the children wouldn't hear.

A boy in the neighbourhood, Yonko's mother whispered back. Kazu and Mitch know who he is. Sometimes he follows them around, and they make fun of him.

Sister Yae nodded. She seemed to be thinking a thousand things at once. At last she stood up.

I'm going to the hospital. To be near Miki-chan. She'll be okay. Look after the kids.

Then she dashed out of the house.

Left alone, Yonko's mother sank into the tatami, confused. Calm down, she repeated to herself. Don't say anything to the children. You can't scare them. Don't say anything.

The four children were silent now, watching her. It was night by the time they got the call from Sister Yae.

It was no use, they couldn't save her, Sister Yae's muffled voice said through the receiver.

Yonko's mother couldn't think of anything to say. She felt tears well up in her eyes, then spill over.

The hospital called Mother Asami, Sister Yae continued, and she's here now. She's going to keep watch over Miki-chan's body until morning. After that, they're going to do an autopsy, but as soon as that's done, I'm going straight back to the orphanage. After three days, I want you to bring the children to the orphanage. We'll have the funeral on the fourth day.

And about that boy, Tabo, Sister Yae added quietly, holding the receiver close to her mouth. I mentioned it to the police. I told them I'd gone to the park with Miki-chan and that I was sitting on a bench nearby, where I could see the pond. And that I thought I saw a boy I didn't recognize standing near Miki-chan. And that I'd gone back to your house first and was just waiting for Miki-chan to come back. That's what I told them, so make sure your story matches mine. I thought it might be bad for us later if we didn't say anything now. I don't think we need to mention the other children. They probably don't even know what happened themselves.

All right, I'll bring them to the orphanage in three days, Yonko's mother replied.

She wasn't sure what else to do. They had to leave the children's world as undisturbed as possible.

But sometime after that, Yonko's mother had a realization. More than one person in the neighbourhood must have seen the four children as they ran from the park that day, flinging tears and snot as they ran, their faces bright red, occasionally tripping but still running at full speed toward the house. And of course, there must have been other people at the park. One of those people had called an ambulance from the public phone near the entrance to the park. What had they seen? That they had seen something was certain. Many people had heard the ambulance. The people in the neighbourhood who saw a group of mixed-race children running out of the park had heard it, too.

That night, and the day after that, the children kept quiet. Perhaps when they were alone with each other they had spoken, but at least in front of Yonko's mother they kept their mouths shut. Yonko's mother went about her daily activities without acknowledging what had happened to Miki-chan. She took a few days off from the pharmaceutical company where she worked, under the pretext that there had been a sudden death in the family.

The day they performed the autopsy on Miki-chan's body, it rained all day. Around noon, a police officer and a detective came by the house and said they needed to interview witnesses. They wanted to hear from everyone, since Miki-chan had been staying at this house when she died. Yonko's mother couldn't hide the children anywhere, so she told them to greet the detectives. They seemed surprised to see four children of the same age who closely resembled each other. Yonko's mother explained that Sachi was from the same orphanage as Miki-chan, and Kazu and Mitch had also lived there until they were three, and that Sister Yae, who had adopted the two of them, was her cousin, so sometimes she brought the children from the orphanage here to play. But yesterday, the children weren't at the park, because they had been at the house. It was just Miki-chan and Sister Yae who went to the park. The two of them were really fond of that place, she said.

The police officer and the detective confirmed the identities of each of the children.

Were you playing at home yesterday? they asked.

Yonko nodded silently. Kazu and Mitch nodded, too. Finally, little Sachi nodded as well, her face contorting as she tried not to cry in front of these strange men.

The detectives didn't question the children any more after that. They would probably interview other people in the neighbourhood, including those who had been in the park that day, who would be considered key witnesses.

But there was no need to worry, Yonko's mother thought, her mind made up. As Sister Yae said, at the end of the day these were children. Five-, seven-, eight-year-old children. And though it was unfortunate this had happened, it had been an accident, not a murder. There was no other possible interpretation. This was all just a formality, and the detectives were just doing their job.

The next morning, a short article had appeared in the newspaper that said Miki-chan was a mixed-race orphan who had been left behind by an American GI, that she had been found floating face-down in the middle of a pond, still wearing all her clothes, that it had been a man from the neighbourhood who had found her, that her death was assumed to have been an accident, that the immediate cause of death was drowning.

Of course, Yonko's mother didn't show the article to the children. The next day, just as she had promised Sister Yae, she told the children to get ready because they were all going to the orphanage. They didn't ask what had happened to Miki-chan. Nor did they ask where Mama had gone, or why she hadn't come back. They packed up their few belongings without a word, as though they understood everything. It was still pouring rain.

One of these days, I'll get the chance to ask them what really happened, Yonko's mother thought at the time. But as each day went by, it got harder and harder to broach the subject, till a week went by, then a month, and, as time dragged on, it only became more difficult to speak about. On the one hand, Yonko's mother had felt relieved. It seemed the lies she had told the police had gone unchallenged. They had settled on the narrative that the children hadn't seen anything. The children, including Tabo, had been saved.

So when she heard the rumours going around at Yonko's school about Tabo and the other children, she felt like she herself had been pushed into the pond.

We couldn't escape them, after all, she thought, biting her tongue. They'll never let this go.

The rumours were much more frightening than being questioned by the police. For the shadow of a rumour never disappears. It warps, bends, propagates of its own accord. And what was most frightening of all was the fact that neither Yonko's mother, nor the children, nor Tabo, nor Miki-chan herself knew what had really happened that day. The only thing that was certain was the fact of Miki-chan's death.

The children never mentioned Tabo's name again, and Yonko's mother never heard it either. And as time went on, it became clear that she would never ask the children: What did you really see that day?

Yonko's mother had never mentioned the fact that she had once made eye contact with Tabo's mother, just for a moment – nor would she likely ever mention it. She didn't want to stir up that sludge of apprehension again. Besides, she thought, the moment had been so brief. Did it even count as making eye contact?

One Sunday evening, eight months after Miki-chan's death, Yonko's mother went and stood in front of the building where Tabo lived. A chilly wind was blowing. Tabo and his mother lived in the corner unit on the first floor. Yonko's mother had confirmed this the last time she'd come here. The cloudy glass window opened, and Tabo stuck his head out for just a minute. Then, just as quickly, he disappeared and the window closed.

Yonko's mother had stood in that exact place four, maybe five times now. She was compelled to keep going back, especially when she thought of how Tabo's mother must be suffering more from these rumours than anyone else. Did she expect to feel something like a mother's empathy? Even now, she was perplexed by the state of mind she'd been in at the time.

One windy day in December, Yonko's mother was standing outside Tabo's apartment as usual. Near the window, she could see a piece of beige cloth, perhaps a pillowcase, that had been hung up to dry, fluttering as though it might fly off at any moment. An hour went by, and she was beginning to think about going home, when the door to the apartment building cracked open ever so slightly. It was Tabo's mother. Yonko's mother knew it was her, from the way she opened the door: carefully, as though she were afraid of something. Yonko's mother immediately craned her neck to try to see her. She thought she saw a pair of glasses glimmering in the darkness for a minute, but the door closed again just as quickly. She stood there in a daze, waiting for it to open once more. The building had lots of apartments, she thought, so surely other people would come and go through the door. But no one appeared again.

Was it for ten minutes, or maybe fifteen, that Yonko's mother waited there, before trudging home with tired, heavy steps? Her tears fell continuously about her feet.

Tabo, you really were at the pond that day, weren't you? Yonko's mother addresses him in her mind. You saw Miki-chan in her orange skirt, didn't you?

What happened after that, of course, no one knows. It's impossible for people not to speculate. But that sharp light in Tabo's mother's eyes communicated something: that there really had been a time when Tabo and Miki-chan crossed paths.

Tabo's mother.

Yonko's mother turned to look behind her as she whispered. She couldn't see the apartment building anymore.

I see now, Tabo, that you have a mother who will protect you. And Yonko has a mother who will do the same for her. But Miki-chan didn't.

As she thinks of the lonely death Miki-chan died, she is assaulted by a pain so sharp she can barely stand it.

6

I can't breathe.

All he can hear is the sound of his own breathing. His feet are caked in mud, and a dark overgrowth of gnarled trees surrounds him.

Is this the jungle they're always talking about?

Something is coming after him. He has to keep running. The mud weighs his feet down, the air feels heavy and thick.

Suddenly the trees begin to sway, leaves and branches rain down upon him. The land is glowing orange as far as he can see. He thinks it is fire, but he senses no heat from it. He has to run away, fast. Fast! Just up ahead, he can see a muddy bog. It must be a crater hollowed out by a bomb. Inside, a woman is lying on her back. No, wait, she's collapsed, unconscious. She is bleeding from the head. But she's not dead. Again the trees in the jungle rustle, swaying violently. The orange light spreads. He realizes there are explosions coming from all around him, that the orange light is mowing down the trees. A deafening roar echoes far above him, and he immediately covers his ears. It must be a combat helicopter.

There is no time to worry about the dying woman, yet he is drawn to her. He enters the muddy bog, approaches her one step at a time. The woman is floating face-up, wearing an áo dài the same colour as the mud.

Careful! If it's a Vietcong, they'll kill you, he hears a voice say. But he can't pull himself away from the woman. He pins her down, they sink into the mud together. The woman's breasts sway softly in the mud. He strips off her áo dài and pants. She bursts into laughter. Her stomach begins to swell, rapidly.

Could this be . . .

Suddenly he is seized with fear. He hears a baby wailing.

Wait, that's me.

The woman thrusts her nipple toward him. Instinctively, he tries to take it in his mouth. Is this woman his mother? Just as the thought occurs to him, he is assailed by another blast and enveloped in orange light. When he looks up, he sees the muddy bog has turned orange, and the body of a small girl floating there – but when he looks closer, he sees that the flesh on her feet and neck and hands is beginning to rot, dissolving into the mud. Fear and despair assail him. He wants to scream, Miki-chan, Miki-chan, but he cannot speak, and tears of frustration well up in his eyes.

Mitch wakes to the sound of his own moaning. As he wipes his tears, he tries whispering her name again: Miki-chan. The fear and despair that assailed him in his dream refuse to fade, and he can't bother to lift his head from the pillow. That terrible colour haunts him. Vietnam? Again? But the Vietnam War is over. And his mother? No, even for a dream, it's too incoherent. Then why was he aroused by the sight of a dying woman? The thought disgusts him.

Miki-chan, please don't misunderstand, he thinks. I promise I don't think of you that way.

He looks around the room nervously. Where is he, anyway? Tangled spiderwebs form dark patterns on the light pink ceiling, whose plaster is chipping off in places. The bed is excessively large. Yes, he remembers now – he'd had some trouble climbing up onto it last night. It looks elegant at first, but the mattress, the most important part, is old and worn out, and the springs dig into him, so he has to be extra careful when he rolls over or changes position. There is an old chair in the room that looks identical to the one in a Van Gogh painting, a table and chairs, a cold fireplace, and a mirror, about one metre tall, that looks like it hasn't been polished for about a century. In the corner is a white washbasin, covered with cracks.

This isn't Yokohama, or Rome, but a cheap hotel in Paris – that's where I've been sleeping, Mitch thinks. A cheap hotel in Paris without Kazu or Yonko.

Just then something begins to ring, shrill and loud. Mitch braces himself, eyes darting around the room, then realizes it's coming from an old-fashioned phone. He picks it up, his heart still beating wildly.

Hello?

Mitch? How long are you gonna make me wait? You're late. Are you still sleeping? I can't believe this. Hurry up and get down here!

As soon as the woman begins shouting at him, a vivid image of Annie's face appears in his mind. Her large black eyes. The shape of her mouth, its delicate expression. It had been a while since he'd seen her, and though her features hadn't changed, and she wore no make-up, she was dazzlingly beautiful. She was studying to become a fashion designer, which is why she was in Paris, a place she'd always wanted to live. Her whole being seemed to radiate happiness. At least that's what Mitch had thought when he'd first seen her.

Hey, Kazu, Annie's really grown into herself, Mitch addresses Kazu in his mind. It's almost like she's been reborn. I'm captivated by her – she's so lovely and elegant.

Right, sorry, Annie. What time is it? Oh, it's four o'clock? And you're at the hotel already?

What do you mean? Isn't that when we said we'd meet? I can't believe this. I've been here for an hour already.

Oh, really? Sorry, I'll be right down, just wait there.

Mitch hangs up the phone and gets dressed in a hurry. He washes his face in the sink, fixes his long hair. He decides to skip shaving, since he's running short on time.

He enters the elevator, which looks like an antique birdcage, similar to the ones he's seen in old French films. As it descends to the small front desk on the first floor, he searches his memories from the night before.

Last night they had gone to a run-down café to welcome Mako and drank until late in the night. Annie hadn't shown up till nine, as she was working late. And today is Sunday, her day off, so they'd made plans to go for a walk in the woods, then have dinner with Mako.

Of course she's angry, Mitch thinks, clicking his tongue. He has a feeling Annie must have escorted him back to the hotel last night. Perhaps he'd tried to invite her back to his room before they'd said goodbye. Had he thrown his arms around her beautiful body, kissed her forcefully while drunk?

God, I'm so pathetic. Did I get rejected by Annie? Is that why I had that dream? What do you think, Kazu?

Mitch grimaces as he continues to search his memory. Mako was there last night, too. But he hadn't come back to the hotel. He'd said something about Annie's apartment being closer. To be honest, Mitch had completely forgotten about Mako, and when a tall, lanky man had suddenly shown up wearing round glasses, with a ponytail and a beard that made him look like Jesus Christ himself, Mitch had wondered who the hell he was. The man was wearing clothes from India, smoked marijuana, and had the dubious air of someone who made psychedelic art – but when Mitch asked him what he did, it turned out Mako was studying architecture at a university in Paris. When he introduced himself, smiling shyly, it suddenly clicked as Mitch recalled the way Mako used to smile as a child.

Mako had been a quiet boy, about two years older than Mitch. And he had memories of his own mother, something that was unusual in the orphanage. The other children envied this and used to taunt him for it.

When is your real mum coming back? You're lying, you don't actually remember her!

No one knew what had actually happened between Mako and his mother, but over time he gradually stopped talking about her. He'd lived at the orphanage until he was thirteen and probably had no relationship with her now.

In fact, Mitch thinks, perhaps the fact that Mako did remember his mother – unlike the other children, who did not remember their parents at all – meant that he was fated to live the rest of his life carrying around something like a small rock or shard of glass inside himself.

When Mitch had first arrived in Rome, it was Kazu who had told him that Annie and Mako were in Paris, and Kazu who had let Annie and Mako know that Mitch would be going there later.

According to Kazu, Mako had been both lucky and unlucky since leaving the orphanage at age thirteen. Two years after he'd become an apprentice at an auto-parts factory, the whole place caught fire and the company went bankrupt. When Mother Asami and Mama found out, they immediately began searching for a way to help him, and eventually connected him with some entrepreneurs who offered to support him as he attended high school during the day. Mako had always been intelligent and worked hard at school, and all the adults agreed he should go to college. He took the entrance exam for the science division at the University of Tokyo and passed on his first try, then began studying architecture, and even managed to study abroad in Paris. But Mako didn't seem too concerned with his architectural studies. The programme in Paris had just been an excuse for him to leave Japan.

Okay, I get what Mako's up to, Mitch had said to Kazu after

hearing about this over the phone. But what are you guys going to do?

We're going back to Japan, Kazu answered bluntly.

But you can't go back by yourselves. I'm going with you. Why do you think I came all the way to Rome? You're responsible for this.

Are we?

Yes.

Yonko will be happy if you come to Paris, Kazu said, a hint of laughter in his voice. Annie and Mako will be, too.

It's not like I came here to have a good time. You know that. You could have waited for me in Rome. Would it hurt you to show some consideration once in a while?

You're right, Kazu said, and hung up. After that, he'd gone back to Japan with Yonko without waiting for Mitch.

Early the next morning, in other words yesterday morning, Mitch had arrived at the Gare de Paris Bercy, sleep-deprived, on an overnight train from Rome. Since he couldn't understand a word of French, Annie came to pick him up at the station. It was his first time seeing her in years, and he was struck by her beauty, teasing her all the way to the taxi, complaining about the overnight train, rambling on about how the air in Rome was cleaner than in Paris. It wasn't until they got into the taxi that he realized: the fact that she had come to pick him up rather than Kazu and Yonko meant that they'd already left. Suddenly the exhaustion from the trip threatened to crush him all at once.

Since then, Mitch has been staying in his hotel room, mostly sleeping, unless Annie or Mako invited him out.

Kazu had gone to the airport with Yonko the day after he and Mitch talked on the phone. Maybe that had been his plan all along, but he hadn't told Mitch any of this. Instead, he'd deceived him. Every time Mitch turned over in bed, he let out a low groan.

Am I really such a nuisance to you? Do you not trust me? he muttered.

Mitch couldn't believe that Kazu would do something so cold-hearted. Maybe it was Yonko who had made the decision. Mitch couldn't endure the thought.

Yonko, what do you have against me? Mitch asked her in his mind. Tears welled up in his eyes. It was your mother and Mama who asked me to come. It's not like I was following you because I wanted to. Are you really mad at me? Are you scared to see me? And, Kazu, why won't you tell Yonko that nothing bad is going to happen if she sees me? Do you resent me, too? Or, worse, do you hate me?

If Kazu and Yonko weren't here, there was no reason for Mitch to stay in Paris. He wanted to go back to Japan right away but couldn't summon the willpower to stop by the travel agency and change his ticket. He didn't feel like sightseeing either. He couldn't decide what to do. He hadn't even called Mama yet to let her know what had happened.

It all started ten days ago, when Mama had got a call from Kazu saying that he and Yonko were in Rome. The line kept cutting in and out, and his voice sounded far away.

Everything's okay, Mama. Yonko just needed a change of scenery. We knew you'd be worried because we decided to go on such short notice – that's why we called. We're planning to go to Paris, too. Can you let Yonko's mother know?

Yonko and Kazu are in Rome, Mama said as she handed the receiver to Mitch.

Hey! You're in Rome? Mitch nearly shouted into the receiver. What the hell? Why would you do that to us? We had no idea what happened to you. Is Yonko okay?

Of course, Kazu answered. Yonko said she wanted to go to Rome and Paris, so that's where we are.

We went to your place in Kyoto, but you weren't there, so

everyone started panicking. I told Yonko's mother that whatever happened, Yonko wasn't the type to commit suicide or anything like that.

What hotel are you staying at? Mama said, taking back the receiver. Mitch is going to pick you up, so just wait there. You're telling us to trust you, that you're not children anymore? Please. You may be twenty-six, but to me you're still a kid who knows nothing about the world. You're the one who just up and left with Yonko, which means it's my responsibility to make sure she gets back to Japan safely. You owe Yonko's mother a big apology. Otherwise, she'll never forgive you. I really don't understand why you'd do something like this.

And that's how Mitch had ended up in Rome. Thankfully his passport had still been valid; he'd used it just six months earlier to go to Hawaii with Mama. He wanted to hop on the next flight out, but he had to get his visa first, as well as the necessary vaccines, which took an unexpectedly long time to sort out, so it was another six days before he was finally able to get on a plane.

After Yonko had graduated from a women's college, she'd got a job, left home, and started living with a man who turned out to be involved with another woman. Then he got into drugs. He kept demanding money from Yonko, who was just an employee at a small publishing house. If she said no, he'd hit her and kick her, or sometimes have sex with the other woman in front of her. Yonko tried her best to deal with things on her own, but at last she reached breaking point, went back to her mother's house and quit her job. Even then, the man tried to follow her, saying he couldn't live without her, that he'd broken up with the other woman, that he'd had a change of heart. He'd ask if they could start over, and every time it would throw Yonko for a loop, but as soon as she'd let her guard down, he'd betray her again, and in the end she felt completely stuck.

Yonko's mother and Mama thought it might be good for her to go and stay with Kazu for a while in Kyoto, since no one was likely to try to pick a fight with him, and Mitch agreed. Kazu had decided he wanted to learn more about Japanese gardens, which is why he'd moved to Kyoto five years ago. Luckily, he'd found an expert there whom he was able to learn from. Mama had given him money to rent an apartment, so Mitch would sometimes go and visit him in Kyoto. And then Yonko moved in.

Come to think of it, maybe the fact that no one batted an eye at the idea of Kazu and Yonko living together was because they were like siblings. After about a month of living with him, she'd grown much calmer, and had even begun working part-time at a soba restaurant that was popular with tourists. Still, Mitch couldn't help but wonder if that was the whole story. He'd even thought that he wanted to – no, must – go to Kyoto and have a long talk with both of them.

But one day, the woman gardener who had been Kazu's boss contacted Mama. Kazu had suddenly quit his job and disappeared. He still owed her some money, so could she send Mama the bill? Mama was shocked. She contacted Kazu's apartment manager. The lease had been cancelled. The furniture was still there, but Kazu and Yonko weren't.

The first thing Mitch wanted to do when he saw Kazu was give him a good scolding. Why would you run off like that? Didn't you think about how Mama and Yonko's mother would react? That they would immediately come to the worst possible conclusion? Did that not cross your mind?

He had no idea what had even motivated the two of them to go to Rome. They had paid for the trip with the money Yonko's mother had given her for living expenses, plus the money that Kazu had in the bank, which Mama had given him to pay the rent on his apartment.

So the two of you used all that money because you wanted a change of pace? Are you children? Or was it because . . . for some reason, that pond keeps reminding you – and me – that it's still there?

I really did adore Japanese gardens, Kazu had said. His voice came back to Mitch as he was nodding off on the airplane. I thought if I wanted to do this, I'd better do it right and learn from a Japanese gardener. But you know how Japanese gardens always have a pond? That always bothered me, though I didn't think about it till now. I couldn't tell my boss, so I just kept it to myself. There are big ponds, small ponds, all kinds really, but I can't stand any of 'em. There's rocks, and moss growing, and that muddy water . . . it's the worst.

What had Mitch said to Kazu then? Maybe he had just nodded and kept silent. For a long time now, neither Mitch nor Kazu – nor even Yonko – had uttered the names Miki-chan or Tabo. They were afraid, yes, that was partly it, but also they didn't need to go to the trouble of verbalizing their thoughts to know what each other were thinking. All they had to do was look at one another and they immediately understood. At least, that's how Mitch felt.

If only all ponds could disappear from the world. And that horrible colour orange, too.

But no matter how much they prayed, the number of ponds in the world never decreased and the colour orange didn't disappear. Meanwhile, Miki-chan drew silently closer and closer.

Mitch flew from Haneda Airport in Tokyo to Anchorage, then transferred in Copenhagen to get to Rome. The whole journey was so long that by the time he arrived, he was completely exhausted. He hadn't slept at all on the flight, his seat was cramped, his back and feet hurt.

You went through all this just to get to Rome? he kept muttering under his breath to Kazu and Yonko.

Kazu, was this how it was when we went to England? How could you bring Yonko on this trip, knowing how brutal the flight from Japan to Europe is? Or had you completely forgotten about it, like I did?

Mama had accompanied them on that flight to England when they were twelve. But when they'd come back to Japan two years later, they'd flown unaccompanied. They were still children then, so perhaps they'd just slept through the flight. Is that why they didn't remember the trip?

Then, too, memories of life at the school in England had grown as faint in his mind as the distant vapour trails left behind by airplanes in the sky. Kazu and Mitch were always huddled next to each other. It had felt like they were trapped in a cramped, dark place. They couldn't have run away even if they'd wanted to – after all, they were in England. Hopelessness crushed them. Still, if they didn't have each other, they probably would have ended up conforming to those around them. They might have been proper British subjects by now, just like Mama had wanted. Thinking back on it, Mitch is grateful they escaped that fate. At the same time, he couldn't help feeling guilty that they'd missed a valuable opportunity.

In those days, taking a trip overseas was no simple matter. Looking back on it as an adult, Mitch is amazed that Mama had decided to go through with sending them abroad. She must have used every connection she had to get them to England, giving the people at the embassy an earful about these 'poor, mixed-race orphans' to elicit their sympathy and convince them to shell out a good amount of money along the way. Mama had accepted that Mitch and Kazu were never coming back to Japan. But less than two years later, they'd started pleading with her to let them return, saying they'd die if they couldn't. Kazu had even fallen ill at one point. Mitch couldn't imagine the disappointment Mama must have felt when they told her that. But she didn't scold them. She listened. Some part of her must also have felt happy that they wanted to come back.

But when they'd returned to Japan, this time it was the Japanese schools they couldn't adjust to. Once again, Mama scrambled to find a solution, eventually sending them to the American school in Yokohama. But they struggled to keep up there as well, not to mention that they couldn't stand being around so many Americans. Still, Mitch and Kazu felt strongly that they didn't want to burden Mama any more than they already had, so they managed to make it to graduation.

After high school, Kazu moved to Tokyo to begin working at a public garden and Mitch stayed behind with Mama. He didn't have to, but he didn't know what he wanted to do, and he couldn't bear to leave her alone. Eventually, he began to help her with her business. After the war, Mama had made a good deal of money by importing American goods on the black market, which had naturally segued into importing food, but the Vietnam War had begun to threaten her livelihood. She considered quitting at one point, but managed to keep the business afloat.

At last, Mitch arrived in Rome. He was exhausted, and his leg felt five times heavier than usual. When he got into the taxi, he was overwhelmed with the loneliness of being unable to communicate as he nervously searched for the address of Kazu and Yonko's hotel.

Rome was much warmer and more humid than Yokohama. It was only May, but he was dripping with sweat. His long hair stuck to his face and neck, and he felt irritated. At last he found the hotel, surrounded by a stand of trees. It had the vague atmosphere of a haunted house. Timidly, he climbed the stone stairs, then inquired at the front desk, which was partially shrouded in darkness, whereupon a plump woman smiled and handed him a sheet of paper. Mitch read the words, written in Kazu's messy handwriting, and nearly fainted right then and there.

We're on our way to Paris. Call Kate. If you need to reach us, call the hotel in Paris. I'll leave the number. We're planning to go back to Japan from Paris. Take care of yourself, Mitch.

Once he'd been shown to his room, Mitch took off his sweaty dress shirt and slacks, then called the hotel in Paris. It was almost ten o'clock at night, and he assumed Kazu and Yonko would be in their room. Sure enough, Kazu picked up on the second ring, as though he'd been waiting for him.

What the hell? Why did you leave without me?

We never promised we would wait for you. Kazu chuckled. You really came all the way to Rome, huh? I was wondering if you would. Well, Kate's still there, so she can show you around.

Who the hell is Kate?

Don't you remember? She went by Kei-chan back at the orphanage. She's an actress in Rome now. She took good care of us when we were there. She's a friend of Joyce's. She and Yonko used to write letters to each other. She can't read or write much Japanese, and Yonko's no good at English, so they mostly communicated through pictures and gestures. Yonko really wanted to see her.

Uh-huh. So Yonko's doing okay?

Yeah, a little better, I think. Kazu's voice grew more serious. She's right here, do you want me to put her on?

N-no, I just wanted to make sure she's okay, Mitch said, flustered. Anyway, I'm coming to Paris soon.

Do what you like. But you should rest first. You don't want to tire yourself out.

Why do you care? Whose fault is it that I'm in this mess right now, anyway? Mitch yelled.

Kazu was silent for a moment before speaking again.

Annie and Mako are in Paris, so I'll ask them to look out for you.

Annie and Mako? So the kids from the orphanage are all over the world now, huh, Mitch muttered.

Yeah. Kazu's voice sounded sad when he answered. They're all over. That could have been us, too, you know, we could have been living in England.

Then Kazu began telling Mitch about Annie and Mako.

Well, I'm glad they're in Paris, at least, Mitch said as Kazu finished explaining. In his jet-lagged haze, he still believed he would see Kazu and Yonko there.

After that, Mitch called Kate, just as Kazu had told him to do. She picked up right away, but her Japanese was so bad that Mitch could barely understand her. She said she'd gone to America when she was four, so of course she didn't remember him. Mitch didn't remember her either. He had a vague memory of a girl named Kei-chan, but that was it.

Mitch? I've been waiting. I'm very happy – Kate said kindly in broken Japanese, but Mitch cut her off.

Thanks. But I actually have to go to Paris soon, so could you tell me the best way to get there?

No! Kate sounded bewildered. You're tired. Rest in Rome. Lots to see here. I'll show you.

No, I can't, sorry. I have to go to Paris tomorrow, Mitch insisted.

At last Kate gave up and promised to help Mitch get on the night train to Paris the following day.

Kate was twenty-one, the same age as Joyce. When he heard she was an actress, Mitch had expected to meet a dazzlingly beautiful woman, but the person who showed up the next day was small and plain, and wore no make-up, just like Annie. And yet the more time he spent with her, the more Mitch began to notice how her gentle features exhibited a curious charm.

The next day he went for a walk with Kate near the hotel. Somewhat reluctantly, he agreed to do some sightseeing. They looked at a large church and some ruins, both crowded with tourists, then ate dinner and drank until it was time for Mitch to catch his train. Kate kept smiling softly as they talked, but she also seemed reserved. She didn't understand what had brought Mitch all the way to Rome. But she seemed genuinely happy that she'd run into three people from her childhood days in the orphanage.

She's a really nice person, Mitch thought. You can tell by her face. Even if her Japanese isn't very good, I think Kei-chan, or Keiko, fits her much better than Kate.

Weren't you raised in America? Mitch asked her. It was the question he'd been wanting to ask the whole time. Why are you in Rome? It seems like a strange place to become an actress.

Kate answered in English. It was American English, so it was hard for Mitch to understand, and he didn't catch everything. But he didn't want to bother asking her to repeat herself.

Kate had been raised by a white American foster father. He had loved her – in fact, she'd been doted on so much that it became a problem. And so Kate had left home and gone to New York first, then Rome. She loved Italian movies. She was starting to make a name for herself as a B-list actress, though she was nowhere close to having the status of someone like Marcello Mastroianni or Claudia Cardinale.

Kate laughed as she told him this, and Mitch laughed, too. He figured that when he got to Paris he'd ask Kazu and Yonko about the parts of her story he didn't understand.

The hotel elevator in Paris rattles in its slow descent, and Mitch feels angry all over again, then disappointed.

I was sure I'd see you both in Paris, he addresses Kazu and Yonko in his mind. I was even planning to ask you about Kate once I got here. You said Annie and Mako were here, too, so I thought it would be like a reunion, that we'd talk about the old days at the orphanage, about Mother Asami. Yonko, I wanted to ask you about Kyoto. And, Kazu, I wanted to ask you about the Italian garden, the one thing you wanted to see in Rome.

But you're not here. Mitch's eyes fill with tears again. You really ran away from me, didn't you? Why? Running away doesn't change anything. Miki-chan and Tabo aren't going anywhere either. I wonder if you're back in Japan by now. When you get there, are you going to talk to Mama and Yonko's mother, pretending not to know anything? What are you going to say when Mama asks why you didn't see me? You know she's going to ask. Let me guess, you'll say something like, I guess Mitch wanted to take his time in Rome and stay a little longer. Maybe you'll even talk about Kate wanting to become an actress. But listen, Kazu, that's not you. You're no good at lying. So what are you really going to tell Mama?

The birdcage elevator screeches to a halt. Just then, another memory surfaces in Mitch's mind. That thing that Mako had told him. Something about Jeff having gone missing? Another outrageous story, surely.

Mitch opens the elevator door carefully with both hands, then steps out. There is a tall woman standing at the front desk. He has trouble making out her face in the dark, but from her frizzy hair there's no doubt it's Annie. Mitch raises his right hand. Annie glares at him for a moment, then quickly steps outside. He hurries after her.

Annie continues walking briskly, never turning around to look behind her. She is well aware that Mitch has a bad leg, but keeps walking faster and faster.

Annie! I'm begging you, slow down.

Mitch is sweating as he walks behind her. But the distance

between them keeps growing. If he loses sight of her, he'll have no chance of finding his way back. Just when he's beginning to worry, Annie stops abruptly and turns around to face him in her large sunglasses. Mitch approaches her with a desperate momentum. The faster he goes, the more his body sways shamefully from side to side. Annie stares. He hates it when people stare at him. He can almost sense her thinking: If he keeps acting like this, it's only going to make me angrier. Which is precisely why Mitch exaggerates his limp. When he finally reaches her, he is so out of breath that he can't speak. But just as he is beginning to catch his breath, Annie begins to walk again. Mitch follows, flustered. Annie stops. Mitch approaches. Annie walks ahead again.

I won't lose to her, damn it, Mitch thinks, beads of sweat dripping from his red face as he continues walking. He begins to cry. A memory flashes through his mind: he is following an adult who refuses to wait for him. He has the feeling that this exact thing has been happening over and over since he was a child.

Kazu, next time I see you, I'm gonna kill you. This is all your fault. I'm gonna kill you, and myself, too. Nobody wanted us to be born anyway.

He feels pathetic chasing Annie. His stomach begins to hurt. Finally they arrive at a park with a fountain in the middle. Annie sits down on a bench and waits for him. Some children are playing nearby, a toy boat floats on the surface of the water.

Oh, there's a pond here. Mitch stops, looks at Annie and then at the pond. But this pond, with its big fountain in the middle, isn't scary. It's perfectly round, and not dark at all. The surface of the water glitters as it reflects the strong rays of the sun.

Mitch sits down next to Annie and wipes the sweat from his face and neck with the sleeve of his shirt, then glares at her as he lets out a grunt.

You know . . .

Annie takes off her sunglasses, glances at Mitch, and smiles sweetly. Two large hoop earrings dangle from her earlobes.

Mitch, look around you. This is one of my favourite spots. Kazu and Yonko liked it, too.

Mitch grunts again, then lifts his head and slowly looks around the park. To his right, he sees a grove of green, glittering trees, and, beyond it, some kind of old building. There is a slight incline leading to the other side of the park, and a large flower bed at the top of the stairs. There are benches everywhere, a couple soothing their baby in a stroller, an old person sitting all alone, staring off into the distance, a young woman reading a book. Above him white clouds stand in sharp relief against a blue sky, just as a child might draw them.

What an incredibly peaceful place, Mitch thinks. Kazu and Yonko came here, too. And they liked it.

It's hot. Feels like summer.

Annie pulls a white towel out of her shoulder bag and hands it to Mitch.

May in Paris is already summer. Here, use this. The nights will get shorter from here on out.

I always thought Paris was cooler than this. Rome was so hot, I couldn't take it.

I've forgotten what May in Japan is like, Annie answers.

The towel she handed him is worn in places, and he keeps wiping his face and arms with it. It smells foreign. It reminds him how far away Kate's and Annie's lives are from Japan now.

I was actually planning to take you to a prettier garden, a real one, but we don't have enough time. It was Kazu's favourite. We went there twice.

As she speaks, Annie kicks her legs out from under her long Indian cotton skirt and holds her arms out in front of her. She is wearing several gold bracelets, which jangle whenever she moves. Her glossy brown limbs shine in the light. The top few buttons of her blue sleeveless blouse are undone, and when Mitch glimpses the top half of her breasts and the thick hair growing from her armpits, he panics and looks away.

You look sloppy, you know. No one would ever believe you're a fashion designer.

Annie looks down at her chest and legs and laughs a little.

You and Kazu say the exact same things. This is just how people dress now. Blue wind of the Andes.

Mitch widens his eyes.

What?

Neruda. He died last year. The military coup in Chile, Neruda's funeral . . . it was all so sad. Everyone at Neruda's funeral sang 'The Internationale', even though they could have been killed for it. That's why the 'blue wind of the Andes' is the most popular thing in fashion right now.

Mitch laughs along with Annie.

Sounds shallow, if you ask me.

Fashion is the voice of an era. What's frivolous is people's desires. Pinochet, Nixon – in the end they're all about money. They kill so many people just for that. How many have been killed in the Vietnam War, in the coup in Chile? All because of a hatred of the colour red. There's lots of people who fled Chile and came here to Paris. There's been a movement to try and help them. This is just a rumour, but people say Allende was killed by the CIA. I'm embarrassed to be here and have American citizenship.

Why would America kill the president of Chile? Mitch asks, tilting his head.

Last year, a Japanese plane was hijacked, Kim Dae-jung was kidnapped, and the oil crisis showed no signs of abating – so when it came to the coup in Chile, Mitch had little capacity to care. Truth be told, Mitch had never been one to care much about politics anyway. In Japan, if you so much as glanced at the news, nine times out of ten it had something to do with America. Which would then remind him that one of those Americans was his father – someone living someplace he didn't know.

American corporations monopolized the copper mines in Chile, Annie continued. And the conditions were terrible. So Chileans decided they wanted Chile to be a socialist country and tried to nationalize the copper mines. But America said, Over my dead body, and mobilized the Chilean military. And then, you know, something terrible happened that implicates us, too. The soldiers who murdered hundreds of Chilean citizens in cold blood – they were wearing khaki military uniforms and orange shirts underneath. The same colour as Miki-chan's skirt.

The Chilean military uniform . . . , Mitch whispers vacantly, shuddering.

I have this dream a lot, about the colour orange, Annie continues passionately. You do, too, right? Kazu and Yonko said the same thing. It's horrible. You know, they just had a presidential election here. France will be a socialist country soon. I can't vote, but I'm so excited. Mitterrand, from the Socialist Party, lost by just a small margin. Kazu and Yonko and I watched them count the votes on TV. We sang that song by Bob Dylan, you know the one, right? 'The Times They Are A-Changin''?

Oh yeah, that one. You said Kazu and Yonko sang it too? That's surprising. Socialism has a bad reputation in Japan. I don't think anyone likes the Soviet Union. There's that group called the United Red Army, you know, and when the Asama-Sansō incident happened, all of Japan went into a panic.

But Mitch, you live in Japan, so you've been shaped by

American culture, too. Don't you feel hopeless when you think about Nixon? Don't you want this world of money, money, money to change?

Before Mitch can answer, Annie begins to sing the first part of "The Times They Are A-Changin'" to herself in a soft voice. It's in English, so Mitch can barely understand the lyrics. He can only listen closely to the melody. It's familiar – he's heard it before, with Kazu.

Do times really change? he thinks. Maybe, but some things also never change, no matter how much he wishes they would.

Which is why we'll never change either, Mitch addresses Kazu in his mind. Right, Kazu? I mean, you came all the way to Paris.

Suddenly Annie stops singing and looks directly at Mitch, as though reading his mind. And then, ever so lightly, she kisses both his cheeks, like a small fish skimming something off the surface of the water.

Your eyes look green in the light, she says. Even though they're brown. How strange.

Mitch looks away. At the same time, he longs to hold her shimmering body.

Why are you telling me this now?

What do you mean? I just looked at them properly for the first time. Remember when I went back to Japan that one time in high school? That was the only time I saw you after your burn.

Really?

Yeah. And I remember thinking how strange it was that Kazu was the only person in the world who you trusted. How it seemed like you couldn't live without him. There's something off about it even now. I mean, I don't get why you're so upset that you couldn't see Kazu and Yonko . . .

Annie pulls away and shifts her gaze to the fountain before continuing.

Mitch, are you jealous of Yonko? It's like you feel she's taken Kazu away from you or something. Do you think that either of them belongs to you? You're like a child.

No, that's not how it is. Mama asked me to come . . .

I didn't hear anything from Kazu or Yonko, Annie murmurs as she brings her large eyes close to his face again. I don't know anything. So don't ask me, okay?

Mitch's green eyes glitter sharply as he gazes back at Annie.

So they told you not to tell me anything? he wants to say. But he stops himself. He knows more or less what Annie can and can't talk about with him, and besides, he doesn't want to pressure her. Annie seems to read his mind.

Well, isn't that a shame, she says, pouting a little as she looks up at the sky. I almost hate you. I wish Mako would hurry up and get here.

Right, Mako's coming.

Of course. We're meeting him at six. But it's not six yet.

It doesn't feel like evening at all. Oh, that reminds me of that thing Mako said yesterday. I was really drunk, so I don't remember exactly, but what's all this about Jeff going missing? Does this mean he got sent to Vietnam after all? I thought he wanted to be a doctor.

Annie sighs and nods.

We don't really know the details either. Poor Jeff.

And then she recounts Jeff's story again, lowering her voice as though to imply that all that stuff about the coup in Chile and the presidential election in France didn't really matter after all.

As he listens to her, Mitch realizes that it was because he'd heard these stories about Jeff last night that he'd dreamed about Vietnam. Mako and Annie thought Jeff had gone to medical school to pursue his dream of becoming a doctor, but all along he'd actually been working at a shipping company. He told Tommy that he wanted to come back to Japan once he'd saved up enough money. But instead he'd been drafted and sent to Vietnam. At first, Tommy and Joyce had got letters from him, but eventually they stopped coming. Had he died in battle? Tommy had tried contacting Jeff's adoptive parents, but they didn't know either.

And then the Paris Peace Accords were signed, meaning that American prisoners of war were released en masse. Tommy and Joyce went over the list carefully, but Jeff's name wasn't on it.

It can't be, they kept thinking as they checked the list of names of soldiers killed in action. But his name wasn't on there either. Jeff's adoptive parents had given up hope. But Tommy and Joyce hadn't. They couldn't. After all, Jeff had been born as a direct result of Japan losing to America during World War II – how was it possible he had died in Vietnam? It was too much to bear. It couldn't be true. Their resentment kept the grief at bay.

It wasn't just Jeff. Many other American soldiers had gone missing, too. No one could find their bodies. Perhaps they'd been killed and tossed into a hole, or thrown into the sea, or maybe their bodies were rotting away somewhere deep in the jungle. There might have been deserters. They wanted to believe that he had escaped. Perhaps he'd fled the front lines, covered in mud, and while he was hiding in a jungle near a village somewhere, he'd met a beautiful Vietnamese girl, and she'd got pregnant, and though he couldn't speak Vietnamese, he'd used pictures and gestures to explain that, yes, though he was dark-skinned, his mother was Japanese and his father was a Black American GI, and that's how he'd been born, and then he'd been adopted by an American family, ended up in Vietnam, was taken in by a village, and was now a father, living a quiet, peaceful life. That's what they wanted to believe.

Mitch hangs his head and closes his eyes. Perhaps he'd heard Mako tell this story last night, felt a headache start to come on, and just kept drinking. He tries to imagine Jeff still alive somewhere, strong, alongside his beautiful Vietnamese wife.

Tommy was almost drafted, too, Annie continues. But he got permission from his adoptive parents to run away to Canada. Now he has Canadian citizenship and works at a bookstore. He's even going to college. But he still blames himself for what happened to Jeff. He thinks he should have brought Jeff to Canada with him. What was he waiting for? He should have made sure Jeff understood just how horrible the war had got.

Listening to Annie retell the story of Jeff, Mitch remembers them playing war as kids, pretending to be American GIs. Never in his wildest dreams could Mitch have imagined that Nobu would be sent to Vietnam as an American soldier and eventually go missing.

Now Mitch has the distinct feeling that Yonko is sitting beside him, and Kazu, too. He imagines Kazu gripping Yonko's hand, pulling her close.

Nobu's not dead, you know, Kazu's voice echoes in Mitch's ear. He ran far away, and eventually made it to India, where his skin blended in with everyone else's. Maybe he's riding an alligator in a muddy river somewhere. Nobu always wanted to do something like that. So you see, he's happy now. He catches big snakes. He rides the swings that hang from the roots of the banyan trees with the long-tailed macaques. There are bright red flowers blooming everywhere. I bet they're hibiscuses. Royal poincianas. Flame of the forests. Bougainvillea. Of course, the white jasmine is in bloom, and the yellow plumeria. But there are no orange flowers there.

In Mitch's mind, Yonko turns toward the fountain and nods.

That's right. I bet Nobu has forgotten all about us by now. It's better that way.

Nobu's as strong as a banyan tree. He can become as fierce as an alligator, too. Now he's a person who doesn't belong anywhere.

Yonko gets up from the bench, approaches the dazzling spray of water from the fountain.

Hey, Miki-chan, she calls out. Do you know where Nobu really went? Will you let us know if you find out? Nobu escaped the war, and we've come all the way here. But we know we can't really escape, no matter how much we try. A person can't escape from their own self.

Maybe Kazu and Yonko have had a call from Joyce by now. Or from Tommy.

We can't find Nobu, he went to Vietnam and never came back.

The two of them couldn't stand living in Japan anymore. Was it because they'd found the newspaper article about the murder in Tokyo? Had the frightening conjecture they'd made all but suffocated them?

Am I wrong? At this point I can't think of what else it could be.

From the park bench where he sits in Paris, Mitch imagines Kazu and Yonko hurrying off to the airport.

When he finds this article, Mitch will definitely come find us.

Is that what you told Kazu in your apartment in Kyoto, Yonko?

We know what Mitch will say: *See, there it is again, the colour orange. A high school girl wearing an orange dress was hit in the head with a rock and killed. Afterward they tore off her dress, though there's no evidence of her underwear being removed. They say the victim had wanted an orange dress for a long time, and her parents had bought one for her birthday. How can we sit here and do nothing?*

And then? How would you respond, Kazu?

I wouldn't know what to say. If we open our mouths, we'll be crushed. We couldn't save Miki-chan. We should have at least yelled for help that day at the pond. That's why we don't want to see you, Mitch.

I should be keeping my distance from you, too, Kazu, perhaps Yonko says.

Kazu – how did you respond to Yonko when she said that?

I'm running away. I have to run away. Mitch is going to show up here, asking us why we didn't try to save Miki-chan that day.

Is that how it happened, Yonko?

Kazu couldn't let Yonko travel alone. Of course he couldn't. She was already a mess as it was. This was the same Yonko who had decided to move in with a man she didn't even like after separating from Mitch and Kazu, the people she was closest to in the world.

Kazu – you really didn't want to lose Yonko, did you?

There is little Tabo, standing all alone on the other side of that dreaded prophecy that's come back again for the first time in eight years. He is standing next to seven-year-old Miki-chan. Neither Kazu, nor Yonko, nor Mitch can approach him. This time in which they are frozen flows on and on, while unknown people in unknown places keep being killed. They imagine that an orange-coloured creature in the shape of Miki-chan has taken up residence inside Tabo, and that, from time to time, the creature begins to struggle violently, tearing Tabo into a million pieces. They feel afraid, but there is nothing they can do. Who will be next? And when?

I can't possibly see Mitch and talk about all of this right now.

Is that what you thought, Kazu?

I can't possibly let him see Yonko. I'll run away. I'll run away for now, and worry about the rest later.

Thanks to Kate and Annie and Mako, you were able to

distract yourself for a while in Rome and Paris, seeing all those beautiful gardens shining with the fresh green of May, eating wonderful food – but when Annie told you the news that Nobu had gone missing, you must have felt pressed, you were worried about me following you here. Isn't that right, Kazu? The Chilean soldiers were waiting for you and Yonko, too – in those orange shirts they were wearing as they carried out a bloody massacre.

As you watched them count ballots for the presidential election on TV in France, you sang 'The Times They Are A-Changin''. And in that moment, the only thought in your head was, We have to go back to Japan, there's nowhere else for us to go.

You'd known it all along, really, but you came all the way here just to make sure, didn't you?

Perhaps you felt the same way, Mitch?

The sound of Kazu's voice reverberates somewhere deep within the recesses of Mitch's body. That's why we're going back to Japan without seeing you – I'm sorry.

Mitch watches Yonko approach the fountain.

Slowly, she begins to walk around the perimeter of the round pond with the fountain in the middle. Kazu, who had been sitting beside Mitch on the bench, also gets up and approaches the fountain, then begins to follow her. The spray from the fountain mingles with their sweat, tiny droplets shine as they sail through the air. Yonko walks cautiously, as though ascertaining each step before she takes it. Kazu walks alongside her at the same pace. There are children playing, floating their toy boats and ducks on the water. Others are splashing in it. Still others are wading into the pond, trying to get close to the fountain. Miki-chan could be one of them. Their laughter ripples across the surface. Suddenly the light reflecting off the water moves and breaks apart. A sharp orange light floods everything, and the pond, and the fountain, and the spray of water, and Kazu, and Yonko, and the children – everything is suffused with an orange glow.

Mitch takes a deep breath, then turns to Annie beside him and speaks in a low voice.

I like it here, too. I wonder when I'll be able to come back.

The wind carries the water droplets along and they strike Mitch's face. He rubs his cheek as he stands up. Then he approaches the pond.

7

She gets off the bus and walks for about twenty metres along the sidewalk, which is protected by a single guardrail. Only then does she see the building on the corner – a beige, ten-storey structure that looks like it was built only recently. The mother doesn't know what was there before, since construction had already begun by the time she moved here. There is a produce shop on the ground floor, while the rest of the building is residential. Though perhaps the shop had been there all along. She'd never bought any fruit from there, though. It was too expensive and, more importantly, too close to the apartment where she and her son live.

The building enters her field of vision, though she has no desire to see it. She begins to tremble, to feel dizzy. Tears well up in her eyes. If she turns that corner, proceeds along the alleyway and makes a left, her son will be waiting for her, the one who has become a cold stone. She wants to keep walking instead of taking that turn. Why does she have to go home, anyway? If only she could abandon her son. She wants to forget all about that cold stone.

When the mother came back to her apartment three days ago, he had already reverted to his stone-like state. Not this again, she thought. This was the third time. He was huddled on his futon, rarely getting up except to get water. It was winter, so there was no chance of him suffocating under the covers. Still, he must have been in pain after staying in that cramped position for so long. But he didn't seem to notice. Only the sound of crying escaped from the futon. After this continued for about a week, the son, emaciated, crawled out of bed to sip the miso soup his mother brought him, tears splashing onto the tatami. He didn't speak. The mother didn't speak, either. This is how it had gone the first time, and the second – surely this time, too, it would be the same.

Slowly, slowly, the son ceased to be a cold stone, began to move around the apartment, until finally he was able to go outside again. It was at least two months until he was able to speak again. In six months, it's possible he will be back to normal, walking his usual bus route. But the mother doesn't want him to go outside. If he went somewhere with lots of people, there'd be no telling when, in what moment, his terrible illness would rear its head again. She didn't want to let him outside for a decade or two – no, until he died.

My son is ill, the mother kept trying to convince herself. All they had to do was cure him. But if she took him to a hospital, would they actually treat him, or turn him over to the police? It wasn't as though the outbreaks occurred that often. Very seldom, in fact, around once every ten years. Eventually they might stop altogether. The son did his best to prevent them, too. So much so that sometimes the mother would wonder if they were gone for good. How happy she would be if God, or Buddha, or whoever, told her that the outbreaks would never occur again, that all they had to do was live the rest of their lives in atonement for what he'd already done.

But that's not how it happened. Just three days ago, he'd had another outbreak, and when she came home, he had turned into a cold stone again.

For some reason, he would always come back home after an outbreak, though she wished he wouldn't. She would always be there waiting for him. She was sure the only reason he came back was to make her suffer even more. Three nights ago, she cursed her son in the darkness, wailed, swore she would kill him, thinking surely this would save them both. But a knife was useless against a cold stone, and if she slammed her head against him like a hammer, the most it would do was create a few cracks in the surface. She wondered how in the world she was supposed to get rid of him. Even now, after the third outbreak, she had no idea how to go about it. It had been eight years since the last one.

There is another version of the mother who does not turn the corner where that brand-new building stands, who does not go home to her son. It is this other mother, dragging the exhaustion of the day's work behind her, who thinks: I don't need to go back to that terrifying room ever again. And in that moment, she feels the sky above her grow taller, her spine a little longer, her feet lighter. The other mother smiles to herself, continues walking along the bus route. Perhaps when she reaches the next stop she gets on the bus. The other mother thinks nothing, gives her body over to the swaying of the bus, almost as though her son never existed at all. Does she eventually fall into a deep sleep as drowsiness overtakes her, riding all the way to the end of the line? If she abandons her son, she can go anywhere she wants – it doesn't matter where. Or perhaps the other mother keeps walking along the bus route, following it to the left and right, wherever it goes, only to find herself eventually near a small pond in a park.

When the news had arrived that her previous building was going to be demolished, she had moved into her current one without complaint. She should have moved further away when she'd had the chance, but in the end she'd settled on a cheap apartment, similar to her last one and not far away, either, located at the end of a road. She had so many horrible memories in the old place. Everyone in town had criticized her and her son. The town became frightening, full of ghosts. Still, the thought of leaving this place, which they knew so well they could practically walk the streets in their sleep, felt overwhelming. She didn't want to move to a completely unfamiliar town.

The other mother continues walking along the bus route, passes her old apartment, and finally reaches the pond. Here it is – the pond she'd resolved never to come near again. What would she do when she arrived? She becomes flustered. Why had she even come here, why, when she'd finally freed herself? She considers jumping into the pond. But even if she did, the water would probably be too shallow for an adult to drown in.

Stupid. The mother shakes her head, turns the corner where the brand-new building is, and proceeds along the alleyway, dragging her feet. Of course, the idea that she could simply abandon this apartment and never come back is nonsense. After all, her son is waiting for her – he can't survive on his own. But what if she really didn't come back? Even if her son were to die, she could be freed of this responsibility if no one knew where she was. Why did her son need to keep living anyway?

She walks through the alleyway, exhausted, finished with the day's work. The seasons continue to change without her noticing, one year following another. But she is still able to work. Thankfully. However tired she may be, however much her back might hurt, she can still move her body. She is worried about what might happen if she becomes ill, or injures herself. Perhaps she is exceptionally strong, or blessed with sheer good luck. Still, she is approaching her sixties, which means that soon she won't be able to work anymore. And when that time comes, how will she and her son survive? She will eventually die, which she doesn't mind, but what will her son do? He is only thirty-five but already looks aged. Her only son. Why had the two of them been forced to keep living? What value did their lives have anyway?

As the mother approaches the apartment, she begins to feel heavier and heavier. With every step she takes, a cloud of white breath escapes from her mouth. It is night now, chilly. Her chest hurts as she regards her own breath. So I'm still alive after all, she thinks.

In the apartment, the son, still a cold stone, is burrowed under the blankets, breathing. He inhales and exhales, his heart beats, his blood circulates through his body. The mother feels nauseous. She can see his blood circulating. She can hear his heartbeat. As for his mind, though, all she can see is darkness. It is a darkness without language. Whatever is happening in that darkness, the fits he suffers there – it is all just beyond her grasp. If she could only understand his suffering, she might be able to save him.

She is careful not to keep anything orange in their apartment. But when he steps outside, it's as though the colour is everywhere. There is orange at the fruit stand. On the restaurant signs, in the pharmacies, in the clothing stores. There are women wearing orange scarves, children wearing orange jackets, men with orange backpacks. Of course, there are subtle differences in shade. Most of the time, her son simply averts his eyes and nothing happens. Even if he sees a woman wearing an orange skirt. But that doesn't mean the mother lets her guard down. No matter how carefully she monitors him, she can never predict what will set him off.

Why had the seven-year-old girl been wearing that orange skirt when she fell into the pond?

The mother pauses, closes her eyes. Tears spill out. What was it that her son had seen that day near the pond? What was it that had smashed his head into a million tiny pieces? No matter how much she tries to imagine it, she can't picture a single thing, just a pitch-black fear that pushes back at her. That is what has caused her to suffer, to be afraid, all this time.

The mother approaches the apartment building. The main hallway is visible from outside, as well as the doors of individual apartments. There are piles of old newspapers in the corners, as well as a number of bikes and a laundry machine. Light spills out of the window facing the hallway. She can see a television screen flickering through one of the windows, most of which are closed, since it's winter. There must be people living in those apartments, but, as a whole, the building is quiet – here everyone lives holding their breath. There are elderly people living alone. Foreigners who can't speak Japanese. Even when the residents pass one another in the hallway, they avert their gazes. The mother isn't sure exactly who lives here, or how many of these hundred-square-foot apartments there are. In one of them is her son, the cold stone, sunk to the bottom of the darkness.

I don't want to go back in there, the mother thinks again.

Why can't she just abandon him? She wants so much to do it, and yet. This life she had birthed. It wasn't as though her son had wanted to be born into this world. But she is afraid of him. She can't stop trembling. As she approaches the apartment, she feels a scream rising in the back of her throat.

Every morning at six o'clock, the mother leaves the apartment, and every night at eight she returns. Mornings and afternoons she spends cleaning other apartments. Monday is her day off, but staying at home is suffocating, so on those days she works a different job at a supermarket. All day she carries crates from the storage unit out back to the shelves inside the store and back again. It is tiring work. When her son isn't in the apartment, she likes to take the day off and relax. But she can't. Even if he managed to go out and get a job washing dishes, there is no telling when he might have another outbreak.

The mother can't stand having to face him every night, and worse, having to share a room with him after an outbreak. She'd much rather be working. No matter how tired she is, she doesn't want to give up this precious time away from him. She has no idea when the next outbreak might occur. There was a time when she used to follow him around, but she soon grew tired of that. She alone didn't have the power to change her son's fate.

Once an outbreak happened, her son would shut himself away in the apartment for at least two months. At six months, he'd be able to go outside again. After a year, he could maybe even work a part-time job. But then three years would go by, then five, and another outbreak would happen. Just three days ago, it had happened for the first time in almost a decade. Where? How? She didn't want to know or even hear about the unknown woman wearing orange who had been sacrificed to her son's rage. He had turned into a cold stone again. That was enough for her to guess what had happened.

When she was in the same room as her son, the mother tried to sit in front of the butsudan as often as possible. A while back, she had made her own butsudan out of a tin box. She didn't care much what it looked like. She'd made it herself, covering it with a flower-patterned cloth. On top of it was the oldest mortuary tablet with the red dot on it, which she'd made out of a kamaboko board. Next to it was one with a blue dot, and another with a white dot. There was also a rice bowl with water in it, and a plate that held a candle and some incense. She'd poured a handful of black sesame seeds into the dish to hold up a stick of incense. She'd have to add another kamaboko board soon. Perhaps she would put a yellow dot on this one. Now there were four boards in total. Even when she sat in front of the butsudan, she was too afraid to look directly at the boards.

Then she'd light the candle using some matches she'd got from her job at the supermarket. The candles had been melted down to stubs – she'd have to replace them soon. They weren't lit for long, but since she used them multiple times a day, every day, she went through them quickly. Then the mother would light the incense and stick it into the clump of black sesame seeds. The scent of the candle would mingle with the scent of the sesame and incense, and though the room was already stifling, a gloom like the stench of rotting vegetables would permeate the air, causing the mother's throat and stomach to convulse.

Then she would rub her hands together, fighting back nausea as she murmured over and over, Nanmaidaa, Nanmaidaa, may they rest in peace, Nanmaidaa. Her voice was quiet, so it was unlikely anyone outside the apartment could hear. Her son could, but he didn't move at all from where he lay on the futon. When he was doing well – in other words, when the effect of his episodes had worn off – the mother would force him to sit in front of the butsudan and pray, once in the morning when he woke up and once at night before bed. But that was impossible after he'd had an episode and turned into a cold stone. Until he emerged from the futon, the mother had no choice but to continue sitting in front of the butsudan alone.

Slowly she walks up and down the hallway of the apartment building. The fifth door on the left is theirs. Unlike the others, the apartment is dark. Her son is in there. The mother knows that. He occasionally gets up to drink water or go to the bathroom while she is gone. Quietly. Treading softly. Crying. The mother, too, treads softly down the hallway. It is an old building, so she has to be careful when she steps on the floorboards, to avoid making any sound. Inside her bag are minced chicken, scallions and eggs. When she goes inside, she'll probably start cooking a late dinner. She wonders whether her son will refuse to eat again.

This son the mother had birthed. It wasn't as though he had been any great source of joy – but when she made the connection between the weight of her stomach during the final month of her pregnancy and the weight of the baby after it was born, she felt an indescribable satisfaction as she realized: So this is what was inside me this whole time. She was still young then. Yes, quite certainly this child was hers – she, and not anyone else, had guarded him, nurtured him, raised him. When he was an infant, his mouth had suckled at her tingling nipples. How pleasurable it had felt. His small ears, which had looked like faintly red, transparent seashells. She had almost been tempted to lick them. The tiny fingernails growing on each and every finger. The whites of his eyes had an almost bluish tint to them, and, when tears would gather, the dark blue of his eyes would grow darker and begin to glitter.

The young mother was fascinated, astonished even, by this infant that had come out of her own stomach, and was glad she hadn't given in to the voice in her head that told her to get rid of it. No matter how much she was cursed at, made fun of, she knew, at least, it hadn't been a mistake to have this child.

But after some time went by, she began to wonder whether it had been a mistake after all. Why had she given birth to a thing like this? When she'd taken refuge in a women's shelter, she'd wanted to abandon him there, take back the time that was rightfully hers. By the time she left the shelter and started living in an apartment, the baby was already a five-year-old boy, and she was beginning to have some time to herself again.

She had been a young woman then. She worked at a cafeteria in Ikebukuro and was friendly with many of the customers. She hoped to eventually meet a man whom she and her son would be able to live with. She believed in that wish wholeheartedly. She was convinced this special man would appear someday.

Why? Because the young mother was here, by herself, holding this healthy child, alive.

Impossible, almost, to believe she had been so naive.

The mother is no longer young. She furrows her brow, clicks her tongue. Sometimes she'd spot those orphans that the American GIs left behind in the neighbourhood and feel disgusted. They were technically alive, yes, but compared with them, her son, loved and protected by his mother, lived like a king, and she would feel good about herself, even if she knew it was foolish. The fact that she'd never abandoned him despite all the times he annoyed her or the moments when she thought she never should have had him, and the fact that she'd continued taking care of him – all this came down to a mother's attachment to her son, even something, perhaps, called love.

One day, when he was nine years old, he'd dashed indoors, his face pale, frothing at the mouth. And then he buried himself in the futon.

Since that day, while maintaining the outward appearance of himself, the boy had transformed into a different being altogether, becoming enclosed in an endless darkness. The mother, too, became trapped in it. But she had to keep working. To maintain the apartment that was his hiding place. She quit her job at the cafeteria and began working at a candy factory in town. There she could hide her face behind a mask, and she rarely had to talk to anyone. The factory was a thirty-minute walk from her old apartment. It made her happy to bring home sweets for her son. In those days, they enjoyed a variety of candy together almost every day. The flavours would melt in their mouths and suffuse their entire bodies, and for that brief span of time they felt they could recover that feeling of ease they used to take for granted. But eventually the factory went under due to redevelopment, and the mother had to take the cleaning job.

After he'd shut himself away in the apartment for a while, the son began to venture out to school once in a while. Sometimes his homeroom teacher would come round and say things like, Everyone's worried about you, why don't you come on back to class. But it was clear her concern was just a pretence. In reality it was a demand, a threat. The mother and her nine-year-old son realized they'd become the subject of fierce gossip. All kinds of rumours swirled beneath their feet as they walked, rumours like schools of rainbow fish glittering in the sun that brushed their legs and sometimes made them fall.

They tried to ignore them. If even one person had reached out and told them that it was about the little girl, perhaps things would have ended up differently. But not even the son's homeroom teacher dared to confront them directly. She was just doing her job – no more, no less.

When her son did go to school, he would spend thirty minutes, or an hour, maybe, wandering around the schoolyard or hanging around the shoe racks near the entrance before hurrying back to the apartment. The mother never said anything to him. She knew he wasn't well suited to school to begin with. No one was particularly surprised when he didn't come to class. As long as he showed up on campus once in a while, the teachers were satisfied. He had no one to play with. He never set foot inside the classroom, so of course he didn't get good grades. Eventually he turned ten, then eleven years old. Years went by. The son grew bigger. The distance between him and the school grew only wider.

But the mother didn't mind. She didn't care about school. She would simply go on living inside the dark time. And protecting her son. She didn't have the capacity to think of anything more than that. Why was she still alive? If someone were to ask her this, she wouldn't have been able to come up with an answer. Today she was alive, so she would live again tomorrow, too – that was all. The days went by like that.

It was right around the son's eleventh birthday when the mother constructed the butsudan out of a tin box. It struck her that they would have to atone for the death of the young girl, which her son had undeniably been involved in. He was alive, the girl was dead. For the mother and son to go on living, they had no choice but to pray for the girl's soul.

Every morning, every night, the mother would drag her son, kicking and screaming, and force him to bow his head in front of the butsudan. The son would tremble as he pressed his head against the floor, wailing. Of course it was painful for him. It was painful for her, too. But the greater the pain, the more it would serve as atonement for the girl's life.

That girl. One of those orphans.

Had she been among those children that the mother had seen in the neighbourhood? The mother had no way of knowing. She didn't remember their faces. All she remembered was the satisfaction of knowing her son was better off than them. Some of the children had dark skin and curly hair. They ran around the streets looking like they owned the place. Surely they had spotted her son a few times, too. Did he want to be friends with them? They were almost the same age, and the orphans were probably excluded by other children the same way her son was. Had he wanted to approach that seven-year-old girl?

She had been standing at the edge of the pond, alone. Did her son call out to her? Did she respond? What did she say?

Go away. Don't come any closer.

And then? What happened after that? Her son's memory was shrouded in darkness, like a lid that has been slammed shut. What if the girl hadn't been standing by that pond alone? What if she hadn't been abandoned by her mother? What if the American GI had never met her Japanese mother? What if the American GIs had never set foot in Japan? What if Japan had never gone to war? The mother had asked herself these questions hundreds, no, thousands of times.

She stands in front of her apartment. The door is unlocked. She looks behind her, then to her right and left. She feels like someone is watching her. Is somebody standing in the hallway entrance? She tenses, staring into the darkness. There is no trace of that woman. The one who was always hanging around the orphans, who looked to be close in age to her. The first time she'd seen her, the mother immediately knew who she was. She didn't know what relationship the woman had to those children, but she always saw the woman's young daughter, with her little bowl cut, playing with the other orphans. The daughter had been nearby that day as well, when the mother's son and the other little girl had been by the pond with the other orphans. And the woman's daughter. But they had been useless. Her son was alone, as always.

Perhaps that was why, ever since that day, the woman would sometimes come by the building where the mother and her son lived and stand there absentmindedly for a while before going home. The mother ignored her. But the woman's presence irritated her. After the second and the third time she came, the mother began to feel uneasy, and she struggled to concentrate.

Why did you come here? What do you want? she wanted to ask the woman. But inside, she already knew the answer. She could never bring herself to approach the woman. And the woman, in turn, never approached her. Over the twenty-odd years they'd lived here, the mother guessed that the woman had shown up at least once a year, though she had lost count a long time ago. Though they hadn't seen her since they'd moved out about six months ago. Perhaps she simply didn't know their new address yet. But eventually she'd find them and come around again – the mother was sure of that. Her prediction was also a kind of hope. She wanted the woman to find them. After all, the mother and her son were living here, in plain sight.

The mother sighs and opens the door. The floorboards squeak like a cat's helpless meow, drawing her inside.

8

A pile of fragrant firewood, burning. On top of the pile is a board, and on top of the board, the corpse of a woman. Instantly the flames leap up, billows of smoke rising into the air. The flames gain momentum, scorch the corpse, melt it, set it ablaze in blue, till at last it becomes ashes.

If only that corpse were Mama, Kazu mutters to himself as he digs with his shovel. Were Indian funeral pyres always so large? Perhaps it was because the person who had died was the great Indira Gandhi.

Last night, Kazu had sobbed alone as he watched the funeral on TV. Alone, he felt free to sob like a child.

I'm so sorry, Mama. We never should have let your precious body burn inside a blast furnace, like one of those incinerators at a steel factory. We should have thought about it more carefully. There was only one of you, after all, and once we burned you, we could never take it back.

The crematorium in Yokohama was a block of steel that glittered black as it sucked in Mama's corpse. There was a window on the lid, and Kazu thought he remembered someone asking whether they wanted to look inside. But of course neither Kazu nor Mitch could bear to do that.

Any last words? the man had asked as they stood in front of the incinerator. But Mitch and Kazu just hung their heads in silence. What were they supposed to say? But now Kazu understood. That had been their last chance.

Wait a minute, no, he should have said. We're not going to cremate her here. Then he would have carried Mama's body out in a hurry, boarded a plane and flown to India. And just like Indira Gandhi, Mama would have burned atop a pile of firewood slowly, delicately, and afterwards Kazu would have scattered her ashes in the Ganges. And then she would have floated down the river, into the Indian Ocean, and travelled all over the world, buffeted along by the current. And she would have smiled contentedly, as if to say: I can't believe such wonderful things were waiting for me after death, as she floated from this to that ocean, the sound of her jubilant voice mingling with the sound of the waves: I'm so glad I got to be your mama. Thank you.

Kazu gives his hands a rest and looks out at the glittering bay. He gazes down at the sea, so calm that it looks like a sheet of aluminium foil. A boat cuts through it, heading toward the offing. Despite Gandhi's death, and Mama's, the ocean will go on shimmering quietly, the trees will stir occasionally in the soft wind, the earth will continue revolving around the sun, and those parts of the earth outside the sun's reach will become night, and the moon and the stars will continue flashing in the sky.

Where am I? Kazu thinks as he gazes upward. The sun is sinking, emitting a pale pink wash of light. The earth is spinning beneath his feet. He feels dizzy. The spinning never stops, it enters the flow of a waterfall called time that pushes us along ceaselessly in the same direction, and just when we think we can see the future beyond the horizon, it slips mercilessly back into the past. We grow older.

Hey, Yonko, where am I? Kazu asks Yonko, who must be in Tokyo.

And where has Mitch gone off to anyway?

It's like we've all been swept along by the wind, become grains of sand flying toward some unknown place. Yonko, is this all because Mama died? Why did we hurl her precious body into the furnace? They say you don't know the value of something until you lose it, but I think that's nonsense. That's not why we've been scattered apart.

Kazu looks down at the hole near his feet, about sixty centimetres deep now. He needs to dig about ten holes to plant his snowberry seedlings. This is the sixth hole. He'll throw some fertilizer in later. The seedlings, spaced some distance apart, are waiting for their roots to dry and settle into the damp soil.

Hurry, put us back in the soil, they whisper to Kazu.

The soil smells sweet and tender, maybe because of all the large ferns that grow in abundance here.

Did you watch the cremation on TV last night, too, Yonko?

What about you, Mitch? Did you think of Mama, like I did?

Kazu adjusts the shovel in his hands and continues digging. He recalls a story he heard a long time ago.

I wonder how old we were when we first heard it. It was a scary story, about a teenage boy who had survived the atomic bomb in Hiroshima. Do you remember it, Mitch? The boy finds his father's dead body, but he can't find the rest of his family. Of course, there's nowhere to cremate the body, and there aren't any adults around to help him, so the boy has to burn his father's body by himself. He gathers the scattered debris, and, over the course of several days, he patiently cremates his father's corpse, which is already beginning to decompose.

Did we hear that story on the radio? I remember one of us saying they'd never be able to do something like that. Just seeing a dead human body would be terrifying enough, let alone watching it burn all by yourself. It's too horrible to think about.

We were just kids then. I wonder what we imagined that

made us feel so afraid. Something impossibly cruel, grotesque? A kind of satanic ritual that, when looked at straight on, would put a curse on us for the rest of our lives? Or was it the discovery that there is no difference between the way a human body and a chicken burn and peel when consumed by fire? Or maybe it was the realization that this is what would happen to Mama when she died.

And then it really did happen – last year, Mama's heart stopped due to a sudden bout of meningitis, never to beat again.

And yet we were so quick to relinquish Mama's body. Even when we saw the hot ashes come out of the incinerator, we just stood there in a daze. Were Yonko and her mother there, too? Did they cry for us? Mama was Yonko's mother's cousin, so she must have been awfully sad. But she wasn't against the idea of cremating her. Yonko's mother's hair had probably gone entirely white by then.

After a few months, it slowly dawned on Mitch and Kazu that Mama's body no longer existed anywhere on this earth, that they'd never find it again, no matter how long they searched. How attached the two of them had been to her. That attachment was extremely physical, even when they were far away. There had always been other women who helped her with her daily tasks, including cooking meals, so Mitch and Kazu didn't necessarily associate her with traditional motherly roles; and besides, they weren't Westerners, so they didn't hug or kiss her. But just the knowledge that she was alive – in possession of a body with blood running through it, bones that moved smoothly, organs that worked properly – had always sustained them, and even though they had no biological connection to her, they had come to rely absolutely on the fact of her existence.

That's what I've come to believe, Mitch. Which is why when that frightening illness took hold of poor Mama's body, an illness we'd never even heard of before, and her blood vessels began to rupture, and haemorrhages the colour of crimson glory vines began to speckle her skin, it only intensified our love for her, and we wished we could mummify her, put her in a glass casket, stay by her side always. Or at the very least, cremate her on the banks of the Ganges. That way, the whole world would know that a great person had died.

When a person dies, the people around them begin to feel what we are feeling. And if the person dies not from an illness but from an accident or in a war, or if the person is murdered, then those around them suffer even more. All those anonymous deaths in the newspaper day after day aren't singular deaths, after all. Though it would be different in the case of someone who lived an extremely lonely life – the death of such a human being would be almost unbearably painful.

Mitch, I can't believe it's taken us so long to realize these things. We're fools. Those incidents with the colour orange. We were too terrified to do anything. Slowly, the wave of fear grew larger and larger, and we became caught in its vortex. We knew that the vortex wouldn't abate, there was nothing we could do, so we blocked it out of our minds. Eventually we pretended we couldn't see it at all – and still, the shadow hovering over us persisted.

Kazu guesses that Mako must have seen Indira Gandhi's cremation on TV too. Maybe Takeshi and Fumi were with him as well. Mako had always wanted to go to India but never did. Still, he would never admit this out loud, especially not to Takeshi and Fumi. Thanks to Takeshi's financial success, Mako's architecture firm had continued to expand. Which meant his dream of going to India had to be stored away in a secret box inside him, where his real mother also lived.

Kazu nods to himself as he looks at the snowberry seedlings, each around a metre tall. Yes, everyone has a secret box. Most people don't let go of it until they die. Mitch's and Kazu's secret boxes had some things in common, but of course there were things each of them didn't know about the other. The same was true for Yonko.

I wish Yonko and Mitch would visit me here, Kazu thinks, sighing. There's so much I want to show them and tell them about. I bet they have lots of things they want to tell me, too.

Sensing evening coming on, the birds around Kazu begin to chirp with abandon.

Chee, chee, twee, twee, kekekeke, chicchon, chicchon . . .

He can almost hear Yonko's and Mitch's voices in the birdsong.

Hey, Kazu, I'm gonna come back to your place. Sonia's coming too, Mitch had said when he called from Denmark two months ago.

But then, shortly afterward, he'd called back in a glum voice.

Actually, can we hold off on that for a while? I promise I'll comc eventually, but something just happened, it's kind of complicated. I'm just going to go back to Japan by myself for now.

When he got back, Mitch met with Yonko and talked with her at length. He couldn't seem to calm down. His voice was high and shaky, his breathing shallow, to the point that Yonko wondered whether he was sick. But Mitch wasn't sick – he was just overwhelmed.

Yonko wrote down everything Mitch told her in a letter and sent it to Kazu, since Mitch hated writing. Afterward, he'd flown back to Denmark to see Sonia. According to Yonko, Sonia was pregnant, and Mitch, as the likely father, wanted to stay close by. But Sonia refused to live with Mitch, or even acknowledge that he was the father of her child. She was an actress, and it was possible that the child belonged to a lover of hers that she'd had a long history with. Though it was also possible he was simply asserting this to hem Sonia in. Not even Mitch knew the truth. But he hadn't given up.

Mitch, how are things now? Where are you?

Kazu begins to dig the seventh hole. Large beads of sweat roll off the tip of his nose and lips and fall to the ground.

I don't even know where I am anymore. Ever since Mama died, it's like we've distanced ourselves from the sun's orbit and become aimless shooting stars. I think that's why you forced your way into Sonia's life, Mitch, why you wanted to have a family with her. But when Sonia got pregnant, that messed up your plans. Right, Mitch? You wanted her to become a mother. You never knew your real mother, and, with Mama dead, you wanted to know how a woman actually becomes a mother and how a man becomes a father. That's what Yonko thinks, at least, and I agree. After all, love, for you, is a kind of curiosity.

Kazu continues digging the seventh hole. He has to finish by sundown. This immense botanical garden in the Southern Hemisphere will close at sunset. Here, unlike in Japan, there is no announcement that the garden is closing. At sunset, the three gates, all in different locations, simply close, and the people in charge go home. No one makes sure that all the gardeners have left, much less someone like Kazu, who is just a part-time assistant. Once it's past closing time, the garden sinks into darkness and grows completely desolate. Anyone who had to spend the night alone in this sprawling place would surely lose their mind from fear. Supposedly there aren't any dangerous animals, but you never know what could happen. Leaves sway in the wind, wriggle their branches and begin to dance; nocturnal birds fly about, their eyes flashing. Hey, look, they clamour. There's a person there, all alone. And then, perhaps, they attack them with their beaks, while the plants crush them with their branches and roots.

Wait a minute, Kazu, Yonko's teasing voice reverberates in Kazu's ear. You love plants. You don't think this would actually happen, do you?

You never know, Kazu answers her silently. Plants are fierce things. I've always been impressed by them. But, Yonko, even if the garden closes, I'll find my way out. It'll be a hassle, of course – I'll have to make my way through the thicket. But I won't be trapped here overnight. If anything, the hardest part will be walking all the way back to town after I get out of here. This place is pretty far out.

If only I could be there with you, Yonko's voice calls back to him like ripples on a pond. I'd like to see it with my own eyes. It's spring there where you are now, right, Kazu? Even though it's autumn in Japan. It's strange, how the seasons are flipped from north to south. It reminds me how far away you are.

It's not far at all. It would be faster for you to get here than to Europe or North America. Come on over. You can see the Southern Cross from here.

I'd love to become one of those plants you care for, Yonko's voice continues. I'd grow taller, you'd be so impressed with me. And I'd never have to speak at all. If only I could live like that.

Don't be ridiculous, Yonko. You're stuck being a human being. However much I love plants, I can't give up on humans. And besides, you're not coming anyway. Though I'd be happy if you did, of course.

I know I'm ridiculous. I've only recently got my life together again, and I can't just up and leave the person I've just married. I wish I could see you, Kazu, but what can we do? Well, at least tell me what kind of plants there are.

I know you can't come, Kazu answers, half in a daze. I mean, you ran off and married another guy who Mitch and I and even Mama hated. It's like you'd completely forgotten about the last time this happened. That was our impression, at least. Though maybe he's much more reliable than we think and you'll never have to work another day in your life.

These snowberries are called papapa by the Maori people. Come autumn, they grow these delicious little red and white fruits. They're seedlings now, but they'll grow to be about two metres tall.

Papapa? How strange! Yonko's voice, laughing, so familiar to Kazu.

The Maori language is really interesting. The pronunciation is so similar to Japanese. And around here, I often get mistaken for Maori because my skin is the same colour as theirs. But then I'm found out right away because I can't speak the language.

Yonko laughs again.

I learned that the Maori people came here during the ninth century. This land must have been a great big forest back then, with giant ferns covering the earth. And there were these huge birds called moas, probably the ancestor of the modern ostrich. They went extinct around four hundred years ago. But when white people arrived, they planted gorse shrubs everywhere to create enclosures for their sheep, and roses for their gardens, and slowly the forests turned into pastures. And then they realized they needed to protect some of the forest that had been here before, which is why they created these botanical gardens. There's little rose gardens, rock gardens and cactus gardens too.

Kazu begins digging the eighth hole as he continues talking to Yonko in his mind. Sweat is getting in his eyes and mouth.

The forest has these giant, luxuriant ferns that grow up to twenty metres tall, crowding each other out. And palm trees, and these giant trees called kauris that are over thirty metres tall. They say kauris live to be four thousand years old. I wonder what it's like to live for four thousand years. There's also these trees called totaras, and others called rimus, that look kind of like red pines, that grow up to fifty metres. The fruit of the karaka tree is orange and poisonous. Yes, an orange poison.

What wrong with that? Yonko's voice, angry, reverberates in Kazu's ears. There are plenty of orange fruits that grow on trees. And some of them happen to be poisonous. That's all it is. There's no meaning behind it.

Kazu stretches his back and uses the towel around his neck to wipe the sweat from his face. A white butterfly flits past him like a scrap of paper buffeted by the wind. A small brown bird dives straight toward him, grazing the top of his head.

Maybe there's no meaning behind it, maybe there is, Kazu murmurs. The fact that we're alive doesn't mean anything either. But it also does. The fact that Miki-chan was once alive doesn't mean anything. But it does. The same is true for the plants that grow here and only here, in this earth. There's no meaning behind it, but there is. I want to become closer to these plants. I want to hear them sing. I wonder what a four-thousand-year-old voice sounds like when it sings. I'll probably have to leave before I've been able to learn much of anything, though. I'm not allowed to stay here long-term.

Yonko, Kazu says, readjusting his grip on the shovel. You can sense the traces of ancient history here in this old forest. That's why it's scary to be here at night by yourself. The forest has such a rich vitality – a vitality that transcends time, which we human beings can never know. I want to walk through this forest with you. During the day, I imagine you running around in it. In my mind, you look like a little girl again, and, at the same time, you look like you do now, with your tall, slender figure. You have that straight, bobbed hair, just like you did when you were a kid, and it fans out around you, and the ferns sway their leaves, mimicking the motion of your hair. The light, glittering green, scatters. Beside you I can see Miki-chan, in her orange skirt. The orange of her skirt is identical to the orange of the karaka fruit, and I feel something pierce me. The pain scatters me into pieces. And then I think of Tabo. The pain he's suffered all this time has probably been so much worse than anything we've felt. Maybe in this forest it's possible to see Tabo as a child, and even ourselves as children. In this forest, time cycles in four-thousand-year loops.

Chee, chee, tsuui, tsuui . . .

The voices of the birds grow in number. The light blue sky has begun to fade to pink.

Pippi, pippi, kekeke, chicchon, chicchon . . .

Kazu begins to dig the ninth hole.

I really have to hurry. The papapa seedlings are getting impatient: Faster, faster, they say. The bird that's singing *kekeke* – is that a kakariki, in the parakeet family, or a kaka, in the parrot family? The kakariki has a vibrant green body and a red head, while the kaka is a reddish brown. Both are friendly and aren't afraid of humans. Sometimes they even pull at your clothes or steal your belongings.

That's right, I have to tell you about the birds here, Yonko. There are lots of strange ones. Many of them don't fly anymore because they didn't have predators. I wonder if they're descended from the moa. Some of the employees here asked me if the birds in Japan were afraid of humans. When I told them yes, they said that must be because Japanese people have a history of killing and eating them. I was shocked. Do Japanese birds really live in such terrible conditions? But then why did the moa go extinct?

Kazu hurries to dig the tenth hole. The last one. His sweat drips onto the ground. An insect similar to a drone beetle brushes against his shoulder, buzzing loudly, then flies off. A cool evening breeze rises up from the sea, blows past the hill, and stirs the surrounding trees.

Hurry, hurry, we can't wait any longer, the papapa begin to shout.

As the day draws to a close, the birds, too, exchange messages with each other: Not a bad day, it wasn't too hot or too cold, there was a gentle wind, no rain, the sea was quiet, tomorrow, too, will be a good day.

Chee, chee, tsuuui, tsuuui, pippi, pippi, kekekekeke, chicchon, chicchon . . .

Something moves in the corner of Kazu's vision. He looks up as he wipes the sweat from his brow. One of his colleagues is waving to him, as though to say: Finish up! The garden's closing soon. Kazu begins to raise his right hand – then, for a split second, he does a double take. Is that Mitch? That thin body, leaning slightly to the left. Kazu can see his glittering green eyes, even from far away. Ah, no. Never mind. That's impossible.

Mitch, where are you right now? Are you holding Sonia's hand as you walk slowly along the beach that stretches out against the shoreline? One of those beaches in Denmark you once told Yonko about?

On that vast beach resembling a desert, Mitch and Sonia are the only ones for miles around. A sandy gust of wind blows so fiercely that they can barely see ahead of them. The beach is on a cape that juts into a strait. Plenty of fishing boats have shipwrecked in this sea, the fishermen thrown overboard, their cold bodies washing ashore. Legend had it that many of them were British or from the Brittany region of France. When fragments of the ship washed ashore, people gathered them and created a small museum.

Mitch, I heard people pray there, too. After learning that their husbands, sons and fathers died at sea, women, young and old alike, come from far away, dressed in mourning clothes, to visit the coast. Some of them end up staying, settling down in a place that overlooks the beach. There they quietly live out the rest of their days, looking out at the sea that swallowed up their husbands, sons and fathers.

Mitch had grown to love this beach and thinks how nice it would be to live here with Sonia and his soon-to-be-born child. He and Kazu had split the money from Mama's inheritance between them – a significant amount, even after taxes, which meant he didn't have to worry about his finances for a while. Sonia is an actress and doesn't make much money, but has been supported for much of her career by a wealthy patron. That situation, however, may not last much longer. The plan is for Mitch to take care of the child while Sonia is working. Quietly, gently, Mitch and Sonia will raise this precious child as they look out onto this sandy beach. Their days will be filled with joy and sorrow as the infant smiles and cries.

That time is sure to be a wonderful one, in which everything around them melts into a supreme bliss.

Mitch holds Sonia's hand as he talks on and on, the two of them walking along the beach. His bad leg feels heavier in the sand, and his movements are clumsy. He can't speak Danish, of course, so he speaks in halting English instead.

Speaking in a language he hasn't yet mastered makes it easier to lie.

. . . My mother's stomach was just as big as yours when she was pregnant. She was all alone at the time. She remembers my father's face, but not his name or military unit. It wasn't one of those rape situations that get talked about a lot. Just a naive, overly eager American GI who my mother met somewhere. He was attracted to her, despite not being able to communicate a single word. The idea that all children in Japan born from American GIs were a result of violent rape is an overgeneralization. There's no denying that there were some tragic cases, but that wasn't true for me. Many American soldiers and Japanese women fell in love. But my mother just lost touch with my father. It was impossible for a woman from the defeated country to keep track of the whereabouts of an American GI who was constantly moved around by the military at will. She didn't even know his name, so she had no way of searching for him. Anyway, he'd probably already gone back to America by then, so she wasn't able to see him again. Still, my mother was set on having the child and raising it on her own. After all, it was already alive inside her, moving with such force. You of all people would understand, right?

Mitch squeezes Sonia's hand. Perhaps Sonia, pregnant, furrows her brow. She must be beautiful. Mitch would never settle for anything less.

Sometimes Sonia glares at Mitch, or sighs to herself. She can't believe anything he says. It's not like he actually cares about this child. He just can't help but project himself onto the unborn child. If anything, she hates the idea of having a family. Still, she goes along with the fantasy he's created, where a man and a woman fall in love, are blessed with a child, and it grows up in a peaceful, loving home. How should she break it to Mitch that this fantasy will never come true, when he himself believes in it so fervently? What is he thinking? Where did he come from, and where will he go?

Mitch continues talking nonsense in English. It's not nonsense, exactly, since he is talking about his dreams, or rather, his and Kazu's dream, one they were able to envision only after losing Mama. Until then, they'd never thought about their own parents. Their real parents. Their biological parents. They'd always thought there was no point in thinking about them.

Just like all the other children from the orphanage. Other than Mako, that is.

There was Mother Asami, and Mama, and that was enough. Fathers? Mitch and Kazu had no interest in them. After all, how could they feel anything about someone who had never existed? Come to think of it, Yonko and Tabo didn't have fathers either. Perhaps that's just how fathers were, they thought. The same was true for insects, birds and fish. Mama, on the other hand, was always there for them, never leaving their side. And they had Mother Asami and Yonko's mother.

Kazu can't help but feel ashamed that he is forced to think this way. He knows it's just an orphan's pathetic bravado but he can't change the way he thinks. After all, it's for his own protection.

After Mother Asami and Mama were gone, Mitch and Kazu finally began to wonder who their biological mothers might have been. They began to invent stories – the kind of fairy tales you might tell to a young child. What kind of woman was she, how did she get pregnant, why did she abandon her child? Maybe these women were still alive somewhere on this earth. For Mitch and Kazu, the fact that their mothers' existence amounted to a distant memory of hidden violence and fear was something embarrassing, intolerable.

Mitch turns toward Sonia and continues his fanciful story, the wind nearly snatching his voice away.

My mother had no misgivings about not knowing her child's father. But in Japan back then, no one liked the children of American GIs, which made many mothers nervous about raising their children there. My mother was timid and cautious, and not very strong. So rather than staying in Tokyo, she went to a seaside town to give birth to her child – that is, me. My mother already adored me before I was born, but once I came into the world I was even more dear to her than before; she thought that as long as she had this child by her side, she'd never need anything else. But then she got sick. And so she put me in an orphanage, thinking it would just be a temporary thing. They said my mother cried when she handed me over, swearing she would come back for me. But unfortunately her illness only got worse, and she couldn't be saved.

Sonia's face stiffens, her eyes fill with tears. It's not that she is moved by Mitch's story, or particularly sympathizes with it. She is simply exasperated. She doesn't know what to say. But he isn't letting go of her hand, so she can't run away.

How can this person tell such obvious lies? she thinks. I bet one day it's all going to catch up to him. He must know this, so why does he keep doing it?

I hate to break it to you, Mitch, but Sonia is probably going to leave you.

Mitch's story isn't much different from the one Kazu made up for himself. They couldn't think of anything original about their mothers. If Yonko were here she'd probably laugh at them. Kazu had never told Yonko his story. But Mitch was telling his to Sonia now. Passionately. Seriously. Why? Because Sonia was pregnant, and Mitch was betting on being the father of her child. He wasn't even thinking about his love for Sonia. And all that business about who the child's real father was? He'd already forgotten about that – even though that was precisely why Sonia didn't want to stay.

Mitch, are you still with Sonia? Was the baby born already? What does it mean to become a father? It's like Yonko said before:

Mitch doesn't understand that being a mother or father isn't a role you can force yourself into. I'm worried about him. But anyway, he's trying to find his new self, you know? He thinks he can wash his hands clean of the past, jump into a different time, live as a different self, and that's what he's trying to do. I'm talking like this is someone else's problem, but really you and I are doing the same thing, aren't we, Kazu? We're just going about it in different ways. We have no other choice.

Kazu finishes digging the tenth hole, puts some compost in it, then places a papapa seedling inside. Now all he has to do is throw soil over the rest of the seedlings and water them. The hose is ready, but the spigot is far away. There's only an hour left. No, half an hour. He still has to put the hose away and walk to the gate. He doesn't have one of those electric carts that his coworkers use.

The branches sway, the ferns sway, rustling and whispering to each other. The birds cry and clamour. The insects hum as they fly about.

Kazu, you need to get out of Japan, too!

Yonko's sharp voice strikes the back of his neck like a bird's beak. Kazu blinks a few times and continues digging.

Kazu, you make up your mind and get out of Japan. Mitch already decided to leave. He's going to Rome first, to see Kate. I can keep living here, but not you. No matter how old you and Mitch get, you'll always be mixed-race orphans. Remember how Mama sent you away to that boarding school in England a long time ago? Not a single thing has changed since then. It's too much for you all to survive here.

Kazu finishes planting the seedlings in their holes and spreads the dirt around. The soft earth smells sweet. Kazu loves this soil. If only he could keep working here forever. But he knows he can't stay here, no matter what Yonko says or Mitch does. In another month or so, he will go back to Tokyo. To be near Yonko. Mitch will probably come back, too. Even though he hates Japan, even though he knows that something horrible is lying in wait for him, he'll come back. Japan, where Kazu and Yonko are. Where Tabo is.

Sunset draws near, and the stirring of the trees and the

warbling of the birds grow more lively. Kazu hurriedly shovels the dirt into the holes where the seedlings are planted, cupping his hands to create small grooves around them, then runs to the water spigot across the garden. He opens the tap, grabs the hose, and runs back to the seedlings, sloshing water over them. The little grooves begin to collapse as the seedlings soak up water from their roots.

I'm sorry I'm being so rough. The water's hitting your roots and hurting you. But I don't have time. I'll do it over again tomorrow, okay?

The little seedlings tremble as though nodding to Kazu.

He runs back to the spigot with the water still gushing out of the hose, holding the shovel in his other hand. He turns off the spigot, twists the hose reel, carries the shovel on his shoulder. Before heading toward the gate, he turns around and pauses briefly to look at the ocean glittering like a sheet of aluminium foil. A number of deep pink cracks run across the surface – no doubt the wakes of fishing boats trying to return to harbour. He can see now that the hill where he planted the papapas is a meadow surrounded by a forest, which begins just where the water faucet is. The view is beautiful.

Inside the dark forest, it's as though night has already begun. The voices of the birds, so noisy until a moment ago, are gone now. A cold, lonesome wind blows, leaves rustle. In the dark, the giant leaves of the palms and ferns look especially frightening. They move dramatically, the leaves brushing against each other noisily. Kazu looks up to find that the overlapping branches of the trees have enclosed him in darkness. A four-thousand-year-old darkness that has piled up and up. An orange fruit glitters inside of it. A poisonous fruit that only Kazu can see.

Get out of Japan. Hurry, leave, get out of here!

He can hear Yonko's voice from somewhere in the forest.

I don't know what's going to happen. But I don't think I'm

going to last much longer. Kazu, get away from Japan, for my sake, too. Just please, get out of here!

Two years ago – one year and ten months ago, in December, to be exact – Mitch had discovered another article in the newspaper about a third murder involving the colour orange and told Yonko and Kazu about it. Were they the only ones who realized this was the third murder? Perhaps Tabo's mother knew, too. And what about Tabo? That, they didn't know. Later they heard that the old apartment building that Tabo and his mother used to live in had been torn down, and not even Yonko's mother had any idea where they'd moved.

In Bunkyo Ward, a twenty-three-year-old woman fell to her death from a cliff. The autopsy found that before she fell, she'd been strangled with a shawl. There were stone steps that led up the cliff, which was about ten metres high – a place where few people went – and the shawl was spotted fluttering across the steps. It was bright orange, quite conspicuous, so someone in the neighbourhood noticed it right away.

Assuming the possibility that the woman was pushed down the stairs after she was strangled, we must turn to the woman's personal relationships for clues . . .

Mitch had been getting by helping Mama with her business of importing food, and he came out to Tokyo that day and called Yonko and Kazu. Kazu was working at a landscape gardening company in Hachioji, and Yonko was living with her mother again and working at a high-end hotel in Takanawa.

Kazu and Mitch each saw Yonko on their own occasionally, but the three of them got together less and less. They'd seen each other years ago, when they'd all been invited to Takeshi and Fumi's wedding. Ever since Kazu and Yonko had gone to Rome and Paris, and returned to Japan on their own without Mitch, there was a certain awkwardness that lingered between them, and they indirectly avoided seeing each other. Mitch assumed that Kazu and Yonko would live together once they got back to Tokyo, but Kazu had moved into an apartment in Yokohama close to where Mama and Mitch lived, and Yonko had gone back to living with her mother. That was the most natural choice for them, but Mitch didn't seem to understand it, instead putting more and more distance between him and Kazu.

Since then, the three of them had tried to live their lives as separately as possible. At least that's how Kazu saw it. Why? Because they felt like the orange poison was swallowing them whole. And because when they saw each other, they would always recall the pond.

Kazu remembers all of them getting together with Mako three years ago, when Annie had been visiting from Paris. Before that, Tommy had come from Toronto to visit Japan. Mama and Yonko's mother had wanted to see him, too, so Yonko, Mitch and Kazu had begrudgingly agreed to meet. But on all these occasions, it was impossible for the three of them to talk about the orange poison. All they did was make small talk about what they were up to, Takeshi and Mako's activities, or Jeff's whereabouts.

Mitch was busy helping Mama with her work, travelling to Hawaii, Hong Kong and Singapore; Kazu was tied up with work at the landscape gardening firm; and Yonko had started her job at the hotel in Takanawa. She had finally found her footing again after separating from the man she'd been with. She seemed to enjoy her new job, so much so that she'd told Kazu she could see herself staying there for a long time.

Thinking back on it now, Kazu realizes that eight years have passed since that second murder. Every day, Mitch had checked all the newspapers he had sent to Mama's office. And for eight years, nothing significant occurred, and they'd been filled with a vague hope that perhaps it was all behind them now. Eight years felt simultaneously like forever and like no time at all. Compared with kauri trees with their lifespan of four thousand years, eight years felt like a brief blip in time. For human beings like Mitch, Kazu and Yonko, who would only live to be around eighty, at most ninety or a hundred years old, it was like standing on a riverbank, watching a current of clear water flow by.

Sometimes the three of them longed to release the tension they held in their bodies, to believe that the fear they'd felt eight years ago was a thing of the past. But deep down they knew the truth: that 'it' would continue happening, that 'it' must keep happening, which was why, perhaps, the three of them had avoided seeing each other all this time.

They met in a room at the Takanawa luxury hotel. Though Yonko's house had been the most logical choice, that would have meant letting Yonko's mother in on their conversation, which Yonko preferred to avoid, since her mother was getting older and she didn't want to worry her. Instead, she reserved an enormous suite at the hotel she worked at. If her boss or coworkers found out she was using the room for herself, she would likely be fired.

Mitch and Kazu were uneasy about the whole thing, but Yonko assured them it was just an official policy, that they would be fine as long as they weren't rowdy and didn't leave the room a mess.

As soon as they got there, Yonko looked like she was about to cry. Kazu became flustered, but her familiar scent, the softness of her body, made him happy. The three of them spent hours in the hushed suite, drinking only water.

Mitch had brought a clipping of a newspaper article with him. Throughout their meeting, Yonko and Kazu would gingerly, fearfully pick up the paper, as though lifting a bomb, read it, then place it gently back on the table. The table in the hotel suite was large, a knock-off of one of those expensive-looking cat-leg tables. A glittering chandelier hung from the ceiling. Mitch kept venturing to the bathroom to smoke. Sitting on the edge of the velvet-covered chair made Kazu's back start to hurt, at which point he would sit on the floor, rest his back against the wall and stretch out his legs. There were fancy-looking beds on both sides of the room, but they didn't dare get anywhere close to them. They sprawled out on the fluffy carpet as though they were kids again. They knew there was no time to indulge in nostalgia, but deep down they also knew that was part of why they'd got together again.

At least, that's what Kazu thinks, almost two years after the fact.

The three of them continued talking in quiet voices, exhausted.

How could this have happened?

They probably won't find the culprit this time either.

Why are the police so incompetent? Why don't they notice that all these cases involve the colour orange? I wish they would catch the person already.

Who, Tabo?

We don't know for sure if it was him. Maybe it was just a coincidence that all the victims were wearing orange.

No, it can't be.

If you're so sure, then shouldn't you report it? Tell them that something like this has happened before . . . ?

No, you can't just go around accusing people of murder without any evidence.

So why don't we find Tabo and ask him?

What about Tabo's mum? We should ask her. That would be better.

But we don't even know where she is.

Maybe we made the whole thing up.

But we saw Miki-chan and Tabo standing by the edge of the pond that day – that wasn't an illusion. And Miki-chan really did die.

People are going to keep getting killed. I can't accept the fact that there's nothing we can do.

As the three of them talked, they'd fall silent, turn red with excitement, grow pale, and just when they were on the verge of bickering, they'd grow timid and their eyes would fill with tears. What had they even done since that day when they were unable to save Miki-chan? Just thinking about it made Kazu dizzy. We're the real cowards, he thought.

I'll go and find Tabo somehow and live with him, Kazu said, desperately.

What are you talking about? Yonko shot back. Tabo has a mother, remember? Or have you just decided that she's dead already?

You always have been the arrogant type, Mitch said, sneering at Kazu. Always trying to be the good boy.

That's not what it is, Kazu asserted. But then he gave up, grew sad and shut his mouth. How pathetic it all was, the three of them getting together, talking on and on, knowing full well there was nothing they could do. As soon as the thought occurred to Kazu, Mitch and Yonko immediately read his mind, and each of their faces contorted in sorrow.

No matter how much they talked, they couldn't find a solution. As five o'clock in the morning rolled around, the three of them parted ways, dejected. After that, Mitch began searching for Tabo on his own, but it was no simple task.

And then Mama died, just three days after becoming sick – something even she never could have predicted. For a while, time stopped for Mitch and Kazu. And a new time began, one where they were trapped inside an empty glass box. On the other side of the glass, they were busy going about their tasks, checking them off one by one, though feeling slightly disoriented. They could hear their own voices, feel their own hands. They could even cry. But on the inside of the glass box, silence reigned. Mama had died so suddenly, without leaving them so much as a will.

After about three months, things finally began to settle down. In the meantime, Mitch had met with Yonko and confessed he felt lost, and Yonko moved out of her mother's house and began living with another man. At the time, Kazu hadn't known about either of these things.

What had Yonko said to Mitch then?

That this time she was planning to marry the man, have a child with him? That if Mitch wanted to go to Rome and see Kate, he should? That she wanted to stay behind in Japan to be near Miki-chan? That that's why she was getting married and having a child? That she had a mother, and she could have a normal family, but that that wasn't the case for Mitch? That Mama couldn't protect Mitch and Kazu anymore, that even now there were people who suspected them of being involved in Miki-chan's death, that all along there had been people like this who saw them as suspicious, that the rumours had never disappeared, that Mitch and Kazu, as orphans who had been left behind by American GIs, would never be accepted in Japan, that at this very moment women wearing the colour orange were getting killed, that this would keep happening? Could Mitch endure all this, and, even if he could, was there any need to?

I'm thinking of going to Rome for a while, Mitch had told Kazu one day. I'll sell the apartment, split the money with you and rent a smaller place. You should do the same. And I'm quitting Mama's business. If I wander around Rome and Paris long enough, I'm sure I'll find something I can do, even with my bad leg.

It was a little while after that conversation that Yonko had called, practically shouting into the receiver.

Kazu, please hurry up and get out of Japan! For my sake, too, please leave!

Remember that, Yonko? Afterward, I talked to Mitch and decided to come here to New Zealand, a place I'd always wanted to visit. I'm not blaming you, of course. Though I will admit that it really shook me when you said that. It felt like a wake-up call.

In his head, Kazu continues talking to Yonko as he switches his shovel from one shoulder to the other, quickening his pace as he makes his way toward the gate. The forest has already sunk into the darkness. An unsettling night wind blows past him, and the leaves of the ferns sway.

I wanted to meet the tree that's been alive for four thousand years. But the orange poison is here, too. Yonko, you heard the rumours from your mother back then, didn't you? You were so worried you almost fainted. That was the first time I understood the meaning of Mama's death. But, Yonko, I'm coming back to Japan. Are you going to get angry at me again? You and your mother are still checking the newspapers, right? You couldn't hide what was happening from her anymore, so now the two of you are looking for Tabo together, aren't you? We weren't supposed to leave Tabo's side. Now that we're all so far apart, I don't know where I am anymore. I want to see you, Yonko. I want to see Mitch, too. I wonder if he's still holding Sonia's hand, Sonia with her big stomach, walking along the sand as he faces the North Sea. Are his green eyes flashing, is a strong, sandy wind blowing past him? This place is very far from Tabo. But he's alive somewhere in this forest, too. And Miki-chan, and you, too, Yonko. Because the time that flows here is a four-thousand-year-old time. From the kauri's perspective, we're alive only for a brief moment, shorter than the blink of a bird's eye.

Kazu walks quickly, almost running now. A bird cries impatiently as it flies over the towering trees, frightening Kazu, who appears, from its perspective, no larger than an ant. Almost to the gate, he breaks into a run. He can't shake the feeling that he is being followed by some large bird that is coming at him full speed from behind.

Is it the moa? Is it angry with me?

He can see Yonko and Miki-chan as children running through the dark forest, their eyes flashing gold like some nocturnal animal. He can see Tabo.

The ferns are angry with me, too, their leaves bristling as they wave in the wind.

The poisonous orange fruits, which usually don't ripen till autumn, are falling to the ground, one after another. Autumn here is spring for you.

Yonko, where have I wandered off to? Where is this place?

Just as Kazu reaches the garden gate, he throws down his shovel and collapses in front of the office. Ten or so visitors who had just exited the garden and were still lingering around the gate surround him, startled. Kazu trembles, the reflection of the orange fruit still flashing in his cloudy eyes.

9

Annie appears at the airport exit, dragging a large trunk behind her. Beside her is a twelve-year-old boy, carefully carrying a box wrapped in a white cloth.

Yonko leans over the railing and calls out to them excitedly.

Annie! Over here! It's me, Yonko!

Does Annie look up right away, dash over to Yonko? Do the two of them embrace? Or perhaps she keeps her cool, nods to Yonko before ambling over to her with the boy by her side. He continues carrying the box with both hands, his face expressionless. A light blue string is draped diagonally across his shoulder and tied to the box.

In Japan, when you carry a box of remains, Yonko had written to Mitch in a letter, the custom is to wear a long white sash around your neck. But Annie and Tommy didn't seem to notice, since they were raised in America. It doesn't matter, though. I always hated that custom anyway. It's much better this way. But it's strange – that light blue string around Hide's shoulder was the first thing I noticed when I saw him, and it bothered me for some reason. Customs are a funny thing, I guess.

Yonko's eight-year-old daughter Sara is standing beside her. She looks so much like Yonko as a child, with her little bowl cut, that it's almost comical. At first Sara looks at the twelve-year-old boy, astonished, then looks up at Annie's bare brown face. In Mitch's mind, the image of Sara is overlaid with the image of Yonko picking him and Kazu up from Haneda Airport when they'd first got back from England all those years ago.

Everything comes full circle, doesn't it? Mitch whispers to Kazu. I don't know what you're doing right now – probably cutting the branches of some tree in Hokkaido or mowing the grass – but I bet you're picturing Annie and Hide arriving at Narita Airport, too. Of course we're in different time zones, so it's late for you now. Maybe you're in a deep, dreamless sleep.

Finally, we're here. Is that what Annie says to Yonko as she sighs deeply, having flown all the way from Paris to Canada to stay with Tommy, then from there to Narita Airport with Hide in tow?

The flight felt long this time because I had Joyce and this little one with me.

Hide, this is Sara, Yonko's daughter. Say hello. You can say it in Japanese, can't you?

Perhaps Hide says hello, lowering his head just a little, looking dazed. From inside the box Joyce, now reduced to a pile of ashes, greets Yonko and Sara, too.

From now on, Yonko will be your mother, Joyce says to Hide from beyond the grave. Now do you understand why I had you study Japanese all this time?

I've always known, Hide addresses his mother, cradling her ashes inside the box. But I'm nervous. Will I be able to make friends in Japan? Was this the right decision?

Perhaps Hide hesitates. What is his expression like in this moment? What is he wearing? For the life of him, Mitch can't picture it. He grows vexed.

Mitch and Kazu had also been around twelve years old when they were sent away to England. Remember, Kazu, how much we suffered during those two years, how we couldn't adapt to our new environment? We'd experienced plenty of awful things back in Japan that forced us to grow a hard shell. But when we got sent to England, it was even worse, because no one was there with us – not Mama or Yonko or the kids from the orphanage. Plus there was the language barrier. Hide is probably going through the same thing right now. But, unlike us, he has nowhere to go back to. He chose to live in Japan, so he has no way out.

And Hide had brought Joyce's remains with him.

When I die, Joyce had told Yonko, I want you to cremate me and put my remains in the ossuary in Kamakura with Mother Asami and Miki-chan. As soon as Yonko had seen Joyce's obituary, she immediately sent a fax to Joyce's adoptive parents as well as to Tommy, who had been like a brother to her. But Hide had made up his mind about what to do even before he'd heard anything from Tommy. He knew what his mother would have wanted for him.

When Yonko sent the fax to the castle in Brittany where Mitch was living at the time, she hadn't bothered to describe what Hide looked like. She probably had her hands full with taking care of the little boy.

Kazu, I heard you're going to Tokyo to see Hide for yourself, Mitch addresses Kazu in his mind. Though I bet the real reason you're going is to see Yonko. I wish it were easier for me to get to Japan. But first I have to go to Indonesia, by way of Thailand. I can't just break my promise to Odile.

Mitch lingers awhile in the entrance to the old church, watching the thunderstorm rage outside. The thunder had begun on his way back from going into town to do some shopping. Then, as he was driving along the country road listening to the thunder, it had suddenly begun to hail. The hailstones were as big as a child's fist, pounding the roof of the car. They sounded like rocks slamming against it. Fearing he might be crushed inside, Mitch immediately pulled over and dashed into an old church he saw just off the side of the road. It had no doors and the windows barely had any glass left in them. These small abandoned churches were a common sight here. Weeds grew up between the cracks in the floorboards, and most of the stucco walls and ceiling, which had once been painted with images of Christ or the Virgin Mary, were now peeling off, so it was easy to imagine a snake or some other creature lurking in the corners.

As soon as it started hailing, the ground turned white. For a while the world looked like it had become winter, though it was actually midsummer. Even after the hailstones had fallen to the ground, they continued to roll around and bounce off each other, never settling. The temperature plummeted.

Mitch is in such a state of shock that all he can do is stand there and watch the hail falling from the sky. After about half an hour, the hail becomes rain, and now there is a vicious downpour, accompanied by rumbling thunder.

He doesn't feel like going back to the car, so he sits in the entrance to the church, waiting for the rain to die down. Just a few days ago, it had been suffocatingly hot and humid, and clouds of small winged insects had emerged, their dead bodies appearing all over the house, on the plates, on the bed. The extreme weather had continued through mid-August.

Odile must be waiting in the castle for Mitch to come home. Mitch doesn't think she is likely to be shaken up by the storm, but if one of the windows in the castle were to break, the rain would get in and soak the floors. And of course, it would be Mitch's job to clean up the mess. He would leave early tomorrow morning and return to Paris, meaning he needed to go back and pack his bags and put away the furniture.

But even as Mitch is thinking this, he can't stop picturing twelve-year-old Hide riding the shuttle bus from Narita to downtown Tokyo. Is Annie sitting next to him at this very moment, with her frizzy hair? Or is it Yonko, his new guardian?

Or perhaps it's Sara who sits beside him, the children being made to sit together?

Perhaps Hide, exhausted from jet lag, half-asleep and pale in the face, gazes at the landscape flowing by outside the window. If he had travelled from America, it would probably already be night-time, and the landscape might be almost entirely invisible by now. What is he thinking about as he glances sleepily out the window from time to time, holding the box containing his mother's remains on his lap?

Joyce had left Japan for America when she was nine. And now her son was coming back to Japan. But this wasn't Hide's first trip here. Once, about five years ago, Joyce had brought him to Japan to meet Yonko and Mitch. Was that around the same time that Yonko had got a divorce and taken Sara, then three years old, to live with her mother? After the divorce, Yonko and her ex-husband had quarrelled for about a year. She seemed to make the same mistakes over and over, never learning her lesson. Yonko might object that it was different this time, since she had Sara. To which Mitch would say, muttering under his breath: No, it was exactly the same thing. Mitch hadn't had a chance to see Joyce or Hide in person. The timing simply hadn't worked out. If he had known that Joyce would end up dying in a car accident, he never would have missed the opportunity to see them – though of course it was pointless to speculate.

Yes, perhaps at this very moment Hide is remembering that little trip they took five years ago, when Joyce was still alive. But he would not, by any means, try to recall the accident in which his mother's car had been rear-ended and crashed into a guard-rail, snapping her neck and killing her instantaneously. After all, even if, with some effort, he could remember the accident, it wouldn't bring back the pieces of his mother.

Five years ago, Hide had visited the ossuary that would someday hold his mother's remains. It was on an elevated piece of land, with a spectacular view of the ocean. Hide knew right away that one of the people buried there, Mother Asami, had raised his mother at the orphanage until she was nine years old. But all Joyce had told him about Miki-chan was that she had died when she was seven.

Was she sick? Hide had asked. Is that why she died? But his mother just put her hands together and prayed over Miki-chan's grave for a long time. Her hands were trembling, and she looked like she might cry, and Hide, too, had felt like crying. That little girl must have died in a tragic way. I'm sure when I'm older Mummy will tell me all about her, Hide reasoned, etching the name Miki-chan into his memory. But then his mother had died without telling him anything.

In Tokyo, they had stayed with someone named Yonko. Sara was still young then, and there was a grandmother in the house, too, but not a father or a grandfather, and he remembered that Yonko and his mother had been absorbed in conversation for a long time. This was a version of his mother that Hide had never seen. He never left her side, and kept a watchful eye on Yonko. He suspected she might try to steal his mother away from him.

Just then, Yonko had smiled at Hide, who was watching her intently with his big black eyes.

What a sweet child. He looks like a little angel. Any chance you'd want to leave him with me? She'd said it jokingly, but Joyce's expression was serious when she responded.

I might ask you to take him eventually, but, for now, I want him with me.

Kazu had been there at the time and told Mitch about it.

When they first learned of Joyce's misfortune, Kazu and Yonko, and of course Mitch, were shocked, then angry, then sad, and when Tommy told them about the funeral that would be held in Seattle, they wondered whether to attend. Eventually it was decided that Takeshi and Mako would go in Mother

Asami's place. Only after the funeral was long over and Takeshi and the others had returned to Japan could they even broach the topic of what would become of Hide.

Five years ago, when Hide came to Japan with his mother, he was just a little boy of seven, but he seemed to remember the entire conversation between Joyce and Yonko. I guess children are sensitive to conversations they know are about them. Yonko was still dealing with her divorce then. She didn't have the capacity to take care of another child, since Sara was still three. But she said that, as she looked at Hide, the idea of adopting him began to grow on her. She said her mother could help take care of the kids, and anyway, one kid or two, what difference did it make? Anyone who looked at Hide was immediately captivated by him. His pupils, like black velvet that sometimes appeared purple, his brown hair, his round cheeks that glowed pink.

Joyce didn't like the idea of her own son becoming American. She said if she could raise him in Japan she would. But Hide's white father would never agree to such a thing, and it would be difficult for Joyce herself to find a job in Japan.

After she died, Hide went to live with Joyce's adoptive parents for a while. There, Joyce's white adoptive father declared he would file a lawsuit against the person responsible for the accident but that he would of course take care of Hide. Hide wondered what right this man, who was neither Joyce's husband nor partner, had to file a lawsuit, since the driver responsible for the rear-end collision had also died. Hide asked Joyce's adoptive father to get the deceased man's remaining family members to pay the insurance money so they could avoid the lawsuit altogether.

Joyce's adoptive parents said that they would hold on to the money for the time being and then send it to Yonko. But Hide was intent on getting away from these people, whom he detested, so he called Tommy and asked to be taken to Toronto.

Joyce's adoptive father threatened Tommy, saying he would appeal to the international police. Tommy invited the father to Toronto and began the process of trying to convince him to give up Hide.

Tommy's a teacher, so he knows how to be persuasive, Annie had said, almost as though she were bragging about herself. Tommy explained everything to Joyce's adoptive father patiently in his quiet, cello-like voice: that Joyce had originally wanted to raise Hide in Japan; that Hide himself very much wanted this too; that Joyce's friend, Yonko, had offered to take Hide under her wing. And to top it all off, Hide had put on a big emotional display and cried his eyes out.

Children are perfectly capable of putting on a performance when they really want to, aren't they? Yonko had said to Mitch, her own eyes brimming with real tears that were very much not for show.

Seems like Joyce's adoptive father didn't feel real love for Hide. I mean, he already had his own family and everything. I bet he was just being stubborn. And jealous, too. Think about it – there was Hide, clinging to Tommy, half-Japanese and dark-skinned. A part of me wonders if Joyce's adoptive father wanted to adopt Hide just so he could get his hands on that insurance money. But Hide's mind was made up. Tommy, who felt a responsibility to Hide, told him that he had the right to decide what happened to him, regardless of what Joyce would have wanted.

I could take care of you, or Kate, or Annie. In Japan, besides Yonko, there's also Mako and Takeshi. Your mum was an orphan, Hide, so you have lots of aunties and uncles who will take care of you. They all love you. Then there's Kazu and Mitch, your two single uncles. Although, because they're single men, it might be a little more difficult for them to adopt you officially. So you can choose who you like best, okay?

Looking out the window of the bus, perhaps twelve-year-old Hide opens his mouth a little and watches the night stream past him as he ponders Tommy's words, recalling the faces of Kate and Annie, Takeshi and Mako, who had all come from afar to attend his mother's funeral. Perhaps he is trying to drive out the image of Joyce's adoptive father's angry red face from his mind, his complete indifference to Japan. And all the while, maybe his mother continues speaking to him ever so quietly from the box in his lap:

Finally, you've made it to Japan. You did good, Hide. You must be exhausted by so many adults telling you so many different things. You know, the fact that you chose to live with Yonko in Japan means you won't have an easy road ahead of you, but you made the right choice. At some point in my life I became an American without even realizing it. It was shameful to me that I couldn't change my fate. After I was adopted by my American parents, I had no choice but to accept myself as the American I had become.

The rain continues falling. The force of it doesn't let up, though since the hail stopped it is becoming gradually warmer. Mitch's leg begins to hurt, and he stands up and wanders around the small church. The layers of grime that have accumulated on the stone slabs of the floor give off a terrible smell. Black insects the size of little beads, so small you can't tell what they are unless you lean in close, are crawling around. Pieces of wood and cloth, fragments of stone, and what appears to be animal fur are all mixed up together in the corners of the building, forming small mountains of trash. Perhaps animals shelter in this church. Maybe there is even animal or human excrement lying around somewhere.

The rain enters through the open windows, and the smell reminds Mitch of Japanese pickles. He's not sure why he suddenly feels so nostalgic for them, since he never really liked them to begin with.

As he looks closely at the peeling walls, he can see a faded brown flower pattern, dark leaves that seem once to have been painted green, a faded human hand and an image of a face. It isn't a human face – is it an angel's? Mitch thinks. Only part of the outline remains, since the eyes and nose are no longer visible.

Odile must know this place well. I wish I could have asked her about it. But I have to leave the castle early tomorrow morning. It takes almost six hours to get to Paris, and I don't have time to make extra stops.

Besides, after the big trip around Asia that Mitch would accompany Odile on, the castle would be put up for sale.

Mitch feels like he's floating as he is enveloped in the sound of rain pounding the church and the surrounding ground and trees. In his mind, Hide's angelic face transforms into the face of Sonia's child, Niels.

So it's Niels I've been thinking of all this time, not Hide, Mitch says to himself. Or is it that, deep down, some part of me wishes Niels were actually Hide? If that's the case, Kazu, then I really am a selfish asshole, just like you said – it means I've been wishing unhappiness on Niels and Sonia all along.

Sonia, a Danish woman who had no connection to Japan, had decided that Mitch was not Niels's father, that instead it was a Danish man whom she had begun living with in Stockholm. And then there had been an accident at some big nuclear power plant in the Soviet Union. Even Mitch knew the name Chernobyl now, and could pronounce it with ease, but at first no one had even heard of the place. There was so little information about the event. But as the radioactive cloud from the plant began to drift toward Sweden, people began to panic. That's when Sonia relocated with Niels, then two years old, to Majorca, where the Danish man had a vacation home.

Kazu, you've heard of Majorca, right? The island that has lots of resorts for rich people? The man who'd been supporting Sonia came from a well-to-do family. I was never going to win that one. I heard they hired a local nanny to take care of Niels, and that Sonia and the man still live in Majorca.

You can see Niels whenever you want, as long as you let me know in advance, Sonia had insisted to Mitch before moving to Majorca. And she was eager to learn about Hiroshima and Nagasaki.

Tell me, what was it like? You're Japanese, so you must know about radiation, right? I've seen the photographs of those poor people who suffered horrible burns. Oh, I'm sorry. I forgot you also suffered a burn on one of your legs, didn't you?

I've never been to Hiroshima or Nagasaki in my life, Mitch responded angrily. I don't know anything about it. Why would you ask me something like that? All the things you want to ask me about aren't particular to me, they're things you could ask any Japanese person.

Come to think of it, maybe there was a time when they had talked with Mama about their fear of radiation, Mitch remembered as he looked at Sonia, and at Niels sleeping in her arms.

Kazu, my eyes are open now. But I was so sad then. Sonia wasn't looking at me anymore, or listening to anything I was saying.

Mitch had pleaded with her to let him be part of Niels's life, but she'd quickly forgotten about him.

After that, Mitch went back to Japan and worked at Takeshi's company for a while. When he got bored of that, he went to see Kate in Rome, and Annie in Paris, but he never saw Niels again. The little boy now lived a completely separate life.

Mitch furrows his brow.

Niels is nine now, the same age as Tabo was that day at the pond. Kazu, it scares me to think about. Time surges forward and keeps blowing back.

Since then, the Berlin Wall has fallen, Bulgaria and Romania and all those countries started seceding from the Soviet Union, and then, shockingly, the Soviet Union itself collapsed. The Gulf War broke out and, completely unrelatedly, Joyce died in a car crash.

Just as Mitch can't imagine what Hide looks like now, neither can he imagine what Niels looks like. Maybe he has blond hair, white skin, blue eyes, like any Northern European child. But Mitch has no idea what the boy's facial features look like, or what kind of personality he has, having known him only as a baby. When he was first born, Mitch was surprised to find no trace of himself in the child. He had no choice but to acknowledge that the boy wasn't his after all. Still, he'd hoped to be Niels's father if possible. The genetic connection didn't matter much to him. He believed that Sonia's feelings alone would make him a father.

After all, she did love me once, Mitch thinks, biting his lower lip. The small hotel in Odense where they'd spent three days together feels like a mirage now. He thinks of the words she said to him on the beach that day as sandy gusts of wind blew past them:

You're just following me around because you have nothing better to do. I might even venture to say you're not actually interested in women. Am I wrong?

Mitch looks out the window, which has grown cloudy from the fierce rain.

Because I had nothing better to do? Preposterous. I was serious about her. I even thought at one point, So this is what it feels like to want to live.

Voices jolt through Mitch's body with the sound of the rain.

Joyce's voice, which Hide is surely listening to now, echoes up from Mitch's feet. But it isn't just Joyce's – it also sounds like Mitch's own voice, and Kazu's voice, and the long-gone voice of Miki-chan.

Ah, that's right. Suddenly Mitch's breath catches in his throat. He'd heard that Hide knew Miki-chan's name. Hide must have realized by now that there was some important secret that existed between Joyce and Yonko, and which involved the little girl.

Kazu, you're going to see Hide pretty soon, aren't you? If he asks you about this secret, how are you going to answer? He'll want to know about her. About that frightening, unnameable doubt that began at the pond that day and continues even now. He probably won't ask Yonko about it, he'll just go straight to you. Though it's possible he'll ask me about it later, too.

You hear that, Sonia? Mitch wishes he could say to her, though he has no idea whether she is in Majorca, or Stockholm, or somewhere else.

Maybe I wanted to be a father to your son, Niels, because of what happened with Miki-chan, which you know nothing about and which haunts me even now, as a forty-year-old man. But you wouldn't have understood any of that, even if I had explained it to you. I mean, I barely understand it myself. I had almost convinced myself I'd forgotten all about Niels, until I heard that Yonko had adopted Hide, and then I couldn't help but remember. Just one decision from you and my life might have looked completely different.

Joyce's voice, speaking to Hide, flows into Mitch's ear like the sound of rain, like a waterfall. The walls of the building are thick, and even though many windows are broken, the floor remains dry in patches. The dark water spreads and spreads, putting Mitch on edge. An ominous feeling comes over him.

*

. . . You already know this, Hide, but my biological father was an American soldier. And whoever my Japanese mother was, he probably raped her and abandoned her. Doesn't being adopted by the country of someone like that amount to stating I should wipe my Japanese mother clean from my memory? I have no way of knowing what actually happened, but I have no doubt my mother experienced some terrible things. And it was all the fault of those American soldiers. I wonder if becoming a soldier makes a person go funny in the head. Still, it shouldn't be so easy for people to abandon their own children. Having you convinced me of that, Hide. I was born in Japan, and raised there till the age of nine. That's because my mother was Japanese. I know that America is a big country, a strong country. You remember, don't you, Hide, the Gulf War that broke out a few years ago? That was a rough time for me. But you know, Japan is a strange, terribly conceited country that hates outsiders, so you have to be careful. You're likely to be bullied wherever you go because of how you look. Terrible things are lying in wait for you. But I want you to overcome those things. I want you to live. Because those are the wounds of my own soul.

Mitch! Hey, Mitch, I didn't want to tell you all this, but I have to. Yonko's voice sounds muffled, as though caught in a spiderweb. It reverberates from the ceiling of the church.

It happened about two weeks ago, when Mitch had just started living at the castle. Yonko's and then Kazu's voices, distorted by pain, had reached him through the fax machine. Not long before that, Mitch had told both of them that he would be staying at the castle that summer. Yonko was officially adopting Hide, and she had even told Mitch the specific date when Hide was arriving in Japan. He was just beginning to settle into his quiet routine at the castle, feeling remarkably unburdened.

I tried to forget about my fear of the colour orange, and about you, Kazu, and you, too, Yonko. I had even begun to forgive myself.

You and your mother checked the newspapers every day. You convinced yourselves that Tabo probably wasn't venturing far from home, and were careful to avoid places like Bunkyo and Toshima Wards, where the killings had taken place, opting to check the local news instead. Of course, it's possible you overlooked something, or maybe the newspapers didn't report on it for whatever reason, but, as far as you knew, no murder involving the colour orange had taken place in Johoku district. And ten years went by like that. You thought that maybe you had nothing to be afraid of anymore. And though it's hard to believe, it's been so many years since this all started. Our souls have paid a high price, but maybe the pain is beginning to abate and our wounds are finally starting to heal.

But Mitch had never said anything like that to Yonko. Even now, he couldn't bring himself to say it out loud. How could he possibly describe this fear that had been with him since he was a child? Childhood, when they could simply be afraid, shrink in fear, cry and tremble, was long gone. And yet, inside each of them was a child who was still afraid, still weeping and clinging to Miki-chan. If they tried to make that child stop crying, it would be unbearably painful. They are petrified inside the fear. Part of them had hoped that Miki-chan might someday fade away like an old photograph. But far from disappearing, her memory grew only more vivid as time passed. Haunted by that smiling, doll-like face, they went on endlessly blaming each other, crushed by the suspicion that another orange murder might occur again at any moment.

But now, perhaps, the time had finally come for them to release themselves from this fear. Maybe Tabo had changed, after all. Maybe it was all just a bad dream triggered by Miki-chan's death.

We wanted so badly to think that, and now, at last, we were beginning to crawl out of the dark, cramped hole where we had shut ourselves away, our ears filled with the sound of a child sobbing.

After the third murder, Yonko told Mitch that he should leave Japan. That it wasn't Tabo but Mitch and Kazu who were suspected of being the murderers.

But that's not exactly how it went, Mitch thinks inside the church, shaking his head and rubbing his face with his hands. Had the three of them met after that? Yes – they didn't even know for sure if this had been Tabo's doing, but they couldn't shake the feeling of unsafety. And then, a year or so after that, Mama had died. Which prompted Yonko's mother to tell Yonko for the first time about the rumours that were circulating about them.

Now that Mama's gone and she can't protect you, it will be too dangerous for you both, Yonko had said to Mitch and Kazu, in her desperate bid to get them to leave Japan.

That was when Mitch had called Yonko and asked whether she thought he should continue Mama's business. He'd barely got the words out when Yonko blurted out angrily: That's what you're worried about right now? Really? Hurry up and get Mama's affairs in order and get out of Japan. You have no reason to stay here. The same goes for Kazu. I'm not a mixed-race orphan, so I'm in a better position than you to stay here. Prejudice and rumours are far more terrifying than you could ever imagine. Mama understood that. There are still people here who suspect you both. The two of you stand out here, a lot. You should never have sympathized with Tabo. Mama even helped you escape to a boarding school in England, but you came right back to Japan. How could you be so ungrateful? You two are stupid, really stupid, you know that?

Mitch closes his eyes. The image of Mama crying on the night of his twelfth birthday comes back to him. She'd decided to send him and Kazu to England to protect them, despite how sad it made her. And then Yonko, moved by the same fear, had urged them to leave Japan. Mitch had stood in front of Yonko and nodded, saying nothing, tears welling in his eyes.

You were right, Mitch murmurs to Yonko as he returns to the entrance of the church. Even if the incident with Miki-chan had never happened, people like us shouldn't be in Japan to begin with. We only exist because Japan happened to lose the war and American soldiers occupied the country and fell prey to their own desires. Isn't it strange how after all this time, even as adults, we're still mixed-race orphans?

What would Yonko do if he said something like that? Would she shoot him that angry look of hers, eyes flashing behind her glasses?

What are you talking about, she'd probably say. Why are you getting all sentimental all of a sudden? Reality is reality, Mitch, and whatever you feel about it is a separate thing. I'm telling you right now, you have to look at the facts and make decisions accordingly. But here you are, still feeling sorry for yourself. It's embarrassing, honestly.

Then Mitch had gone to Rome to see Kate, and Kazu had gone to New Zealand. The three of them had begun living their separate lives, in distant places. But gradually Mitch and Kazu began to realize that physical distance didn't hold much meaning for them.

Right, Kazu? Wherever we were, the three of us always sought each other out, shared our fears with each other. Our world still revolved around that stagnant pond that swallowed Miki-chan's life. Sometimes when we were in countries where no one spoke Japanese, we felt like we were the ghosts, not

Miki-chan. That's why you came back to Japan, isn't it? Not to Tokyo, where Yonko was, but to Hokkaido, where you started working on a farm. I'm sure you wanted to be near Yonko, but you wouldn't let yourself. Yonko had her own mother to take care of, and Sara.

I have to be careful, Kazu had said to Mitch. If I so much as go near that house, I'll put Yonko in danger too.

Maybe, Mitch had answered. I wonder if it's really necessary to go that far, though?

You didn't say anything, Kazu, just nodded. Even now, I'm not entirely sure. Were we really in danger? Were we overthinking it?

Mitch, how much longer are you going to keep wandering around like this? Annie's voice closes in on him from somewhere inside the church.

He'd spent a lot of time in Paris with Odile lately, and had got plenty of chances to see Annie. And she'd scolded him plenty of times.

I'm not just wandering around, Mitch had answered. I swear it's that time just slipped away from me and now, somehow, I'm in my forties. I can't believe it. But I guess that's how it's going to be for the rest of my life, getting older and older, one year after another.

But Annie, who was being worked to the bone by her job in Paris, wasn't sympathetic.

While you're standing around, the clouds are going to sail past you, the sun will set, then rise again, and before you know it you'll be an old man. If you want to go back to Japan, you should just make up your mind and do it. If not, then get serious and actually find a job here. You've gone through life just mooching off other people, haven't you?

Odile's hoarse voice, too, echoes through the splashes of rain. Even though she lived in Paris, Odile was originally from the Netherlands, so she spoke English with Mitch, though that had as much to do with Mitch's poor grasp of French.

There are rabbits around here, and squirrels, weasels and wildcats, wild boars even. Though I've only actually seen rabbits and squirrels. Wildcats are nocturnal, after all. You know, Mitch, sometimes when your eyes flash green they look just like a wildcat's. Yes, of course I'm sad you won't be helping out around the castle anymore. But what can I do?

Castle? You said castle?

Mitch heard his own voice echoing back to him when Kate had first told him about a seventy-year-old woman named Odile who was looking for a helper. Mitch had imagined a castle like Cinderella's.

Wow, a castle, Yonko had written back immediately in a fax. That's incredible.

Kazu had said something similar. I guess that's Europe for you. If it's being put up for sale anyway, why don't you have Takeshi or Mako buy it? They have plenty of money, so I bet they could do it, he'd said, half jokingly.

They'd been writing each other more frequently. After all, for ten years, not a single murder involving the colour orange had occurred in the Johoku district of Tokyo.

Perhaps *fortress* was a more appropriate word than *castle* for the surly-looking stone building. When Mitch had first arrived from Paris by car, he was secretly disappointed: the stone was already crumbling, and it looked gloomy and haunted. It stood in the middle of the woods and according to Odile had once been the property of a feudal lord. The surrounding area must have been quite open and spacious back then, but eventually the entire family was killed during the revolution and the building was abandoned, and over time weeds sprouted up, and trees, until at last it had become surrounded by a vast forest. It was about fifteen years ago that Odile's husband had bought the property on a whim for dirt cheap, and after that they had renovated part of it and begun spending their summers here.

Still, it was surprisingly spacious inside, with so many rooms that even Odile hadn't explored them all, much less Mitch, even after he had been there for two weeks. Sometimes Odile would tease him, telling him not to be surprised if he saw a ghost around every now and then, and get a kick out of Mitch's reaction. If Odile hadn't been there, Mitch would have run far away from the place a long time ago. At night there wasn't a single light for miles around, and when the moon was hidden, it was completely shrouded in darkness. Sometimes Mitch would hear the cry of an owl or some other animal and wonder if it was a wildcat. Thankfully, there were no wolves or bears in this forest, at least according to Odile, but still he had no desire to set foot outside the castle at night. He was even afraid of sleeping in his own room, separate from Odile.

Every morning, Mitch would think about how much Kazu would like it here. And when the bright summer sun illuminated the early morning, the transparent green of the forest enclosing the castle would glimmer and the branches sway as the light bounced off the evening dew and made the grasses dance; and the pink hyacinths and white wild roses, which usually bloom only in spring, sprang up around the castle, and little birds twittered happily – yes, the view of the forest from the castle was beautiful, so much so that even Mitch, who usually preferred life in the city, couldn't help but be enthralled by it. But unlike Kazu, Mitch didn't know what kind of trees grew here. The only thing he knew for sure was that there were chestnut trees, from all the old shells he found lying on the ground. That and willow trees – those he could distinguish, too.

How should he tell Kazu and Yonko about these things, Mitch wondered. Odile was letting Mitch use her personal fax machine, which made him hesitant to use it too often, and faxing wasn't much different from writing a letter, which was a pain, so he rarely got around to it. He'd sent them one fax to brag about the fact that he was living in a castle, but after that he couldn't be bothered.

And anyway, you two are probably busy taking care of Hide. I'll tell you everything the next time I see you. Just wait. I'll tell you about the time I took a walk at night and suddenly found myself surrounded by a pack of wildcats, or how I'd wander up to the watchtower at the top of the castle every night and see a ghost wearing all white, who would call out my name in an eerie voice – yes, I'll make up eight hundred lies to entertain you all.

But just as Mitch was thinking this, a stream of faxes from Yonko and Kazu was beginning to roll out of the fax machine, like a long shriek.

. . . Kazu said we didn't have to tell you. When are you coming back again? If you're not sure, then I think we should tell you now. The idea of you not knowing is just unthinkable.

. . . It was Yonko's mother who first noticed the newspaper article, since Yonko was too busy to read the news carefully. They faxed me a copy of the article right away. It felt like having the rug pulled out from under my feet. Why is it happening again, why now? I feel like I can't breathe.

. . . It happened in Bunkyo Ward again. They said it was a woman in her thirties. I'm going to send you a copy of the article, too. The woman's skirt was torn up, and some of the fabric was scattered in the grass around her. It was a park, so there were kids playing there, and at first they mistook the pieces of fabric for flowers and ran over to them, only to discover a corpse. I didn't see it myself, but the images of those torn pieces of orange fabric are burned into my retinas, they haunt me, fluttering, in my dreams. Mitch, I'm scared. I'm ten, twenty, a hundred times more scared than before. I feel like it's crazy for me to take care of Hide right now. I wonder if I should tell Tommy.

. . . But Hide already knows Miki-chan's name. He senses our secret, or rather, the spell that's been cast over us, the shadow of that pond. Once he finds out about it, I have a feeling he'll suffer even more than us. But we can't hide it from him anymore.

. . . I told Kazu not to come back right now, though he can eventually come and see Hide. Mitch, I don't want you coming back to Japan right now, either. We'll wait for you, I promise. We don't know what will happen in the future, do we? Mitch, do you think this is going to keep happening forever? When is it going to end?

. . . I wonder where Tabo went. I'm thinking of renting a room in the area so I can try to find him. Tabo's mother is getting up there in age, so maybe I'll give them a call pretending to be a social worker, then approach Tabo and try to find out if he's been involved in these incidents. If he has, then I'll pretend to be his friend. I won't leave his side, no matter how he reacts. We can't just leave him to die. He must be suffering more than anyone else right now.

. . . Kazu is being ridiculous again. Mitch, say something to him, please. Why is he making himself vulnerable like this? Finding Tabo is going to be no easy task, and if Kazu hangs around his apartment, clearly someone is going to call the police on him. And if he's really unlucky, he might even get accused of being the murderer. After all, it wasn't Tabo but Kazu who was close to Miki-chan. Even now, there are plenty of people who remember Kazu simply because he's darker-skinned.

The sound of the thunder grows more distant, and the rain begins to abate.

Odile must be worried. I should get back to the castle soon, Mitch thinks. As soon as he makes up his mind, he takes off running from where he has been crouching. Just then, a torrent of large, furious raindrops comes pelting down, almost as if they had been waiting for him. Mitch's left sandal plunges into a puddle of water, and he almost falls. Some grass that has fallen into the puddle twines around his foot. The straight path through the meadow has become a rivulet. In an instant, the back of his polo shirt is drenched. Rain drips from the pine trees, blurring his vision.

Where are the animals that live in this forest? Are there wildcats hiding between the tree roots, their golden eyes glittering? He is suffocated by loneliness. Is this how Jeff had felt in the jungles of Vietnam? Where is he now, anyway? Where is Tabo?

Mitch runs through the torrent of rain, then jumps into his car, thoroughly soaked. He doesn't care about the seat getting wet. He wishes he could take off his pants, his polo shirt, even his underwear. But he can't, so he removes just his shirt, takes out a towel from the shopping basket he'd put in the passenger seat, and wipes down his head and chest, then his legs.

Earlier, when he'd gone into town to buy some crepe flour and apple wine to bring back to Paris, a magnificent blue sky had stretched out above him. The sun was so strong he'd regretted not bringing his sunglasses. He wrinkles his nose and puckers his lips. At least he'd brought this towel for wicking away sweat. He turns on his windshield wipers and starts the engine.

Let me get back to the castle. I just need to get back to the castle.

What's wrong? Did something happen? Odile had asked earlier when she saw Mitch reading the faxes from Yonko and Kazu. Normally Odile didn't meddle in Mitch's affairs, even if she was worried. But given how long the fax machine had been rattling away, she must have sensed that something was really off this time. If the fax machine hadn't been such a common device, the castle would have remained quiet, Yonko's and Kazu's voices never would have reached him there, he never would have known anything, and he wouldn't have had to worry Odile.

Mitch had apologized to Odile, but when she still looked worried, he began, hesitantly, to tell her the whole story, beginning with what had happened at a pond in a park in a corner of Tokyo. He had already told her the circumstances of his and Kazu's births. How at three years old they had become Mama's children and left the orphanage. This time, he told her about the other children at the orphanage: Miki-chan, Sara, Joyce, and Yonko, the daughter of Mama's cousin, and about Tabo, another child in the neighbourhood. But when he began to tell her about the rumours in the neighbourhood, about Yonko and the mixed-race orphans, he hesitated. It wasn't easy to find the words to describe what had happened after that.

Miki-chan died a long time ago, Mitch said. But even now, there are people who suspect that we were the ones who killed her, which is why Yonko thinks I shouldn't go back to Japan. Recently Joyce died in a car accident, and Yonko adopted Hide, the son Joyce left behind, but she's worried this might cause people to talk even more. In Japan, mixed-race people like us become objects of curiosity, and orphans in particular are a reminder of the American military occupation, so it's not easy for us to be there.

Odile listened to Mitch's story with her mouth halfway open, looking like she wanted to say something, but she just sighed and kept quiet.

That's it? perhaps she wanted to say. Are you sure that's the whole story? It feels like you're hiding something, Mitch. But it's all right, I'm sure you'll tell me in due time.

Odile herself was mixed-race, too. That had been the first thing she told Mitch when they'd met. That's why she was interested in Mitch's upbringing and the children from the orphanage. She was already close with Kate because of Kate's job in Rome, and Kate had introduced her to Annie, but she wondered about the other children she hadn't met, about Tommy and Jeff, and Joyce, who adored Yonko, and the intelligent Mako, and Takeshi, who had made a lot of money from his company. And most importantly, she wanted to know about Kazu, who was like a twin brother to Mitch, or perhaps a younger brother.

Odile was a quarter Indonesian. When the Dutch had colonized Indonesia, Odile's grandfather had a child with an Indonesian woman, and when the Japanese military came to Indonesia, the grandfather took the child back to the Netherlands. That was Odile's father – she had no idea what had become of her Indonesian grandmother. Mixed-race children were not particularly rare in Europe. As a mixed-race orphan himself, Mitch had come to realize this over the course of his time there. That history had left a peculiar shadow over Europe.

As a kind of conclusion to her life, Odile had planned to go to Thailand and then to Indonesia. Of course it would be impossible for her to meet her grandmother now, but she longed to know the land, the air, the faces of the people there. After that, she would go to Japan, Mitch's homeland. When they'd agreed that Mitch would accompany her on her trip to Asia, Odile had suggested they stop in Japan. The two of them would part ways there, and she would go back to Paris alone.

For Mitch, the prospect of having his flight back to Japan covered by Odile, not to mention the opportunity to go to Thailand and Indonesia, seemed too good to pass up. Odile was worried about going on such a big trip all by herself. It would be her first time in Asia. She was old and had trouble carrying her own luggage. She had asked Kate whether she knew anyone who could work as a personal assistant, which is when Kate had introduced her to Mitch.

This person isn't young by any means, Kate had told Odile.

But he doesn't have a stable job, and he has plenty of time. The reason he doesn't have a stable job is simply because of his personality. But you can trust him.

They'd decided that Mitch would also help organize the documents that Odile's late husband had left behind in Paris.

I'm going to die soon, so I want to have all my papers in order, Odile had said to Mitch. This is my last summer here. I'm going to sell the place next year. I have two sons who live in London and Milan, but they've been telling me to get rid of this old place forever. Even though their father loved it.

Outside, the rain continues falling, and the rainwater that Mitch had brought into the car makes the inside feel like a sauna. If he opened the window, more rain would get in. Odile's car, of course, doesn't have air-conditioning. Though, unlike in Japan, it wasn't particularly rare for cars not to have air-conditioning here. Just twenty more minutes of this, Mitch tells himself. Moments ago, rainwater had been dripping from his hair, but now beads of sweat are beginning to drip onto his arms and thighs. Even if he wanted to drive faster, he couldn't. The country road is bumpy, there are pools of rainwater here and there, which create little rivulets, and the branches of the shrubs to either side are sagging under the weight of the rain, blocking the way ahead. Mitch has no choice but to crawl along at a pace not much faster than a person walking.

Kazu, of course you have no idea that I'm in the middle of a forest right now, getting rained on. You're on a farm in Hokkaido, probably cutting and gathering grasses in the pasture.

Mitch imagines Kazu's muscular body glistening with sweat beneath the blue Hokkaido sky. But Mitch has never been to Hokkaido. He'd simply conjured up a landscape in his mind that he'd seen on a poster somewhere, and superimposed Kazu onto it. Besides, Kazu might already be in Tokyo by now. He could be at Yonko's house, meeting Annie and Hide, kneeling in front of Joyce's remains with tears in his eyes.

Kazu, I really want to see you. I want to see Yonko, too, I want to speak in Japanese. Odile is a lovely person, and I like her a lot, but she can't understand Japanese. Sometimes it annoys me. Even though I know it's selfish. You know, it's strange, Kazu, ever since we've been at the castle, Odile and I have been talking a lot. In Paris I couldn't have a real conversation with anyone. Here it feels like we have all the time in the world. Sometimes we talk in the kitchen while we're cooking together, or while we're wandering aimlessly around. If we drive into town, we'll stop in a café and talk. It's funny, with her age and my bad leg, we end up walking at about the same pace. Maybe I really do have a mother complex. But you do, too, you know. Though it seems weird to say that when we never even knew our real mothers.

I told Odile about what happened with Sonia. It was embarrassing, but I wanted her to know that I had a woman I wanted to marry at one time. She told me about how she used to work as a radio announcer when she was younger, and how her husband was the president of a radio station and a newspaper, about how they met, and how he died a couple of years ago. That's what made me want to tell her about my life, too. So then I ended up telling her the story I'd heard in Denmark, about the body of a fisherman that was found on the beach.

Do you remember, Kazu? How a group of fishermen set out for Hokkaido from the coast of Brittany and got caught in a storm and shipwrecked, and how their bodies washed ashore on the northern coast of Denmark? The local people held a memorial service for them, and some of the fishermen's wives and mothers who'd heard the news came as well, and just never left.

When Odile had first heard that story, her brown eyes had

grown wide with fear. Now Mitch hears her voice again in his sweat-drenched ears.

Is that so! I've heard that many fishermen in that area got caught in storms and died at sea. And some got all the way to Hokkaido only to die there. They say this area was extremely poor, so there were plenty of men who had no choice but to go to sea, knowing full well how dangerous it was. And the women in Hokkaido spent the rest of their days gazing at the sea, waiting for their husbands or sons to return. Sometimes I feel jealous of them. I wish I could keep watch over my husband's death, just like they did. But nowadays, urban life doesn't afford that kind of luxury.

And then, Kazu, after that, Odile told me all kinds of ghost stories that have been passed down in this region over the years. Of course there are ghosts, since so many fishermen died at sea. Some rise up from the offing at night and make their way toward the shore, shouting as they wander along the beach, soaking wet, till morning. Some manage to find their sleeping wives and kidnap them. Younger ghosts call their fiancées to the sea and have the wedding they've always wanted. On stormy nights, the dead scream and cry. Some villagers even say they've seen Death itself riding along the shore on a white horse. Odile says there are demons who play tricks on people, too. One girl in the village made a deal with the devil and sold her own child to him. The money that the devil offered her burned a bright red, and you can still see where he placed the money on the stone. The mother was immediately struck by lightning and killed. And then there's a famous story about an entire village that got swallowed up by the sea, and every night people heard the church bell clanging, clanging from the bottom of the sea, and all the people on land had insomnia. Maybe there was a big tsunami or something.

Kazu, maybe it's the way Odile talks, but every story she tells me is so interesting. Sometimes she'll be telling me a ghost story and I feel like I can sense all the animals in the forest around the castle quietly gathering, listening. I bet animals are more familiar with ghosts and demons than we are. One time I told Odile that there was a wildcat outside our door.

The wildcats are listening to your story, too, I told her. She just grinned and nodded, then continued speaking in her hushed tone.

I'm starting to think I'd like to come back here someday. I wonder when that will be. Kazu, I'm going to keep talking to Odile every night. And on my last night in the castle, I'm going to tell her about how we are haunted by a little girl named Miki-chan, and about all the dead women who were killed on account of the colour orange, about the vague fear we live with, about our sadness. You don't mind, do you, Kazu? I know Odile will understand that this story can't leave the forest. That's right, Kazu, I want Miki-chan and all those women to feel at home here, along with the fishermen who died at sea and all the animals of the forest. I want to leave Tabo's suffering and our fear behind in this forest, far away from Tokyo. If only I could bring Joyce and Jeff here. Your forest seems great, too, but I've never been there, and besides, this is where I am now.

Suddenly everything grows quiet outside the car. The world brightens. Mitch opens the window. The rain has left behind a fog of tiny droplets. In front of him, grey rain clouds are breaking open and a bright blue sky is peeking through. He stops the car for a moment, rolls the windows all the way down, and sticks his head out.

Rain falls from the branches of the surrounding trees. A rainbow appears in the blue swathe of sky. The colours, almost too vivid to be real, float against it in sharp relief, as though inviting Mitch to some other, faraway place.

10

The peach blossoms are the first things that greet Yonko as she approaches the flower shop. She is numb with cold. That's right, it's almost Hinamatsuri, Girls' Day, isn't it? she thinks as she gazes at the pink blossoms clinging to an assortment of branches hastily thrust into a tin can. In some warmer region of the world, there must be buds like these already swelling to full blossom.

She parts the branches and enters the shop. Yellow forsythia flowers enter her field of vision, then Thunberg's meadowsweet. There are mimosas here, which she never used to see but which seem to be popular lately. Red and white magnolias are already beginning to bloom, announcing an early spring. Yonko proceeds to the back of the narrow shop. On the wet concrete floor, potted hyacinths and Japanese primroses stand in a row, with some cyclamens mixed in, though it's still a bit early for them. In the glass case in the very back, a bunch of stiff tulip buds are crowded together. They seem to be watching Yonko. She can just barely make out their colours: a mix of red, yellow, white and purple. Some have tiny frills on the edges of their petals. Some of the buds are long and tapered, others round and full, others slightly twisted. Recently the shop has begun to import flowers from the Netherlands, and there are new varieties of tulips that she's never seen before.

The young shop owner approaches Yonko and opens the glass case.

Is this a gift for someone, or are they for you?

Yonko doesn't reply, but shifts her gaze from the tulips to the roses. There are small and large roses of all different colours, and they seem to turn toward Yonko and make eye contact with her, crying: Us, us, buy us! See, look how pretty we are! But Yonko isn't interested in the roses. She looks at several other types of flowers. That's odd, she thinks, tilting her head. They all look so artificial for some reason. Since when have the flowers in flower shops looked like this? Suddenly she feels like crying.

Kazu, ever since you died, the roses and tulips all look so cold and distant. It's been six years since you passed, but I'm still so sad.

Yonko turns towards the employee and smiles.

I'll take the peach blossoms and Thunberg's meadowsweet. Could you give me three of each, please?

Yonko exhales as she watches the woman.

Kazu, do you see her hair? It looks just like Miki-chan's. It was that exact shade of red, all fluffy and frizzy. Miki-chan always hated her hair, wished it were black, but nowadays it seems like everyone dyes their hair some other colour. I've actually started dyeing my hair, too, to hide the grey. You were starting to get some grey hairs yourself. With curly hair like yours, I assumed you wouldn't have to worry too much about that, but I remember looking at you after you died and noticing them.

Yonko can hear Kazu chuckle in her ear. She continues addressing him in her mind.

Kazu, do you remember that time we celebrated Girls' Day? I'd almost forgotten about it, but then it came back to me all of a sudden. Each time I think I've uncovered every memory of you, I find there are still more. I was so happy that day. Miki-chan was there. I think we were six. And you and Mitch were seven. You two were on your best behaviour.

Kazu's laughter echoes in Yonko's ear again.

The employee with the reddish-brown hair carries the six stems of peach blossoms and Thunberg's meadowsweet over to Yonko in both hands and shows them to her, as though seeking her approval. Yonko purses her lips, her expression stern, regarding the pink and white buds.

Kazu looks at the buds. I like them, he whispers to her.

I like them, too, Yonko answers. These flowers are for you, Kazu. But I like them so much, I almost want to get some for my mother, too. Though I don't know whether she'll approve.

Excuse me, Yonko says to the employee. Would you mind adding two more of each? They're not a gift, so they don't have to match or anything.

The woman quickly grabs two more of each type of flower out of the tin cans, gathers them into a bouquet, and shows them to Yonko again. She nods and smiles. The woman smiles back, then heads to the register at the back of the store.

An image of the children appears before Yonko's eyes. They are kneeling on the floor in front of the paper Hina dolls and artificial peach blossom branches, sipping on amazake. Kazu, Annie, Mitch, Miki-chan and Joyce, who must have been very young still – perhaps they were all there. Maybe it wasn't amazake but orange juice that they drank? Some kind of tangerine juice that her mother had made for them, perhaps.

If I'm remembering right, I think they made you and Mitch sit on special shiny cushions and greet us girls in an overly formal way, and of course we teased you for it, but you were both so nervous and uncomfortable, you just sat there drinking your tangerine juice and shovelling roasted mochi into your mouths. Do you remember?

Kazu shrugs as though to say, Maybe, who knows.

I guess my mother had decided to do the whole Hinamatsuri thing on a whim that year. We didn't have a proper

Hina doll set, so I used some pastel crayons to draw an odd-looking emperor and empress on some drawing paper, stuck it on the wall, and put up some fake peach branches next to them. I remember I started sulking because I couldn't stand that gaudy pink colour. I hate fake flowers, I remember grumbling before everyone came over, and I hate these Hina dolls, too. Though maybe there was something else bothering me that day. Anyway, that's all I remember. Kazu, you were seven then – do you remember anything else from that day? Like the chirashizushi my mother must have prepared, or what games we played after we ate? Sadly, all those details escape me now.

Yonko senses the sharp light of Kazu's dark eyes behind her. The scene of the Hina dolls from all those years ago comes back to her again and superimposes itself on the yellow forsythia branches.

Did I leave something out? Yonko tilts her head, gazing at the scene again. Annie was there, and Kazu and Mitch, and Miki-chan, and . . . oh, right, there was another boy next to her. Tabo? But why would Tabo be there? Yonko stiffens. Does that mean Tabo and his mother were there that day, too? Did you and Mitch invite him over? No, that never happened. Right? Kazu, are you trying to alter our memories so they include things you wish had happened? If Tabo was there when we were celebrating Girls' Day, then that means Miki-chan might still be alive now, and Tabo, and you, too, Kazu – is that what you're thinking? I don't think it occurred to any of us to invite Tabo that day, though we easily could have. I mean, none of us had any idea that something so awful would happen a year later. If only we could go back and change that one decision.

The image of the children dissolves among the forsythia branches, and Yonko suddenly feels dizzy. Pain shoots across the back of her neck. For a moment she wonders if it's Kazu's cold breath she's feeling, stabbing her like an icicle. The pain turns to tears, which well up from somewhere deep inside her.

She takes the peach blossoms and Thunberg's meadowsweet, wrapped in beige paper, from the employee and decides she may as well buy the potted primrose, too. She fishes her wallet out of her shopping bag and pays, then steps out of the store with Kazu, the exuberant voice of the employee calling out behind them: Thank you for shopping with us! The peach blossoms and Thunberg's meadowsweet have made for a bigger bouquet than she'd anticipated, and she has to carry the potted primrose in one arm. The wind is chilly, and Kazu keeps his head down. Though it has been an unusually warm winter – it hasn't snowed even once – spring is still a long way off. She's heard the United States has been hit by heavy snow this year.

Yonko readjusts her moss-green scarf around her neck and sets off toward home. The flower shop is midway up a gently sloping path that leads to a main road. There used to be a soba shop on the corner of that road. The food and the atmosphere were good, and Yonko had been quite fond of it, but it had been replaced by a fast-food chain. Next to it is a bento shop, another chain. Yonko waits for the light to change. As she looks around, she realizes that almost everything in sight is a chain store or restaurant. There are two convenience stores. She can't remember what shop was there before the chain bakery that's there now. Memory is an unreliable thing, isn't it? Yonko wrinkles her brow faintly. Still, when had hers become so hazy?

Kazu, I want to say it's because you're gone, but I know that would just be an excuse.

Kazu doesn't respond, just stares vacantly out toward the other side of the road. It is a six-lane road, so the light takes a long time to change. Yonko looks up at the sky. It is only four o'clock, but already the shredded clouds scattered across the sky have begun to absorb the colours of the sunset.

Those colours are the only things that haven't changed, she thinks. That and the way the length of the days goes on changing little by little each day.

Setsubun is already coming up next month, you know. Then the days will start getting longer and longer, and before you know it the summer solstice will be here. For now, though, Earth is still gently orbiting the sun. Remember when we talked about how the sun has a lifespan of its own? How long was that, again? For those of us living on Earth, I guess it must be a long, long time.

. . . Hey, Yonko, didn't there used to be a streetcar that ran through here? Kazu's whimsical voice strikes Yonko's ear. Remember when we were kids and Mitch wanted to ride it so badly? Whenever we went to your house from Yokohama, he used to beg Mama to let us ride it, even though it was out of the way, so we'd take the Sobu train line to Suidobashi station and get on the streetcar from there. We were captivated by the driver's movements. How he'd turn the small steering wheel that came up to his waist, or pull the string that dangled from the ceiling to ring the little bell. Mitch used to brag that when he grew up he was going to drive a streetcar, too.

That's right. Yonko nods. Miki-chan and Ami-chan and I used to laugh and make fun of him. It was a mystery to us why boys loved trains and cars so much. Girls think boys are simple-minded. That reminds me, Kazu: Ami-chan is probably leaving her apartment right around now. She stops by my place sometimes. Maybe there's a homemade blueberry tart in the passenger seat of that white Citroën that her company bought for her. I wonder if she remembers those Hina dolls, too.

A while back, Annie, who had been working for a fashion designer in Paris, was transferred to Tokyo after switching to the sales department. She didn't end up becoming a designer like she'd dreamed about, but had no complaints about her current job. Her company had appointed her assistant manager at a store in Ginza since she could speak Japanese. Annie had told Yonko that she'd give her a discount on any clothes she wanted if Yonko came to visit, but she'd rarely gone. Everything in the store was too pricey, and it didn't seem like the items would go with the clothes she already had. Annie told her that the clothes didn't used to be from such high-end brands, but, with the onset of globalization the fashion world had become increasingly cut-throat.

Today was Sunday, Annie's day off, so she likely wouldn't wake up till noon.

That reminds me, Kazu, Yonko says. You know the place where I work, right? That furniture showroom in Hibiya? Annie owns one of those queen-size beds we have on display. Those beds are so expensive – I bet you'd never guess how much they are. Her company rented a luxury apartment for her. I guess they're doing well. She says the apartment is too big for one person. She seems a little lonely, actually – she invited me to come and live with her, but I have to stay with my mother. Tommy and Kate stay with Annie when they come to Tokyo, and Mitch goes to visit her sometimes, too.

Finally, the light turns green, and Yonko and Kazu cross the street. She holds her arms at a ninety-degree angle as she carries the bouquet, careful not to let the stems drag on the ground. She'd got greedy and bought ten of them in all, plus the potted primrose, and now she is beginning to regret it. If only Kazu could help me, she thinks. The shopping bag on her shoulder is getting heavier. Inside is the wagashi she bought for Annie, and the mango pudding she wanted her mother to try, and some bread for breakfast toast.

Kazu, did you know Annie is coming to pay her respects to you? Well, I guess it's not 'paying her respects' really – she just said that she wanted to see you while your remains were still with me. Mitch has been keeping you in your old apartment, which he's now taken over – you know how stubborn he is. He keeps saying that, when he dies I can scatter both your remains together somewhere, or put you in an ossuary. He says I can do whatever I want, but, as long as he's alive, he's not letting go of you. I don't get it, it's not like your soul is attached to your remains or anything. But anyway, he asked me to hang on to your remains while he went to Vietnam. He made plans to meet up with Kate there. Not that this is anything new. Mitch has always been the sentimental type. But he also can't sit still. One minute he's going on and on about holding on to your remains, the next he's at my door announcing that he's taking off somewhere. And then, suddenly, he's back again, saying, Merci, thank you, Yonko, and bringing you home with him.

Kazu places his hand on Yonko's shoulder gently – she is wearing a wool half-coat – and wraps his hand around her waist. She feels a slight ticklish sensation, and wiggles her shoulders and shakes her waist in response. She smiles, amused, as she pictures what she must look like. She meets the gaze of a taxi driver waiting for the light to change, blushes and lowers her head. Then a smile breaks out on her face again.

Stop it, Kazu. Anyway, I was going to tell you that Mitch and Kate are in Vietnam right now. They've become really close lately. As long as he's with her, he feels secure. I'm starting to feel like maybe he'll be able to go on living without you after all. I wanted to ask him, Why not me? I'm the one who stayed with Kazu the whole time. But Kate feels comforted when she spends time with Mitch, eating with him, sleeping with him, walking the streets with him. Especially since Jeff, the person she'd trusted most in her entire life, isn't here anymore.

Kate had been adopted by an American couple when she was only four years old, so it was only natural she'd become closer to Jeff and Tommy, who both went to America, too. She became especially close to Jeff, who was there for her when her adoptive father began sexually abusing her. Jeff and Tommy felt responsible for the kids from the orphanage who were being raised in America. They wanted to protect them from all the misfortunes and disasters and sadness they were sure to face. Kate's difficulties had begun when she was around ten, but it wasn't until a few years later, feeling like she had no other option, that she reached out to Jeff instead of taking her own life. Jeff immediately explained the situation to Kate's adoptive mother, and, after much back-and-forth, Kate finally moved to New York City, where she was able to live on her own before graduating from high school. She'd been living in nearby Princeton until then, so it wasn't too far of a move, and her adoptive mother was able to visit her frequently. But it was really thanks to Jeff that Kate was finally able to get back on her feet, which is why, when Jeff went missing in Vietnam, she wanted more than anything to go and search for him.

After crossing the road, Yonko and Kazu turn onto a smaller street they'd often walked together in childhood. At least half the homes have been rebuilt since then, and the owners have changed hands, too. A ray of winter sunlight illuminates the road up ahead, and Yonko squints as she walks. The sunny patches are warm, but, as soon as she steps into the shade, she feels cold again. The westward road begins to slope downward.

Last year, Tommy had taken his wife and child to visit Vietnam for the first time. First they went to Hanoi, in what used to be called North Vietnam, and then to Hue.

Of course we couldn't go to the jungle, Tommy had written Yonko in an email. *We just wandered around like the rest of the tourists. But it does feel like we got a little closer to Jeff, even though we didn't find him.*

Can you believe it, Mitch had written to Yonko sometime

after that. People can actually go to Vietnam as tourists now. I'm going to see Jeff, and Kate in Rome, and then Annie in Paris.

They thought of Jeff. Was he still alive somewhere in the jungles of Vietnam? Those jungles had been decimated by napalm and Agent Orange, leaving the trees scorched and withered.

Six years ago, Kazu had been cutting down some tree branches in a park, lost his footing, or else had a sudden fit of dizziness, and fallen from a large chinquapin tree and died. After that, Mitch had become empty inside. Even now, he sometimes finds himself crying, unable to accept that Kazu is really dead.

Hey, what are you all doing? he'd say sometimes out of the blue. We have to hurry up and find Kazu.

When Yonko would look up in surprise, he'd grin and say: Don't worry, I wasn't serious. But then he'd mutter under his breath: Although maybe we should try and find him anyway.

Sometimes when the phone would ring, he'd turn to Yonko with a serious face and say: I bet that's Kazu.

Every time, Yonko's heart would do a somersault, and for a split second she'd expect to hear Kazu's voice on the other line. But he never called.

Suddenly Kazu is standing next to her, crying, too.

I guess even spirits cry when they're sad, Yonko thinks, reaching her hand out to wipe his face. But the tears dissolve before she can touch them.

Kazu, I couldn't believe you were gone. I stayed with Mitch in your old apartment for a while. It felt like you'd just gone away somewhere and we were waiting for you to come home. I didn't mind it, really. After all, just because you died, it didn't mean you'd ceased to exist. I still think that. Because you're still here, Kazu, aren't you? You're right by my side. The same goes for Miki-chan, and Tabo, and Joyce – they never left. No, you feel even closer to me now than you did when you were alive. You're always illuminating me from the inside, like a sharp light – inside my arm, behind my ear, in my stomach, in my chest. I know you're here, I really do. It's like you're trying to trick me into being brave again.

Yonko begins to walk again, motioning for Kazu to follow her. A ray of afternoon sunlight illuminates the slope in front of them.

We have to hurry. I don't want Annie getting there before us. Listen, Kazu. I know I told you this before, but Mitch took your remains and moved into your old apartment. He never went back to Hokkaido, to the radio station where he used to work. And to think he'd finally found a steady job there. Summer break was just beginning when you passed, so Hide went up to the apartment Mitch was renting in Chitose to cancel the lease and pack up Mitch's things. And then he sent a few boxes to your apartment in Tokyo. There was a tape in one of those boxes of the Ainu and Breton singers that he'd just begun to record by the shores of Lake Shikotsu. Yes, the one you were supposed to hear, Kazu. The young employee made some last-minute calls and they were finally able to play the song on the radio. It didn't get much recognition, and they weren't able to sell it as a CD. But the Ainu singer performed in Breton, and I think she even met with Mitch a few times after that. There were recordings of the song being played on other radio stations. And several CDs' worth of Breton music that Mitch had brought back to Japan. What else was in there? Mitch's clothes, I guess. We haven't touched any of your things. Even though Mitch didn't bring much with him, your apartment is pretty cramped now.

. . . Yeah, I bet. I mean, I was living there by myself, so it must be tight with both of you there.

Yonko can hear Kazu's voice from inside the shimmer of the setting sun. She grows flustered and opens her mouth to speak, then changes her mind and nods silently.

At the time, that's all we could do. Can you imagine how shocked we were? My mother was still doing well then, and Hide and Sara were staying with her. So I was able to spend time with Mitch. But I had to keep working. Hide was fine, since he had some money left over from the settlement from Joyce's accident, and he was already twenty by then. Sara was sixteen, though, so she still depended on me. My mother did, too. She had her pension, but with the cost of repairing the old house, and the dentist and hospital bills, things were adding up.

About two months after you died, Mitch finally admitted that he needed to get a job, too.

Maybe Takeshi will let me work at his company again, he said. But I don't want to beg.

Why don't you ask around? Yonko suggested. Maybe Odile will have some ideas. Or maybe you could find something in Brittany? What about the sorcerer? You haven't seen him since he kicked you out, right? I think you should tell him that two of his predictions actually came true, and ask what he thinks you should do. I mean, thinking about them now gives me the creeps. I'm scared of what the third one will be.

He might be dead by now, Mitch said. And even if he is still alive and I can see him, he'd just mock me and make some more absurd predictions. Maybe they were just to intimidate me, but I've had enough of that. What can I do? I can beat him to a pulp, but that wouldn't bring Kazu back, and it wouldn't save Tabo either.

But the last prophecy hasn't come true yet. What's going to happen? Who is the sorcerer, really?

Kazu sighs, and his cool breath grazes Yonko's earlobe.

You know, it was 10 September when Mitch and I had this conversation. A huge typhoon was headed toward Tokyo. And then the next day, 11 September, around noon, the typhoon passed, and that night the terrorist attacks happened in America. Hide called us and told us to turn on the TV immediately, so I turned it on, wondering what was going on. I remember seeing the same footage replaying over and over of the airplanes crashing into the World Trade Center.

Was this the third prophecy? I said to Mitch in a trembling voice.

Of course not. The sorcerer was talking about Japan, not America.

But maybe he just got the location wrong. I heard the Pentagon was attacked, too. And other places. Maybe the evil spirit that the sorcerer was talking about was war.

Mitch was silent for a while.

If only I had a magic power that would let me break the curse, he muttered to himself.

To me, watching those attacks on TV was apocalyptic. But you know, Kazu, the strangest thing was that they seemed to have the opposite effect on Mitch. He started getting better after that, going out with Mako and Takeshi and even talking to Hide again. He started visiting that garden you used to take care of, watering the flowers so they wouldn't wilt, pruning the branches in his own clumsy way. Of course, it wasn't his garden, no matter how much he pretended it was. I think a few times he even went to the apartment where Tabo's mother lived. He wanted to offer some incense for her son, who had killed himself two years earlier, and tell her that Kazu, too, had died, in an accident this summer. But he could never bring himself to do it. Just looking at the place terrified him, and he'd always come home dejected. Finally, he got in touch with Odile, and started talking to Tommy, Annie and Kate.

Do you remember, Kazu? The way the three of them dropped everything to come to your funeral? We didn't bother going to a funeral parlour – Takeshi and Mako arranged everything themselves. Mitch was a husk of his former self. He got drunk and didn't help with anything. Kate cried the whole time. But she delivered a speech in Japanese for you, Kazu. She read a few poems that you'd learned when you were in Rome. They were by some Spanish poet named Lorca, I think? Kate's Japanese was halting and I couldn't understand everything she was saying, but her voice was beautiful as she read, and we were all moved to tears.

In the setting sun, Kazu strokes Yonko's straight black hair and whispers:

Little black horse
Where are you taking your dead rider . . . ?

Yonko opens her mouth, stops in her tracks.

Yes, that was the poem. An image of Tabo as a child, riding piggyback on Kazu as they ran through the grass, appears before her. Where were they going?

Kazu's funeral took place at a restaurant on the edge of a forest in the middle of Tokyo. Yonko felt Tabo's presence there, too: next to her and Mitch, near the table, in a corner of the room, hovering near the ceiling. Everyone at the ceremony remembered him, but no one could speak about him.

Yonko tries to recall the altar that Mako had hastily prepared. In the middle was a photo of Kazu, and on either side, vases of sunflowers in bloom, and a photo of all of them taken at the orphanage long ago. In the photo, Kazu resembles Tabo. Then his face morphs into Mitch's – strange, since Mitch is still alive.

I don't know what's wrong with me, Yonko says to Kazu. I'm getting confused about who actually died: you or Mitch. Now it's Mitch I see carrying Tabo on his back as he runs, even though his bad leg would make that impossible.

Yonko reaches out to grab Kazu's arm like she used to, but

her right hand swims through the air in vain, her face contorting in sorrow.

Mitch, are you thinking of Tabo too, wherever you are in Vietnam? Remember how we used to shoo him away whenever he followed us? Tell him he was strange and to go home? We never really talked to him. So why do we still feel his presence, why does regret haunt our dreams, why does the pain only grow deeper and deeper?

After your funeral, Kazu, Mitch finally came to his senses and began to look for work. And then boxes began arriving from Indonesia, full of local goods made of cotton, teak, bamboo and rattan. After Mitch reached out to Odile about needing a job, she came up with the idea of procuring goods in Indonesia that Japanese people might like to buy, such as Indonesian kasuri fabric, batik dyed in the roketsuzome style, which Mitch could then sell in Japan. He agreed to try it, and Odile began shipping goods to him right away. With the help of Mako's company, he began selling the goods online. This was a moment when 'Asian goods' were becoming all the rage in Japan, so the Indonesian fabrics sold quite well. Still, since the items were sold fairly cheaply, Mitch didn't make much of a profit, just enough to provide him with a bit of spending money. But it was better than nothing. When he thought about it, he realized he was basically continuing the same kind of work that Mama used to do. For her part, Odile seemed to enjoy buying the local goods in Indonesia, and Hide and Sara, who helped Mitch with the business, found the work interesting.

Since she'd visited Asia for the first time eight years ago, Odile had gone back a number of times on her own, and finally ended up renting a small house on a hill in Lombok. The place seemed to suit her. Perhaps she felt less lonely there. She visited Japan, too – Nara and Kyoto – and even the Noto Peninsula. Although she'd heard plenty from Mitch about the curse, she'd never broached the topic. Instead she talked about the ethnic cleansing that was happening in Sarajevo.

I remember you liked Odile, Kazu. You said she spoke very beautiful English, that she had an elegant way of carrying herself.

Yonko senses Kazu nodding slightly. She readjusts her bags, faces the western sky and begins to walk again, the flower stems in her left hand, the potted primrose cradled in her arm.

And then, before we knew it, six months passed since you left us. Finally I had to tell Mitch that I couldn't stay at your apartment anymore, that I had to go back and be with my mother.

No, please don't say that, Mitch cried, holding me tight. Don't leave me here alone. Let's keep living together just like this, you and me.

I did want to stay with him, of course. But I couldn't keep neglecting my mother and Sara. Plus, Hide was already a college student, and I felt a responsibility to Joyce to take care of him, too. I never wavered in that decision. But of course it was terribly difficult to leave Mitch and go back home.

It sounds ridiculous to say now, but we both stood there and wailed as we held each other. There was your death, Kazu, and the incidents with Tabo on top of that. And then Joyce's death, and Jeff disappearing, and Miki-chan, and the five anonymous women who died because of the colour orange: everything was just so sad, and the tears seemed to flow out of us endlessly. I think the two of us had been waiting for the right moment when we could finally cry together without holding back. So that we could each go on surviving on our own time.

Yonko trails off and takes a deep breath. She senses Kazu doing the same.

Kazu, I loved you. Remember that time when we lived together? I was so happy then. We went through periods of being closer and more distant after that. When we embraced, our scents would mingle and become something that smelled like a cross between fresh apple and cypress trees. But then the smell of Mitch would come welling up from within that scent, something like a cat or a squirrel that had been rained on. Did I hug Mitch recently? I'd think. But when I opened my eyes, it would just be you. And it was the same when I'd embrace Mitch. You were always somewhere near. I think Mitch felt it, too. That's why I didn't want to leave him. But whenever I'd think about how wonderful it would be to live with him, I'd think of Miki-chan, and Tabo, and the five murdered women. And I'd realize it was impossible.

Yonko and Kazu continue walking down the hill, following the road as it bends to the left, squinting into the last rays of sunlight. The widened road appears sunken in darkness, out of reach of the setting sun. A middle-aged woman passes by on her bike. A boy who looks to be in high school walks toward her, talking on his cell phone, then passes her, too. Two businessmen come out of an apartment on the right side of the road, both wearing long black wool coats.

The building next to the apartment is where Yonko's old house used to be. Though the entrance is narrow, the building extends back quite a bit. Yonko and Kazu stand in front of the glass door. On either side are potted azaleas. Above is a metal sign that says CLOVER'S HOUSE in black lettering. Yonko nudges the door open with her shoulder and goes inside. Kazu follows her. She greets the woman in the front office, then heads toward the elevator. The heat isn't on, but thankfully it's warmer inside than outside. The lobby is spacious. There is a planter covered with white tile in the middle, and a decorative plant. Beside the elevator is a long, vertical stained-glass window. Mako's architectural firm had designed the building, so it didn't feel like just any old nursing home. Yonko listens as she waits for the elevator. Voices echo from afar that sound like animal cries, which only accentuates the silence in the building. The elevator display flashes 4, then 3, then 2.

Somehow, Mitch and I have managed to swallow our sadness and go on living during the six years you've been gone, Kazu. Since you died, the Iraq War started. The world is becoming a terrible place. Mitch isn't exactly enjoying his new job. He worked for two years, then lost all motivation, quit and left everything to Hide. After visiting Odile in Indonesia, he went off to Paris. He left your remains with me, of course.

The elevator doors open. No one comes out. Yonko and Kazu step inside and Yonko presses the button that says 8. She places the potted primrose on the floor and holds the flower stems against her chest. Kazu squeezes her shoulder. She smells fresh apples and cypress, and a single tree leaf twirls in front of her. As the elevator climbs up and up, the leaves grow more and more numerous. She hears them rustling in the wind.

Yonko pictures Mitch and Kate somewhere in Vietnam. Maybe they are wandering through the town of Hue. Or setting off on an adventure, approaching the jungle. When she thinks of Vietnam, only images of the war come to mind. Photographs of naked girls crying, running down a dirt road in a rural village. Photographs of men getting their heads blown off by guns. Images of forests burning as they are blasted open with bombs, emitting an orange light. She saw that in a movie once. Combat helicopters spraying Agent Orange from far up in the sky. But those things don't happen anymore. Mitch and Kate are holding hands as they stroll through a quiet suburb, or maybe a village somewhere, hoping to get as close as they can to Nobu, who disappeared into the jungle during the war.

Maybe Mitch is whispering to Kate, telling her how he used to get mistaken for Vietnamese when he was in France. Lush tropical plants grow in abundance. Some unfamiliar brightly coloured bird flies overhead, and, in the village, the soft sounds of Vietnamese echo through the air. Otherwise, the town looks like it could be somewhere in France, a reminder that this place used to be a colony.

In Yonko's mind, Mitch morphs into Kazu, and Kate becomes her.

Maybe the two of them are disappointed. Maybe Nobu feels further away than ever.

The last thirty years blow past them. They are overwhelmed by the thunderous roar of time. This must be the sound of Earth turning, Mitch (or Kazu) whispers to Kate (or Yonko).

The boxy elevator sways a little, and the doors open. The leaves that had been swirling around inside the elevator fly out one by one into the long hallway of the eighth floor.

Finally, we're here, Yonko says out loud.

She waits for a moment, but doesn't hear Kazu reply.

She pauses, adjusts the flowers in her arms again, and begins to walk down the hall. At the end is a large window, and a strong western sun shines through it, the light reflecting off the linoleum floor. The shadows of the leaves dance upon it.

The room where Yonko's mother spends all her days now is at the very end of the hallway.

Her mother's health suddenly began to decline about two years ago, during the summer. Yonko, her only child, then had to choose between quitting her job to take care of her, and putting her in a facility. Wanting to help her, Hide and Sara decided to consult Takeshi. By then the two of them had moved out of the house. Together, Takeshi and Mako came up with a plan. First, they'd put Yonko's mother in a nursing home, then Yonko would rent an affordable apartment nearby. Next they'd tear down the old house, and finally build their own nursing home that included hospice care. Patients under hospice care would die as natural a death as possible, not pursuing any unnecessary medical treatments apart from painkillers or bedsore prevention. Takeshi's company would pay for the initial expenses, then they'd hire another company to take over and run it after that. Of course, Yonko wouldn't need to pay for any of it herself.

Now Yonko's mother is on the eighth floor of this building, in a private room with a lovely view, spending most of her time sleeping, while Yonko lives in an apartment nearby.

It is to that apartment that Annie is headed now, speeding along in her white Citroën. How far away is she? Annie had loved Kazu dearly since she was a child, and had always wanted to live near him. But she'd kept her distance, since Yonko was always nearby, greedily keeping watch over both Mitch and Kazu.

I could never tell what you were thinking, perhaps Annie mutters to herself as she drives.

It's Sunday, so the roads downtown are nearly empty. Would Annie call Yonko in just a little while on her cell?

Yonko slowly walks the hallway, which shimmers in the afternoon light. Kazu drifts away from her and melts into the setting sun.

Where are you going? Yonko calls out instinctively. The entire hallway is awash in bright orange. More and more leaves gather in the hallway, their shadows dancing toward the light, and suddenly she feels like she is in the jungle in Vietnam. But that's just her imagination. She's never been to Vietnam, after all. She sways with the leaves, unable to resist their motion. The sound of her footsteps echoes in the light, and she hears Kazu's voice in the shadows, faintly at first, then louder, undulating toward her. It is a dry laugh, the voice of a child.

Yonko, it wasn't Tabo who pushed Miki-chan into the pond all those years ago – it was me, I swear. And then, because Miki-chan was wearing an orange skirt, I killed five women who were all wearing the same colour – yes, that was me, too. Yonko, do you believe me? I'm begging you to believe me.

As she walks down the hall, she hears Mitch's voice, too, high-pitched, ten years old again.

No, it was me that pushed her in. And ever since, that orange skirt followed me everywhere. That's why I ended up killing those five women, though I did feel sorry for them. That's right, it was me all along, you just didn't know it, Yonko. Do you get it now?

Yonko . . .

A hole opens up in Mitch's voice, and the faint voice of a little girl flows inside it.

Miki-chan, it's you, Yonko whispers as she continues walking, straining her eyes as she searches for any trace of the girl among the shadows of the leaves. She looks at Yonko in the dazzling afternoon sun. The orange of her skirt melts into the light, so that she is only half-visible. Her red hair flutters in the swirling leaves.

. . . No, Yonko, that's not how it was, no one pushed me into the pond that day. It wasn't Tabo's fault either. He just happened to be there and see me fall in. My foot got caught on a rock. I fell in, swallowed muddy water, and that was it. I was only seven, so I didn't suffer at all.

Yonko continues walking in the orange light. The shadows of the leaves cross her body, collide with larger shadows and disappear.

Is that you, Kazu? Yonko calls out. Miki-chan?

If you're all going to come out and say it, then I will, too. I'm the one who pushed Miki-chan into the pond, I'm the one who killed those five women. There is a Yonko inside me that I don't even know, that no one knows, and one day that Yonko got caught up in the orange-coloured fear and couldn't escape. Sachi knows. She was near the pond that day, too.

She reaches the last room in the hallway. The shadow of another person. No, not one but two. They are standing next to each other, watching the door. As Yonko walks, she squints into the brightness of the setting sun. As soon as she notices them, the shadows disappear into the room.

Was that Tabo? And Tabo's mother?

She had never really seen their faces, and had only a vague sense of what they looked like, but she had seen them from the back a few times. That image was seared into her memory, so that sometimes when she walked through the neighbourhood she would be convinced she'd seen them silently steal past her, just as they did in her dreams. The mother was very small, and Tabo was thin – they had the same rounded back, the same shuffling gait.

Yonko pauses and looks at the door of the room where her mother is sleeping. It is closed. She trembles, and all the light vanishes from around her. Is it possible her mother had asked Tabo and his mother to come and pick her up? When her mother was still clear-headed and could walk with a cane, Yonko had thought about how Tabo had died all alone, hanging from a sakura tree. Who knows what kinds of thoughts his mother had lived with after that? Yonko had only caught glimpses of her through the window. She had never talked to her.

She doesn't want our sympathy, Yonko's mother had said. We'd only make her sad or angry.

I can't help but feel it's still happening. I'm too scared to even read the newspaper closely, but they say that women are still being killed over the colour orange.

Suddenly all the strength goes out of Yonko's hands, and the bouquet of flowers falls to the floor. The sound hits her body and unleashes an unbearable pain. A cold stillness seeps toward her from the inside of the room.

Mother?

Yonko cannot move from the spot on the floor where the flowering branches are scattered. Her phone begins to ring cheerfully from inside the shopping bag. She wants to scream.

What happened? Yonko wants to ask her mother. Why did you want to see Tabo? Why did you ask Tabo's mother to bring him to you? Did you want to apologize to them?

Excuse me, yes, I think something has happened to my mother. Could I ask you to come and check on her? Something is off, please . . .

The sound of her own voice begging for help from the office staff on the first floor sounds far away. She can't move. She stands among the white and pink blossoms and regards the stillness inside the room.

II

Inside the aspic jelly, Mitch knocks twice on the plywood door, then pauses for a moment to listen. Yonko stands behind him, hiding. They are both wearing masks, the heavy-duty kind that are pointed in the middle, making them look somewhat like ancient tengu.

Outside, the flood of sunlight makes it feel like midsummer, but inside the cracked corridor of the building total darkness reigns, indifferent to the changing seasons, and their eyes struggle to adjust. Sound warps, the outlines of things wobble inside this jelly-world. Here it is again. That suffocating feeling he associates with the radioactive jelly comes back to him all at once.

When Mitch first arrived at Narita Airport, he'd been terrified of setting foot in that irradiated world – but once he did, his fear gradually began to dissipate, and as he watched the people around him going about their daily lives, calm and composed, the young children running around outside without masks on, he began to doubt whether nuclear fallout had ever landed on Tokyo at all. Perhaps there really was nothing to worry about.

But, of course, sinister radioactive clouds are probably gathering over Tokyo at this very moment. And every time an earthquake rattles the land, he remembers the aspic jelly and chides himself for his foolishness – after all, it was radioactive fallout, which human beings cannot physically sense, that was responsible for creating this grotesque world in the first place.

Mitch knocks on the door again, a little harder this time. He is careful not to knock too forcefully, though, since it looks like it could fall apart at any minute. He listens again for any movement on the other side. It is strangely quiet, considering how many apartments there are in this building and how many people live here, and he wonders if the foreign residents have all gone back to their respective countries to escape the radiation. Or maybe they've moved out because the old building is finally getting torn down. After the earthquake, it is clearly on its last legs. Mitch can't help but wonder. He can hear Yonko's voice faintly but can't make out what she is saying.

. . . Leave? Yonko had shot back, puzzled, when Mitch had first asked her. I'll admit I am afraid of the earthquakes. And it's true I'm not in the best shape right now. My heart won't stop pounding. I think I have post-earthquake vertigo, though it might just be stress-related. It's possible I was exposed to radiation back in March. Though they did say people over sixty would probably be okay. I can't believe I'm saying all this out loud. Just the other day, I was drying my futon on the veranda, enjoying a nice stroll in Hibiya Park on my lunch break. Even back in March there were people jogging around the imperial palace without masks on. So of course you see that and think everything must be fine. They weren't reporting anything on TV in Tokyo, but some people still evacuated right away. I guess everyone has different ways of dealing with their fear, but that's exactly what makes you feel crazy.

Suddenly Mitch remembers what the sorcerer had said. *It hurts me to think of what's become of Japan.*

It was Annie who had conveyed his message in an email to Yonko once she'd got back to Paris after visiting the sorcerer in

Brittany. He was barely able to sit up, but when she said Mitch's name, he narrowed his eyes and asked her to convey these final words to him:

I'm sure you probably despise me, though all I did was relay a prophecy to you. That doesn't mean I have the power to change it. Prophecies are always vague. Even I can't always decipher them. I'm just an ordinary Breton who possesses a certain degree of spiritual power. There are plenty of others like me. A while back, an acquaintance of yours, an Ainu woman, visited me with a Breton singer. That Ainu woman possessed a similar spiritual power. I'm sure she'd explain it to you if you asked. That said, I don't have much time left to live, so I wanted to make sure I apologized. I take full responsibility for letting my personal feelings inflect what I shared with you. I truly regret that and will go to the grave with it. And when I die, I'll be buried someplace unknown to you. You still have quite a while left to live, Mitch. You'll probably live to the age of ninety or beyond. So I'm telling you now – though it will be a miserable life, you must live it anyway.

In March, the two singers who had visited the sorcerer some years back emailed Yonko from Finistère and Chitose, begging her to leave for her own safety. Annie also reached out to Yonko around the time she was visiting.

Run away, quick! It's not too late. Come to Paris for now. You have no reason to stay in Tokyo! Just the thought of you being in a crowded city is terrifying. If there's a big aftershock from the earthquake and the nuclear power plant explodes again, that'll be it for Japan. At least, that's what everyone is saying over here.

If Kate were still alive, she'd be so angry with you, Mitch, Annie had said to him. *What are you even doing,* she'd probably say. *Hurry up and get out of Japan with Yonko.*

Kate had died the previous year when she had suffered a

heart attack while she was shooting a film somewhere near St Petersburg.

How come everyone close to you keeps dying? Odile was already pretty old, but people don't usually have heart attacks at Kate's age. What if Yonko dies next? I'm worried. You need to stay close to her so you can protect her. She's always cared for you.

Ever since he'd learned of the disaster that had struck Japan, Mitch had been thinking about what Annie had said. How was Yonko doing in the aftermath of the earthquake? Maybe she felt like she couldn't leave because he had left Kazu's remains with her for safekeeping. He knew he had to go back for her, but the prospect of entering a radioactive zone terrified him. He spent April fretting and fussing, until finally he made up his mind in May and headed to the airport.

Yonko was sitting alone in her apartment in Tokyo, perplexed. Near the end of March, Hide and Sara had moved to Chitose, where the Ainu singer was waiting for them, leaving Yonko all by herself. She feared the aftershocks of the earthquake, but continued living her life more or less as usual. Hide had been researching folk music, which eventually put him in mind of becoming a singer-songwriter, and before long he was able to earn a decent living performing duets with Sara, thanks in part to his good looks.

Chitose might be contaminated, too, Hide had told Mitch on the phone, but it's probably safer than Tokyo. I'm going to take this opportunity to really learn about Ainu songs. I'm not Indigenous, of course, I'm just a wanderer, but I plan to stand by my Ainu and Breton friends and continue protesting nuclear energy. There's been a growing anti-nuclear movement for a while, but I'm embarrassed to say I didn't know anything about it until now . . .

*

Did you really come back just for me, Mitch? Yonko's voice, slightly hoarse. I mean, I wanted you to come back, of course. But can't I stay in Tokyo? I have my job and everything here. Moving is so stressful. I'll admit, sometimes leaving seems like it would be a relief. But when I think about going through with it, all the strength goes out of me. My thoughts always come back to Miki-chan.

But don't you remember when you told Kazu and me to leave Japan? Mitch argued back. Kazu would tell you the same thing if he were still alive. We listened to you then, so why won't you listen now?

Tommy and Annie had tried to convince Yonko to leave, too. Go to Toronto, they insisted. There's nothing stopping you. You can figure out the rest later, once you get there. Maybe most Japanese people have decided the radiation's nothing to be afraid of, but that's ridiculous.

All of us were duped by a gang of politicians who love nuclear power. And they'll try to dupe us again. America and Japan and France, too!

Please get out of there. I mean it. To survive, you first have to get yourself someplace safe. What's holding you back?

Yonko finally relented after a week. Fine, she said, her face contorting the way it did when she was a child. But I'm leaving Kazu's remains with Mama. Though I'll set some of them aside for Mitch, of course. I'm worried about Tabo's mother. Ever since Tabo died, she's been living all by herself in that apartment my mother found.

Mitch lost no time contacting Hide.

Sorry to bother you with this, but could you help us find an apartment? We want to leave Japan, we're just not sure when. Takeshi and Mako? Yeah, they're worried, too, and they want to leave, but when you've got a company as big as theirs, it's not that easy. Plus, they said they've taken a pretty big financial hit. Once that happens, you may as well change course completely. Sure, he could just retire. He's getting older. I'll talk to him about it one of these days. You could always live like Mother Asami.

*

Mitch turns the round doorknob and pulls it toward him as he listens to the voices inside the radioactive jelly. The door opens more easily than he expected, causing him to bump into Yonko behind him.

Instantly, the jelly becomes heavier, denser. The room is sunk in total darkness, and it's impossible to see anything. Mitch enters hesitantly, feeling his way forward. There is a strange smell. Even through their masks, they can smell mould and sewage, incense and candles. Yonko squeezes his hand. He squeezes it back. Just as they thought, someone still lives here, someone very, very old.

Mitch and Yonko remove their masks and venture forward as they call out quietly to the person: Hello, excuse us, sorry to bother you.

They have no choice now but to face their fear of radiation. Small flies are buzzing about.

pish pish pish pish

Mitch remembers the sound of the beetles greedily devouring the leaves. But they can't reach him here. At the other end of the room he can see a window with the curtain drawn. The radioactive jelly is more concentrated beneath the window, where he hears the faint sound of a person weeping amid the buzzing of flies.

Three steps, then four. He takes a fifth step, nearly choking on the jelly, then a sixth, carefully moving forward, exhaling deeply, still gripping Yonko's hand. Then he collapses all at once onto the floor. In the darkness, there is a futon spread out on the floor, a pair of broken glasses, and in the back of the room, two small white glittering dots. The gleam of human eyes. They turn toward Mitch and Yonko. Mitch says nothing, simply looks at them. Yonko doesn't speak. The weeping voice wraps itself around the two of them.

Mitch speaks to the person in his mind, gasping for breath.

Tabo's mother.

The sound of the weeping, layered atop the buzzing of the flies, is coming from the ceiling, and from beneath the tatami, and from the walls. Tabo's voice, crying. Even though he is dead, his voice is still trapped here. His wailing, and his mother's, too, has piled up and up, filling the room, and over a long, long time, the jellied darkness has become trapped inside their weeping voices.

Tabo's mother, Mitch says again, though not out loud.

Just then, from out of the jellied darkness comes a faint, quivering voice. It isn't audible, but it pierces directly into Mitch.

Tabo . . .

Water drips down in a single stream. The low weeping voice becomes so many droplets of water, dripping from the ceiling, pouring out of the walls, bubbling up from the tatami mat. Mitch's and Yonko's hands and faces become drenched.

How come? Why? Tabo's droplets ask Mitch and Yonko, over and over, opening up holes in their bodies, one after another. Their faces contort with pain.

Tabo . . . that child is no longer here.

From inside the darkness, a white wooden mortuary tablet and a few old kamaboko boards float to the surface, drawing Mitch's and Yonko's eyes toward the ceiling. The white tablet has Tabo's name written on it, and a red, blue, white, yellow, green or purple circle has been drawn on each of the six other boards to differentiate them. Though the incense has been extinguished, the scent lingers, clinging to the white tablet and the six boards. The buzzing flies, the weeping voice and the dripping water, heavy as mercury, create a whirlpool, and Mitch realizes that the silver jelly is also Tabo's pond. From the time they were children, the small droplets had accumulated, one by one, into a murky pond, and still the droplets continue to quietly drip, drip. Everyone was afraid of it, keeping their distance, but all this time, Tabo and his mother had been living alone at the bottom of this pond.

Mitch and Yonko watch as Tabo's dark shadow sways like algae. The child Tabo. The fifty-year-old Tabo. The twenty-year-old Tabo. Though his body appears in different sizes, his childlike face remains unchanged. The oldest kamaboko board, with the red dot on it, drifts up toward the surface, and, at the same time, seven-year-old Miki-chan appears, embracing the board as though it were a prized possession. She floats gently in the water, just like Tabo. She isn't smiling, but she isn't crying either. Her eyes are open wide, and her mouth, too, as though she is captivated by something. Only her orange skirt is floating in the leaden pond, gleaming brightly like the tail of a goldfish. Why does Mitch find the view beautiful, though the water is turbid and he is enveloped in the scent of incense and candles? He shakes his head. And then, unbelievably, he notices radioactive material falling here, too, clinging to the droplets of the weeping voice.

Our soil, and water, and grasses and trees, and insects and birds, everything without exception – the animals, the humans, our dreams, our sadness, our pain, our anguish – has been contaminated by the radiation, Kazu's voice whispers to Mitch and Yonko from somewhere inside Tabo's pond. And time has stopped.

Let's get out of here, please, come with us, Mitch says.

Kazu whispers from somewhere inside Tabo's pond, voicelessly, into the depths of the dark jelly. The two eyes flash again.

That child was waiting for you. But it's too late now.

Let's get out of here. In any case, you can't keep living in this crumbling apartment.

And leave Tabo?

Tabo will come with us, too, of course.

To where?

We have a temporary spot picked out, but we're not sure where we'll go after that.

But the world has already disappeared.

But you haven't, and neither have we. We're still alive, see? Please, spend the time you have left with us in the places that remain. Let's get out of Tokyo, this monstrous, horrifying, inflated city. It's all right, we'll worry about the rest later.

But everything is over already, I'm as good as dead.

No, you're alive, even in this world where time has stopped.

I want to die here. Please, let me die.

But you can't. Time has stopped here. In order to die, you have to go where time is still moving. The same goes for us. Even though we might die soon, we want to die a proper death. Please, we're begging you, as Tabo's friends.

Tabo's friends?

Yes, Tabo's friends . . . Mitch nods, guilt-ridden.

Suddenly the radioactive jelly begins to wobble. The water in the pond dashes darkly against the sides of the room, becoming denser, and Miki-chan and Tabo disappear into its murky depths. Another earthquake. Instinctively, Mitch pulls Tabo's mother toward him. Yonko clings to his back. The sound of something falling, then crashing. The walls and ceiling shriek. Mitch's eyes flash green, like the eyes of a scarab beetle, and he holds tight to Tabo's mother.

Then, just as quickly, the sound stops, the water in the pond grows quiet.

Thank God the building didn't crumble. Mitch sighs and looks down. He is shocked to find how small and thin Tabo's mother is. Like a child, her delicate bones almost weightless. Her body is burning hot.

Yonko steps away from Mitch and begins to pick up the kamaboko boards and rice bowls that have fallen to the floor. For the first time since entering this room, Mitch speaks out loud.

Let's get you out of here. You can't stay here anymore. We have to go. For some reason the three of us survived. So we have to leave together.

Tabo's mother furrows her wrinkled brow, shakes her head helplessly. Tears well up again in her eyes, which are buried in wrinkles.

Don't worry, Tabo and all of us will be together.

Tabo . . . , her husky voice says through the weeping.

Yes, that's right. Mitch nods slowly. Gently he strokes her shoulders, which look like they might crumble at any moment. He and Yonko help her to her feet as they imagine the pond filling up with tears over a long period of time. Parting the dark forest of algae and water weeds, the three of them make their way to the surface of the pond, where the sunlight glimmers. Tabo approaches, and seven-year-old Miki-chan, her orange skirt swaying in the water like a goldfish, and Kazu and Joyce and Jeff – all of them are young again – and Kate, and the women who were sacrificed to the colour orange, all gather around. Mitch pictures the radioactive jelly gradually shrivelling up, then sinking down, down to the bottom of the pond.

He glances at Yonko, who is still frightened from the earthquake, then addresses Tabo's mother again.

Let's get going now. Tabo and everyone else are waiting.

She nods, trembling, tears welling in her eyes. Yonko nods back, her expression childlike.

Mitch smiles and gently wipes away the mother's tears with the tip of his finger. The low weeping sound continues, mingling with the buzzing of the flies, and Mitch realizes that even when they go outside, no matter how far away they go, that sound will forever cling to the mother. And the radioactive jelly will cling to the ground, the stones, the houses, causing them all great pain. It will be washed away by the wind and the rain, and will continue changing without rhyme or reason over a long, long time, inflicting a quiet, cruel suffering on the grasses and trees, and the birds and beasts and insects and fish, and the people. It is impossible to run from it.

Why? How come?

It should have been Tabo's voice asking these questions, but it sounds like Mitch's own voice. And Kazu's voice, too, and Jeff's.

Why? How come?

The wailing voice goes on and on.

Author's Note

From 1945 to 1958, the United States conducted nuclear testing not only on Bikini Atoll but also on Enewetak Atoll, in the Marshall Islands. The people who lived there were forcibly relocated and were not allowed to go back until 1980, when the US military completed decontamination work. When the residents returned, however, they found that some of the islands had disappeared due to the nuclear tests. Moreover, a huge concrete dome called 'Runit Dome' had been constructed on Runit Island to collect the enormous amount of contaminated material that had accumulated during the decontamination work. Around the dome, signs were erected in Marshallese and English that said 'Warning! Do Not Enter.' But after twenty-five years, the words had already faded and become difficult to read.